She raised the pistol and waited, trying to stay calm. She felt the warmth of his body behind her and flinched slightly when his hands grasped her shoulders, moving her so that her body faced more squarely down the lane.

"I know this will feel strange to you," he said calmly. He was so close she could feel his breath, warm against her nape. His hand moved to her upper arm, just closing on it gently, urging it back.

"Move your right foot forward just a bit and lean your shoulder back. Your arm should be at an angle to your body, like this."

She obeyed but she could feel her arm start to shake and took a deep breath, trying to focus on nothing but the pistol.

"Relax." His voice was soft and low, soothing. "Remember, this is easy for you." His hand moved down her arm slightly, steadying it. It felt warm through the thin fabric of her dress. He was mere inches behind her now and the contrast between the coolness of the underground cavern and the warmth radiating from his body was disorienting.

Author Note

My first week as financial analyst at an investment bank, I sat in a large room with twenty young men and one woman. Amid all the information bombarding us (including the admonition to us two females not to wear pantsuits—and this was in the '90s!) I started thinking: What must it have been like two hundred years ago for women whose skills placed them in predominantly male environments? I had already spent two years in the military and here I was again—surrounded by confident, aggressive, ambitious men.

That evening I sat in my little flat in Fulham, London, and began writing about a young woman thrust into the male world of espionage in Regency times—a world being shaped by men like my hero, Michael, the Earl of Crayle, who is driven by the dark cost of that privilege and the deep scars of war.

Sari Trevor, my unconventional heroine, has no such traditions to either ground her or limit her. She has to invent herself in a world intolerant of female initiative, so when she enters the earl's world she is both deeply insecure and fiercely determined to succeed. The inevitable clash between them is also at the core of their attraction—it lays bare each other's scars and needs and allows them (eventually) to find salvation together.

The first draft of this story lay dormant for many years alongside others in my writing drawer until my mother, a wonderful poet and editor, drew my attention to Harlequin's So You Think You Can Write 2014 competition. With her inspired help we dusted it off and submitted it and now *Lord Crayle's Secret World* is about to be revealed.

Lara Temple

Lord Crayle's
Secret World

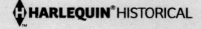

HARLEQUIN® HISTORICAL

Recycling programs
for this product may
not exist in your area.

ISBN-13: 978-0-373-30734-0

Lord Crayle's Secret World

Copyright © 2016 by Ilana Treston

This edition published by arrangement with Harlequin Books S.A.

For questions and comments about the quality of this book, please contact us at CustomerService@Harlequin.com.

Printed in U.S.A.

www.Harlequin.com

Lara Temple was three years old when she begged her mother to take dictation of her first adventure story. Since then she has led a double life—by day an investment and high tech professional who has lived and worked on three continents, but when darkness falls she loses herself in history and romance (at least on the page). Luckily her husband and two beautiful and very energetic children help weave it all together.

Lord Crayle's Secret World
**is Lara Temple's exhilarating debut
for Harlequin Historical!**

Visit the Author Profile page at Harlequin.com.

Chapter One

Hampstead Heath, March 1817

Sari rubbed her gloved but frozen hands together as she and George hid among the beeches lining the London road. It was past midnight, and even as she watched the limp leaves were turning crisp with frost. She wondered once again what on earth had convinced her that highway robbery was a good idea. Madness was the only reasonable explanation for resorting to such extreme measures, no matter how desperate they had become.

It was partially George's fault. As children, she and her brother had been captivated by his tales of the robber gangs on the Heath and he had taught them both how to ride and shoot, much to her parents' chagrin. As she had stared at the last few copper coins in their deflated purse, the Heath had seemed a viable means of escaping debt and starvation. But now, as George stood by her side in the dark, looking as defeated as she felt, but showing the same loyal doggedness that had kept him by her family's side, she knew she could not do this.

She was just opening her mouth to speak when she heard it—a distant rumble, separating into the staccato

of hooves and the uneven rattle of wheels. George gave
a quick nod and swung into his saddle as if mere days
rather than twenty years had passed since his last raid.
Sari scrambled into hers, her heart jerking unevenly and
her body alert. This was it; there was no turning back.
When the carriage was close enough for them to see the
mist rising from the horses' breath, George dug his heels
into his mare's flanks, and Sari urged her horse after him,
just as they had practised.

'Stand and deliver,' George called out as Sari's horse
skidded to a halt in the middle of the road. The coachman,
finding himself staring straight down the silvery rim of
a pistol, pulled hard on the reins. The four horses twisted
and whinnied in protest, but finally the whole steaming,
huffing contraption shuddered to a halt barely two yards
from her extended pistol.

The back rider diligently jumped off his perch, weapon
at the ready, but George clipped him on the head with his
musket and the man crumpled. The coachman made a fu-
tile grab for his shotgun, but Sari disabled it with a well-
aimed shot. With a horrified look at the mangled wood and
metal, the coachman raised his hands shakily.

Sari turned her attention to the carriage, moving her
mare to cover George. She heard a muffled shriek from
inside and smiled grimly. A woman. Hopefully well jew-
elled. Perhaps this would be their lucky night after all.

The two inhabitants of the carriage hardly shared Sari's
optimism. Lord Crayle was tired and the tedious social
rituals at the Stanton-Hills' ball had reminded him why
he tried to avoid such events as much as possible. Unfortunately, his sister Alicia's debut in society required his
occasional attendance. The last thing he felt like dealing
with at the moment was footpads. It was sheer ill luck that

these particular footpads had chosen that night, that road and their carriage. He had spent a third of his life getting shot at by the French and would have been happy to remain on the right side of firearms for the rest of his life. Unfortunately, fate apparently had other ideas. His only consolation was that at least he was better equipped to handle this unpleasant situation than Alicia and her usual chaperon, Lady Montvale.

'Do something, Michael,' Alicia squeaked from the corner of the carriage to where she had shrunk at the explosion of the shot.

Michael sighed. The blinds were drawn, but he had little doubt the momentary silence would soon be rudely interrupted.

'What precisely do you suggest I do, Allie?'

'I don't know. You always think of something.'

That last statement was a depressing truth. As head of the large Alistair family he had indeed always 'thought of something'; as major in the Ninety-Fifth Rifles during the Peninsular War he had always 'thought of something'; and now as advisor to the government and one of the founders of the Institute aimed at preventing foreign intrigue on British soil he always 'thought of something'.

'There is no need for heroics, Allie,' he said reassuringly, reaching over and giving her hand a squeeze. 'I had rather hand over my purse than get into a shooting match, especially with you in the carriage.'

'But, Mama's brooch! I would never forgive myself if they took it.'

He groaned inwardly as he registered the brooch pinned to her lace of her bodice. It had been their mother's favourite ornament and the thought of some greasy footpad wrenching the delicate and very ancient Celtic cross apart for its emeralds and diamonds was repugnant.

'What the devil did you wear that for?' he said impatiently even as he moved into action. He tugged off his greatcoat, tossed it in an ungainly pile on the seat facing him, and plucked a pistol from the coach pocket.

Alicia was about to retort hotly when the door was pulled open and a giant of a man filled the frame, musket in hand.

'Your valuables, if you please, sir,' he said in a deep voice.

Michael considered how best to deal with this rather large-looking person.

'My purse is in my coat.' He nodded at the lump of cloth on the seat opposite. 'If you will allow me to reach for it…?'

The giant grunted. 'If you don't mind, sir, I'll do that myself. If you'll sit well back, sir,' he continued, keeping his musket trained on them.

Michael did not mind in the least. Polite chap, he thought sardonically as the giant cautiously leaned over to reach for the coat, allowing Michael a view of the other rider illuminated by the carriage lamps.

Michael took a deep breath before he moved. It took no more than a few seconds to slam the butt of his pistol against the back of the giant's head with his left hand while he grabbed the man's weapon with his right. He took aim at the other rider outside and fired the musket.

The giant slumped to the floor at his feet, but to his frustration the rider was still in the saddle, his pistol now trained straight at Michael. Michael quickly switched his own loaded pistol to his right hand, aiming back. He cursed silently. He was sure he had scored a hit.

'It throws right, sir,' said the rider calmly. 'It is always risky to borrow someone else's firearm.'

He almost faltered at the voice and he heard his sister

give a faint squeak of surprise. It was deep and intentionally husky, but most definitely a woman's voice and a cultured one... He contained his surprise and focused on the
problem at hand.

'It seems we are at an impasse,' he said after a moment.

'Indeed,' the robber replied laconically, not appearing
the least bit concerned. 'Still, I am sure we can reach an
understanding.'

He marvelled at the steadiness of her aim. It was no
simple feat to keep a pistol firmly trained for any length
of time. Nevertheless, he had little doubt he had the advantage. He heard a moan from outside, no doubt from his
servant reviving. Surely she realised there was no way she
could win this standoff? And yet she sat there calmly, apparently unconcerned. An 'understanding'. An outrageous
idea flickered through his mind. The giant groaned at his
feet. Obviously, he had not hit him hard enough. The man
must have a head like a rock.

'An understanding?' he queried politely.

'It is late, sir. I have no doubt you and...the lady...are
anxious for your bed.'

Michael's hand tightened on his pistol at the insinuation.

'You let my friend go and toss his musket after him and
we will let you be on your way.'

'That is a rather generous hand you are dealing yourself,' he replied.

'You have some use for a pre-war musket then, sir?'
she asked mockingly.

He paused, interested in testing this further. The idea
had settled like a butterfly on a blade of grass. It was still
tenuous, but it had potential.

'What would you say to another arrangement? You run
along and I will keep your big friend. I will even give you

a pound for him. You could buy two better highwaymen
at the price—'

He was cut off as a bullet tore through the squabs,
inches from his head. He had to hold himself back from
returning the compliment, with more extreme effects. He
kept his arm firm despite the heat of sudden rage that
surged through him.

'I don't sell out my friends,' she bit out.

Her voice shook slightly as she swiftly pulled another
pistol from her saddle and cocked it. He saw her arm waver
again as she raised it. She was tiring, he realised, his calm
returning. He had tested her and he should be happy that
she had exceeded his expectations.

'Miss, now be good and take yerself off, as the gentleman said,' the giant said from the floor, surprising them
all.

Michael decided to cut to the chase before they got into
further unnecessary arguments.

'All right, enough nonsense. You, man, get up and step
back. The three of us are going to have a little talk.'

The giant hauled himself up and groggily stepped back
onto the road. Michael stepped down after him. He knew it
was a risk, but he had a feeling he understood the param-
eters of this particular game. As he descended, he noticed
the mangled remains of his coachman's rifle that lay on
the road and his brows rose in appreciation. So that shot
had not been mere luck.

'Higgins, unhook a lamp for me and back on the coach
with you. And, McCabe—I want you to pull up the road
some twenty yards and wait for me there.'

'My lord?' The coachman faltered.

'I believe I was clear, was I not?'

'Yes, my lord.' When he employed that tone his men
knew it was best to act swiftly and without argument.

With a lamp in one hand and his pistol in the other, Michael faced his assailants. He surveyed the woman first. She had lowered her firearm and was resting it on the pommel of her saddle. In the lamplight he caught the glint of light-coloured eyes above a black kerchief. He bent to set the lamp carefully at their feet and noticed something else. A small dark puddle on the ground just by her horse. The giant noticed it at the same moment.

'You're hit, miss!' he exclaimed.

'Not hit. Grazed. I am perfectly fine.'

Michael stared at the rider. Up close he could see she was smaller than he had expected. And she had sat there holding him marked throughout this whole episode with a bullet wound. His resolve grew. This could prove extremely interesting.

'You should see a doctor,' he said mildly.

'Of your offering? Make sure we go healthy to the gallows? No, I thank you. What the devil do you want?' The veneer of politeness faded and he could hear the edge of pain in her voice. He decided to move quickly to his proposal before she fell off her horse. He had much rather they depart under their own steam.

'I have no intention of seeing you to the gallows. In fact, I have a business proposition for you, young woman. I would like to offer you a job at a government institution I help operate and where I believe your particular skills may be…useful. It is all above board, if that has any appeal. And with good pay. Twenty pounds a month to start with and more if you prove suitable.'

Sari stared down at the madman standing before them. Now she knew what they meant when they said 'mad as a lord'. Or was it 'drunk as a lord'? And yet he had hardly appeared mad or foxed.

It had seemed endless, but the whole affair had probably not lasted more than a few minutes. The numbing throb of pain in her arm told her she would pay a price for her bravado in holding her ground. This man had knocked out George and taken his shot with a speed that had completely taken her off guard. If it were not for George's relic of a firearm, they would both either be dead or be on their way to the local magistrate. The thought sent a chill through her. Not merely for them, but for her brother Charlie.

From her limited experience, she'd thought of all aristocrats as indolent—men more concerned with cravats than with fighting skills. This man was probably an officer from the wars. Trust her to hold up someone of his calibre.

She inspected him more carefully. Until now she had focused on him so intently she had hardly registered anything about him apart from the most crucial facts such as his firm aim. Now she could see he was tall, a few inches short of George's six and a half feet. In the half-darkness she could only make out the main lines of his sharply cut features. The lamp at their feet accentuated deep-set eyes, a tight mouth and clearly defined chin and cheekbones. She tried to lock all of those into one image, but it escaped her. She knew she was tiring. The throb had spread to her fingers and deep into her chest. She wished he would go so she could get home and lie down.

But a job, above board, with good pay. Offered by a man, a lord according to his servants, whom they had just tried to rob and whose carriage now sported a bullet hole courtesy of her pistol. He was clearly demented. She decided to humour him. Anything to get rid of him.

'It sounds most appealing…my lord,' she added as a slightly mocking afterthought.

Ignoring the nervous movement of her gun, he reached into the pocket of his coat.

'This is my card. I am usually in during the early morning. And you may bring your…friend here if you feel the need for protection,' he offered drily.

He moved to hand her the card, then with a glance at the rigid way she was now holding herself he handed it to George, who took it promptly.

'I am quite serious about this. If, however, you decide not to accept my offer, I hope you have memorised the coat of arms on my carriage as I would rather not run into you two again.'

The smile he gave them made Sari's hand clamp on to her pistol more firmly. It was neither pleasant nor unpleasant, but it was unequivocally a warning.

'What on earth were you doing? What if they had killed you?' Alicia demanded as he re-entered the carriage.

Michael gave her a reassuring hug and settled back into the relative warmth of the carriage. He didn't envy the poor devils. Highway robbery was cold work.

'I do not think they were intent on blood.'

'Not…*not intent on blood*? What on earth is that then?' She indicated the hole by his head.

'That, my dear, is ventilation,' he said lightly, but he relented as she began to splutter. 'It was a good foot from my head, as it was meant to be. I thought them quite… interesting. I merely wanted to find out more. And you still have Mama's brooch, which, if you do not mind, I will put in a nice deep safe at my bank.'

Alicia turned away with a huff, her beauty marred by the petulant moue on her lips. She had not even been ten years old when he had left to join the army and he sometimes felt he didn't really know her. He sighed and turned his mind to the two highway robbers. It was about time the Institute recruited a woman. He would discuss it with Anderson when they met for their game of chess the following day. His lips curved in anticipation of his friend's response. Poor Anderson.

Chapter Two

'By all that's holy, Michael, you were lucky to have escaped with your lives!'

Michael frowned ruefully across the chessboard. He had tried to keep the story to the barest minimum, but perhaps it was the fact that Alicia had been with him in the carriage that had shocked Anderson. He was well aware that his mild-mannered friend was becoming increasingly enamoured of his spoiled little sister. Under other circumstances he would have been delighted at the connection. John St John Moncrieff Anderson, or Sinjun to his friends, was possibly the best man he knew, but his sweet temper might not be the best match for Alicia's wilful nature.

He and Anderson had been friends since going up to Eton as children and they had both served in the army, though in very different capacities. Anderson had been one of Field Marshal Wellington's aides-de-camp, and while he had witnessed much of the carnage of war at the great commander's side, unlike Michael he had not participated in its bloodier aspects. It was precisely for this reason that Wellington, aware of the connection between them, had asked Michael to take a role in setting up the 'Institute' for the War Office.

'I've been campaigning for thirty years now, Crayle, and I've no stomach for another war,' Wellington had told Michael. 'You know what I mean more than Anderson would. He's a good man and one of the best minds for organisation I've had the pleasure to work with, but I need someone on the spot who knows what it means to get over rough ground as lightly as possible. I know you have other fish to fry now you've decommissioned, but this new venture needs everything you learned with the Ninety-Fifths. You've always been able to get your men to follow you into the mouth of hell, the devil knows how, and some of the men you'll be recruiting won't be easy to manage. Will you do it?'

Faced with this direct approach, Michael had found it impossible to say no. He sympathised with Wellington's wish to avoid future wars more than he would have admitted to the commander he admired so much. He was still paying a heavy price for going into those mouths of hell, as Wellington had called them. The thought of being responsible for other men's lives again, and the inevitability of failing them, was something he preferred not to contemplate. The nightmares had mostly faded, but not the memories. He had consoled himself with the thought that this was a substantially different battlefield.

He shook off these thoughts and inspected the chessboard. Apparently Anderson had been even more distracted than he.

'Pay attention,' he remonstrated. 'You just left your poor bishop completely exposed.'

'Never mind the bishop! You might have been killed!'

'For heaven's sake, Sinjun. I told you they had no intention of shooting anyone. They were damn amateurs.'

'It didn't sound so amateurish to me.'

'Not in execution, perhaps, but I would have heard, and

so would you, if there was a woman highway robber on the
North Road. They cannot have been at it long.'

'Well, from what you said, she was not the one who was
supposed to be doing the talking. For all we know she may
have been at it for years…'.

'Unlikely, but still, that is beside the point. We both
agreed after the Varenne incident that you could use some
females at the Institute. She is perfect for our troop of
spies.'

'Agents, not spies,' Anderson corrected absently as he
withdrew his bishop. 'And I was thinking along the lines of
an actress available for the odd job and so were you. What
the devil will we do with a female criminal?'

'The same thing we do with the male criminals. Train
her and use her.'

'They are not *all* criminals!' Anderson protested.
'And…hell, between setting up the Glasgow office and
taking care of that business in Birmingham we're too busy
and shorthanded to deal with new recruits anyway. And
now we find out from the Foreign Office that two Austrian mercenaries are apparently on their way to London.
You yourself said that finding out what they plan to do
here is a top priority.'

'Any more information from the Foreign Office or from
the ports?' Michael glanced up from his inspection of the
intricately carved wooden pieces.

'None. Stimpson assured me he has his best Austrian
contacts on alert for information, but all we know is that
they are being sent on behalf of one of Metternich's closest friends and that they are to receive their orders from
someone in London. And he said it was the merest chance
they found out even that much. Apparently someone is
being very careful.'

'I don't like it. Junger and Frey are the best, or the worst, of their lot. We need to find out why Metternich is sending particularly vicious mercenaries onto English soil and who they are working with here. I came across Junger's work in France once and it wasn't pretty. The thought that they might even now be in London... We need to find out what they are here for. And who on our side of the channel is paying their shot.'

'Well, you see why we can't be distracted just now,' Anderson said, almost imploringly.

'Well, with any luck, she won't show up,' Michael said reassuringly and drained his port. 'Come, it is no fun winning when your mind isn't on the game. We need to leave anyway or we'll be late for our meeting with Castlereagh.'

Anderson stood up swiftly, clearly happy to dismiss the thought of being saddled with a female highway robber.

Sari would have been happy to dismiss the idea as well, but the throbbing of the bullet graze to her arm was a constant reminder. George, too, had become uncharacteristically obdurate. He had placed the lord's card prominently on the single table in the seedy rooms they could barely afford at the poorer edge of Islington and for two days she had done little but stare at the stark black letters proclaiming 'Michael Julian D'Alency Alistair, Viscount Northbrook, Earl of Crayle, of Grosvenor Square, London'. The name had begun to take on a singsong quality in her mind. It was madness, she told herself. They would probably find it was a hoax at best, a trap at worst.

George had disagreed. Two evenings after their failed escapade, he had come home from his job at the hostelry and had sat with her and his wife, Mina, at the table as they mended their well-worn clothes to the accompanying noise from the tavern next door.

'I've done some asking, miss, and he's solid. I know it's

not what your ma would have liked, but she never thought we'd find ourselves in such a tangle, neither.'

Sari felt the familiar mix of guilt and panic rise up in her again like a sickness. She let her throbbing arm rest for a moment before picking up another shirt from the pile.

'If only Papa had lived, we might still have been able to earn enough to get by.'

'Aye, and I'm sorry Mr Trevor's gone, but he never was the same after your ma passed. I've as much reason as anyone to be grateful to him and your ma for taking me in all those years ago, but I call a spade a spade and he had no business leaving the work and the worry to you all those years while he drank himself and his money under every night. He should have at least seen you married and then you might have had a husband's helping hand with Charlie.'

She smiled somewhat crookedly.

'To be fair, he did try when we returned to England after Mama died. We have it on excellent authority that I'm not marriage material.'

Mina snipped a thread and reached for another pair of socks from the pile before her.

'Mrs Ruscombe and her kind are no authority you should be listening to, Miss Sari,' she said in her soft voice. 'Now put that down and let your arm have a rest, do.'

Sari shrugged and laid down her sewing thankfully. 'Everyone else listened. Hector certainly did.'

'Moresby was a weak young fool,' George said roughly. 'And your father was an even greater fool for not taking him to account for shying off instead of having at you for not being more ladylike like your ma.'

She flinched. Even four years later, the memory of that confrontation still hurt.

'It wasn't completely his fault. He was…still upset about Mama.'

Mina, usually taciturn, surprised her by looking up with unaccustomed fire in her brown eyes.

'Don't wrap it in clean linen, Miss Sari. He was dead drunk most days and nights and feeling sorry for himself. If anyone had the right to feel sorry for themselves over your ma's passing. it was you, miss. I'm as grateful as any for what your pa did for my George, but it was the outside of enough watching him neglect his duties and you having to do all them translations when it should have been him all along. You are more a lady than that snooty Mrs Ruscombe ever was, even when you was in breeches and going on about politics and the like with your pa's cronies in the desert. Your ma knew that well enough. No one knows better than me she wanted back to her life in England, but I know she was prouder of you and Master Charlie than of anything on this sainted earth and never regretted a moment of what she had with you two. And if that Mr Moresby was fool enough to have his mind made up for him by the likes of Mrs Ruscombe, well, good riddance, I say. So!' she finished, plunging her needle into the pincushion with alarming violence.

George grinned appreciatively at his beloved's outburst.

'That's right, love. You have at them.'

Sari wiped away the tears that had welled up. She hated crying, but she was just so tired. She knew George was right—she had to do something. George's meagre pay as an ostler was barely enough to cover their living expenses and certainly not enough to continue to fund Charlie's schooling. Whatever his commitment to her and Charlie, Sari knew it was not fair to expect George to support her and her brother indefinitely. The headmaster of Charlie's school had agreed to give her more time to cover his fees 'in consideration of Charles's significant intellectual promise and personal integrity'. But he had made it clear there was a limit to his generosity and they were fast approaching it. There would be no choice now but to default. Charlie was old enough to work, but Sari felt sick at the thought of him having to give up his dreams. She knew he would never blame her, but she couldn't stand failing him like this. She wanted so much for him.

It was not that she herself had not tried to find employment, but no one was willing to trust a mere woman with the translations her father had undertaken. Her claims that it had been she and not he who had actually done the work had been greeted with amused incredulity. And the employment agencies had been quick to point out that she had none of the skills required to be a governess—she could not sketch, or embroider, or play the harp or pianoforte. It appeared they shared Mrs Ruscombe's doubts as to her suitability as a lady of quality.

It had been desperation bordering on lunacy that had made her suggest highway robbery as a means of survival. More proof that Mrs Ruscombe and her friends had probably been right about her—no matter if her parents had once been, she wasn't quality. Certainly no young woman of quality would contemplate such an offer as the one made by this peculiar Lord Crayle. But twenty pounds a month seemed like a fortune to her after these lean years; it was more than most servants could make in an entire year and much, much more than she could ever dream of making as a governess. It would mean Charlie could stay at school and she could even afford to help Mina and George…

'All right, George. You're right. We'll go to London tomorrow and hope our luck takes a turn for the better.'

George smiled.

'It will, miss. I feel it in my bones.'

Chapter Three

Lord Crayle had just sifted through his morning mail when his butler knocked gently at the library door.

'Two…ah, individuals to see you, my lord,' he announced calmly, staring at a point beyond Michael's left shoulder, a clear indication that these visitors were slightly out of the ordinary, but that he was well accustomed to his lordship's sometimes peculiar choice of guests.

Michael nodded absently.

'Show them in, Pottle.'

At first Michael just stared at the couple that walked in, perplexed. If not for their relative sizes he might not have made the connection with his Hampstead Heath assailants. Michael was above average in height and breadth, but the man who stood crumpling his cloth hat nervously easily outstripped him.

Despite the giant's size, it was the woman who captured his attention. At the moment she looked like a slightly dishevelled schoolmistress. Her pelisse was ridiculously outmoded and, contrary to convention, she had removed her simple straw bonnet and held it dangling by its ribbons. She might at one point have been wearing her hair in a bun, but the golden-brown hair appeared to have rebelled and unwound, and was now held back tenuously with a ribbon. It looked surprisingly lush against the drab grey pelisse and it framed an unusual, heart-shaped face with a determined chin. But her eyes were her most arresting feature. They were gently slanted beneath arched brows and a strange mixture of blue and green. Right now they were narrowed as she seemed to be caught between apprehension and nervous amusement.

Michael realised his guests were becoming increasingly uneasy at his silence and he waved them to the two chairs that faced his desk.

'Please sit down. I trust your arm has healed?' He turned to the woman, one brow cocked.

Something flashed in her eyes, but she smiled politely and took the seat he indicated.

'Perfectly. I thank you for your concern.'

He ignored the slight sarcasm in her tones and focused on the voice. His memory had not deceived him. It was deep and cultured. Without the asperity it could be seductive. It was hard to reconcile her obviously high-bred tones and perfect posture with the highway robber who had placed a bullet a whisper away from his temple. But it was most definitely she and she was turning out to be better than he had expected.

'Good. I am glad you decided to accept my offer. I admit I was not certain you would.'

'We have accepted nothing yet, my lord. You were rather sketchy about the details…'

He almost smiled at her haughty tones.

'I can see this may be as arduous as it was back on the Heath. I apologise if I am being difficult,' he said with mild amusement.

To his surprise, instead of raising her hackles further, she appeared to relax.

'Surely, my lord, you can appreciate this is a rather... uncomfortable situation for us? Perhaps if you told us what you want, we could all proceed more quickly?'

Very good, he approved silently. Perfection, down to the faintly coaxing smile that tilted up one corner of a rather pleasing mouth. Not a bad little actress at all.

'Very well. My offer is simple.' He continued, 'I am part of a government agency and we need a woman in the ranks. I think, given your skills, you might be suitable.'

'What precisely would I be required to do?'

'You would take part in certain official operations aimed at protecting crown and country. We will obviously train you and develop the necessary skills, but most importantly, you would be expected to follow whatever directives your superiors give you. If you accept, I will provide more details. Until then I am afraid you will have to take my offer at least partly unseen, as I am accepting you rather on the same terms. Which reminds me, I would like to know your names. Your real names.'

He saw the hesitation in her eyes.

'My word on it that I have no intention of handing you over to the authorities.'

He met her probing gaze evenly, watching as doubt changed to resolution in the peculiar green-blue depths. But as she still hesitated, the giant leaned forward and spoke for the first time since they had entered.

'My name is George Durney, my lord, and this is Miss Sarah Serena Trevor, but we have only ever called her Miss Sari.'

Michael smiled at the annoyed look the young woman shot her companion. Obviously she would go by nothing as commonplace as merely Sarah and Serena was as inappropriate a name as he could imagine for such a mercurial creature.

'What if I agree, but you then decide I'm not suitable for this…agency?' she asked abruptly.

'If we decide at any time during your initial training period that you are not suitable, we will give you three months' salary and part ways.'

'And the pay?'

'As I mentioned before, twenty pounds a month to start, including whatever costs you incur as part of the job. You should find accommodation close to the Institute…'

He paused, wondering if they might be lovers. He didn't know why that possibility had not occurred to him before. The man was older, but probably no more than forty. It was possible.

'Is it just the two of you?' he asked brusquely.

'Also my wife, sir, and miss's younger brother, but he's away at school,' George stated.

Michael ignored his faint relief at the giant's response. He noted the woman's change in expression, her shoulders pulling downwards, as if the weight of responsibility was physical. Her lips parted slightly, but she said nothing and he noticed for the first time the soft fullness of her lower lip. He shifted slightly in his seat, annoyed by the sudden tension in his body. He was assessing her as agent material, not as a potential mistress.

'Very well, the pay should be enough for all of you. If…' he deferred to her with a faintly sardonic bow '…you decide to accept our offer.'

Sari forced herself to straighten in her chair, inspecting the man facing her. In the dark, with her nerves singing with fear and pain, he had appeared to be a giant and a devil. His size was still formidable, but in daylight his threat was more refined.

Firstly, he was too handsome…no, perhaps *handsome*

was not the right word. In the dark the shadows had painted his face in harsh angular lines. The full light of morning streaming through the windows only softened those lines a small degree. His eyes were deep-set and glinted with a strange grey she found hard to identify. His mouth was tightly held, the tension apparent in the grooves that bracketed it. He had a perfectly sculpted nose and cheekbones, the only features that she could actively label handsome. The rest of him was far too forbidding, too challenging.

His black hair was cut short and simply, unlike the artfully curled fashions that were now common, and his clothes were equally subdued and tasteful. There was no ostentation about him or about the room in which they were seated. It was blatantly his space. The walls were lined with books, but there was none of the haphazard air that had characterised her father's studies. Apparently he controlled his environment with as much rigidity as he held himself. A sudden twinge of pain throbbed in her arm. Seeing him in the light of day made her all the more aware that he could have killed her that night.

'Had I not been a woman, would you have taken that second shot?' she asked suddenly.

'Yes,' he replied, his mocking air disappearing instantly, his eyes unequivocally telling her the same. Their colour was not as dark as she had thought. A rim of slate grey held in a paler ice. The combination was disconcerting, almost feral.

Sari shifted back slightly in her chair, removing herself from the intensity of his gaze. She rather thought it was not the smartest thing to do, putting her fate in his hands. He would use her thoroughly for his own purposes with little thought to the consequences. He was a man with an agenda and she was merely a small means to his ends.

Still, what option did she have?

'Very well.'

He lifted one eyebrow at her laconic response. Then he half-smiled and pulled a sheet of paper from his desk.

'Good. I will give you an address. Arrive on Monday morning and ask for a Mr Anderson. He is responsible for the new recruits. Meanwhile, here is a draft on my bank for twenty pounds.'

It was Sari's turn to raise an eyebrow—she was surprised he trusted them not to simply disappear with his money. Then she saw the faintly disdainful look in his eyes, as if he knew precisely what she was thinking. Her sense of helplessness and fear shifted into a surge of anger at this cold, unyielding man who dangled salvation with little concern whether she took it or took herself to perdition.

A perverse, rebellious demon took hold of her and she stood up and strode briskly to the desk. Even as she saw his disdain turn to wariness, she extended her hand, the abruptness of her gesture making a mockery of its polite antecedents.

'A pleasure doing business with you, my lord,' she said.

Michael stood up, unhurriedly, inch by towering inch, making her hand look very small indeed. Just as she thought she would have to withdraw it, he reached out and grasped it in his. A rush of heat rose up her arm and she was peculiarly aware of the texture of the large hand that held hers; it was firm and warm and calloused and it seemed to engulf more than her hand. She was swamped by the same mixture of fear and anticipation that had rushed through her on the Heath. She tried pulling away, but he did not immediately let go. Finally, he released her hand slowly, and she felt each finger as it grazed her palm.

Despite the fact that she stood closer to him now than she had ever been, his voice sounded distant.

'As you said: a pleasure.'

Sari breathed in deeply, picked up the address and draft and strode out without another word, followed by George.

Michael remained standing after the door closed behind them. He flexed his right hand. That had been a mistake. He had merely been responding to her aggravating bravado, but the moment he had grasped her hand every nerve-end had gone on alert. He had felt for a moment just as he had before a battle, every sense and instinct ready, focused on danger and survival. It was a ridiculous response to a mere handclasp.

He had a premonition that perhaps this was not his best idea. She was too independent for their purposes. They needed someone who could follow orders. Then he remembered her stone-cold focus as she had aimed the pistol at his head, even as blood dripped down her arm. He had to face the fact that she was as good as they were going to find. The fact that she brought out the worst in him and that she clearly disliked him was beside the point. After all it was Anderson who was primarily responsible for new recruits, not he. Hopefully, by the time she went through her training she would have learned some discipline. He turned back to his correspondence. He would keep an eye on this experiment. Just enough to make sure she didn't turn the whole Institute on its head.

Chapter Four

That evening he found Anderson at Brooks's Gentlemen's Club, lounging behind a newspaper in his favourite chair in a quiet corner by the tall windows overlooking St James's Street.

'My highway robber paid me a visit today, Sinjun,' Michael said casually as he sat down next to him.

'You sent her away, of course,' Anderson said hopefully, folding his newspaper.

'Not at all. We are to expect a visit this Monday morning. Unless she absconds with my twenty pounds.'

'Michael, you cannot be serious. What on earth are we going to do with her? I thought we agreed it wasn't suitable.'

'We agreed to no such thing. I merely said that with any luck she would not show up. It seems your luck is out. Don't be so negative, Sinjun. She might prove useful.'

Anderson leaned his forearms on his knees morosely, and Michael tried not to smile. Unlike Michael, Anderson had no sisters and he had always been diffident around women. Though he had frequently professed to being in love with some pretty girl or other in his youth, he conducted his liaisons the same way most men dealt with the nursery—he enjoyed himself once he was there, but usually found an excuse to postpone his next visit.

'Then you take responsibility for her,' Anderson said finally. 'You always seem to know what to do with women... and stop grinning, that's not what I meant. I mean they're always comfortable around you and you just don't seem to care.'

Michael's grin widened.

'But I care a great deal, Sinjun. That's why they are comfortable with me. And I don't know why you say you don't know what to do with them. I seem to remember you falling in and out of love with some fair maiden or another every term whilst we were up at Oxford.'

It was Anderson's turn to grin.

'Everyone was falling in love then. Except you—I remember how offended I was when you told me to stop making a fool of myself and just go and get the job done.'

Michael laughed.

'Well, it was damn exhausting, listening to you go on about Jane, or Sophia, or Anthea or whomever. I was trying to study and you'd be reading your maudlin poetry out loud. You were lucky you *were* too timid to ask any of them to marry you, otherwise you'd probably have at least ten children by now.'

'Anthea! I'd forgotten her. Lucky is right. She'd have made my life a living hell. But I still want to get married. Do you really not want to?'

'Thankfully, I don't need to, now that Chris has two healthy sons. He's much better suited to managing Crayle Hall anyway. He lives and breathes estate management. If the estate and title weren't entailed I'd hand them over without a qualm, except that he's too proper to consider such a flouting of convention.'

'For heaven's sake, one doesn't marry just to produce

an heir. I mean, there's love, and companionship…and I don't mean the kind of companionship provided by someone from the muslin company,' he added with asperity.

Michael smiled affectionately at his friend.

'I have no idea what you're talking about when you talk about love. And frankly neither do you. I would wager you can't even remember the names of all the women you've been in love with. It's just a fancy name for unrequited lust.' The smile faded. 'And when it's something more than that it's usually destructive. My father was in love with my mother and look where that got them. All I can remember was his jealousy and her misery. You saw what it was like when they came to the Hall. Sometimes I think you had the best of it with your parents being away in India for all those years. You only had to see them once a year.'

'If that. I much preferred spending the school holidays with you lot, though I do admit your parents did put a damper on our fun when they would come down from London. I never understood why your father always was so jealous. She was far too sweet and timid to ever stray.'

'They were both fools,' Michael said dismissively. 'Thankfully they rarely stayed for long.'

Anderson laughed suddenly. 'I just remembered how he used to line you and Chris up the first day they arrived and quiz you about your achievements at school like a drill sergeant. No wonder you always excelled. I was always terrified he would put me in the line, too.'

'If we'd had any courage we would have told him to go to hell,' Michael said with a self-deprecating smile.

'Well, you did eventually, I suppose. Enlisting in the army amounted to the same thing. It definitely wasn't what he planned for you. But that's not the point. Not every marriage is like your parents'. And even if you don't believe in love, then what about children? Isn't that a good enough reason to marry?'

Michael could indulge him no longer.

'It was bad enough being responsible for Letty and Christopher and Allie or for my men during battle, but at least they are their own masters in principle. I've done my share of being responsible for other people and a damn poor job of it too often. I have Lizzie and my father and more of my men than I care to count on my conscience and I don't need any more opportunities to let people down, especially not those who are wholly dependent on me for their survival and wellbeing.'

Anderson gaped at him.

'Good God, Michael, your father had a heart attack and overturned his curricle with Lizzie in it. If anything, it's his fault that your sister broke her back in the accident. You weren't even there!'

'I might as well have been. He was so furious when I told him I was joining the army that if he could have disowned me he would have. He made it clear that if I left I wasn't to come back. Don't tell me the fact that he had a heart attack the next day was unrelated.'

'It's still not your fault. And as far as I can remember he'd already had one heart attack years earlier and the one that killed him in the end happened much later when you were already in Spain. Were you responsible for those two as well?'

Michael shrugged. Even with Anderson he had no intention of touching this particular wound. He had already said too much.

'We are straying from the point, which is that there is no reason why you can't deal with Miss Trevor. In fact, she might be just what you need.'

'You make her sound like a medication, or a trip to Bath to take the waters.' Anderson grimaced.

Michael laughed. 'I hope it's not as bad as that.'

'Fine. At least tell me what she is like. Big and vulgar?' Anderson asked despondently.

'Not at all. I would wager she is a gentleman's daughter, though I haven't the faintest idea how she ended up on the wrong side of the Heath. I will leave the family history exploration to you. I have a feeling she will answer your questions more readily than mine since she and I did not exactly hit it off. As for size, she is a small thing, a couple inches shorter than Allie, I would say.'

He sipped his whisky, watching with amusement as a faint bloom of colour spread across Anderson's cheeks at the mention of Alicia. He wished his friend had more stomach when it came to women so he could follow through on his obvious attraction. No wonder he was horrified at the prospect of being saddled with Miss Trevor. Michael wondered how he could make her sound more acceptable, then decided it was best for Anderson to be forewarned.

'She is quite pretty which could be useful. Very direct—in fact, painfully direct. A bit of a shrew, I think, but clever and quick to grasp what is good for her. From her behaviour on the Heath she appears to have an inordinate amount of loyalty for her silent giant friend. I have no idea how they ended up working together in such dubious circumstances. Another piece of the puzzle for you to uncover...'

Anderson sighed. 'I hate puzzles.'

Chapter Five

Sari stared at the neo-classical grey building with its simple entrance. There was no distinguishing plaque. Just a number—eleven—by the wooden door. She glanced up at George who stood beside her, hands on hips.

'I'll go in with you, Miss Sari.'

She patted his arm. 'No, George. If this is the place, I'm going in alone. I won't have you be late for work. It's a long way back to Islington.'

George frowned down at her, wavering.

'It's all right, really it is,' she said with much more confidence than she felt. 'You can wait here and see me safely inside, but it is about time I stood on my own two feet.'

Without waiting for his response, she crossed the narrow empty street and pulled at the bell pull by the door. The door opened so promptly Sari took a step back in dismay.

A very tall, elderly man inspected her, not unkindly.

'Ma'am?'

'I…I was told to come… My name is Sari Trevor and…'

'Ah, of course, Miss Trevor. Do come in.' He stood back, indicating a long corridor. Sari glanced over her shoulder, sending George a quick smile before stepping inside with an assurance she was far from feeling.

'My name is Penrose, ma'am. If there is anything you need, you have only to ask.'

'I...thank you, Mr Penrose.' Sari smiled nervously at this rather sweeping statement.

'Here is Mr Anderson's office.' He knocked on the door and opened it. 'Mr Anderson? It is Miss Trevor. And Lord Crayle asked to be informed if she arrived. I will go and fetch him.'

Even in the midst of her confusion, Sari noticed he said 'if' rather than 'when'. Clearly the earl had not completely trusted her not to just disappear with his money. She took a deep breath and tried to focus on the man who had stood up from his desk. She had expected someone like the earl, but he was almost his antithesis. He was good-looking, but in a pleasant, unthreatening way, with kind blue eyes and very light brown hair. He did not look at all like a government agent.

'Thank you for coming, Miss Trevor. Please sit down. Did you have any trouble finding us?'

'I... No, we found it quite readily.'

'Ah, good. Very good.'

He hesitated, and Sari realised in surprise that he seemed as nervous as she. Her own thumping heart calmed slightly and she smiled encouragingly.

'It was a bit of a leap of faith. I was afraid I might arrive and there would be nothing here.'

He gave a short, surprised laugh, visibly relaxing, and sat down again.

'A leap of faith indeed, then. Knowing Michael... Lord Crayle, I assume he was less than forthcoming with details?'

Sari smiled at the understatement. It was a relief that this man was so different from the earl.

'He mentioned something vague about being agents for

crown and country—' she replied hesitantly and broke off
as the door behind her opened and Lord Crayle stepped
into the room. She straightened slightly and nodded at him.

'Lord Crayle,' she said properly.

A faint look of amusement glimmered in his eyes as he
came to lounge against the bookcase by Anderson's shoulder. Then the light from the window was behind him, en-
casing him like a dark monolith.

'Miss Trevor,' he responded with equal politeness.

Anderson cleared his throat and smiled.

'Good. Well, let me be a bit more explicit. First, what
do you know about the state of Continental Europe today?'

Sari gathered her thoughts. Growing up in politically
sensitive parts of the Continent and the Levant had made
her very politically aware and she hoped she was not too
far out of touch with Europe's rapidly changing landscape.

'It seems rather chaotic to me at the moment. Napoleon
is still causing trouble, even from St Helena. The Bour-
bons are struggling to make believe they control France.
Metternich is playing the Prussians against the Russians.
And Tsar Alexander is hoping to transform Russia into a
linchpin of the Continent's security through a Holy Alli-
ance. And we in our turn have our finger in every pie, trying to make sure none of them succeeds in their attempts
to run the show.'

Sari saw Anderson cast a quick glance at Michael but
his friend's gaze was on her, inscrutable.

'That is a pleasantly concise and accurate summary of
our murky political environment,' Anderson said appreciatively. 'Part of our role here is to help nip in the bud any
attempts to foment trouble on British soil by any of these
European powers. Now that it is no longer so clear who
the enemy is, some of our statesmen are becoming easy

prey to manipulation for one cause or another. Our role is to identify potential troublemakers and limit the damage.'

The significance of what he was saying, of what she was being offered, hit Sari with almost physical force. She hadn't even known such things existed. Compared to the possibility of being part of such an organisation, her wish to become a governess seemed hopelessly tepid. She had no idea yet what might be required of her, but she wanted to be part of this with an instinctive passion. She had always wanted to do something significant, meaningful, but it had never seemed a feasible possibility. And now, in a mere few sentences, a whole world had opened up before her and she knew her life was never going to be the same. She stared at the sweet, soft-spoken man offering her salvation and bit her lip against the surge of unaccustomed joy that was thrusting up from inside her like a butterfly struggling against its chrysalis.

'Now, why don't you tell me something about yourself? A bit of family history and how you ended up robbing people on the Heath?' Anderson continued. There was no condemnation in his tone, and Sari, still caught up in wonder at the gift that had descended on her, was surprised by her willingness to answer his question.

'There is not much to tell. My father was an orientalist and we grew up travelling between antiquity sites in the Levant. We were supported mostly by another orientalist, Emilio Cavalcatti, a Sicilian who used to be a successful mercenary. Emilio and my mother both died during a typhoid epidemic when I was sixteen and my father, my brother and I returned to England. My father took in translations for a while. He…died three years ago. By then there wasn't much left. We sold what we could, and George worked, but it wasn't enough for us all.' She dropped her gaze as shame dimmed her excitement.

'It might seem strange that I…that I allowed George to support us, but he and Mina have always been family. He was part of a robber gang when he was a boy and it was thanks to my parents that he escaped that life and met Mina. He and Mina insisted Charlie remain in school, no matter what it cost us. And I did try to find employment, but I was unsuccessful. But matters… Anyway, we were about to sell a few of our last belongings, including the pistols Cavalcatti had given us, when I told George we could make more money using them than selling them. After all, he already knew what to do… I know it sounds mad and immoral, but we were desperate. It actually made sense at the time. That is all.'

She ended her story and glanced up. Anderson's kind blue eyes were full of compassion, and she ducked her head again for a moment, feeling suddenly weary and close to tears. Anderson extended a hand as if to comfort her but withdrew it as Lord Crayle moved closer to the desk.

'What skills do you have?' he asked abruptly, and she drew herself up.

'Skills? I… Well, I can't embroider or play an instrument if that is what you mean.'

Michael laughed. 'Drawing-room accomplishments aren't quite what we are looking for here. I meant anything that might be useful. I already know you are a decent shot. Anything else?'

'I believe I am more than a *decent* shot, my lord,' she stated with some hauteur, and his smile deepened for a moment. 'Aside from that, I am very good with languages and I can fence…*decently.*

'I can pick locks, too. I suppose that may be useful?'

'Very useful indeed,' Anderson replied faintly.

'Where precisely did you learn those skills?' Michael asked levelly.

Sari wished he would move away from the window so she could make out his expression. He was hard enough to read as it was, but standing there like a shadow only made him more intimidating. She was used to reading people, but she had no idea what he was thinking.

'Mostly from George and Signor Cavalcatti. Cavalcatti taught us all how to fence and how to pick locks. He had a Smith-Caldwell safe he would travel with and we practised with that. It was a bit smaller than yours, Mr Anderson,' she added with another mischievous smile.

Anderson sat back in surprise.

'How did you know…?' He glanced from her to the bookcase that hid his safe.

'You didn't secure the bookcase fully. I can see the gap reflected in the window behind you. Cavalcatti had a safe with just that distinctive grooved dial with the silver rim.'

Michael considered Anderson's clearly admiring gaze. Given his initial reluctance, he had fully expected to have to ease his friend's way through this interview, but he had clearly underestimated her. He wondered if her behaviour was calculated. If it was, it was brilliant—that mixture of forlorn waif and mischievous young woman was very effective in exciting Anderson's protective instincts. Calculated or not, objectively she suited the Institute's needs. But her disclosures were highlighting some serious problems as well. Despite her rather peculiar upbringing and unconventional skills, she was clearly less experienced than her performance on the Heath had seemed to indicate. Her obvious intelligence might also be as much a drawback as a benefit. But it was more than that. Something less tangible was bothering him. There was something too intense, too driven about her.

Out of nowhere he remembered a children's book he

used to read to his brother and sisters. It had been about the adventures of a young page, Cedric the Small, an unlikely little hero whose determination to save his family from the evil Knight Mercur led him both into and out of trouble. It was a classic story about brain over brawn, but it had been Cedric's mix of warmth, vulnerability and mischief that had made him so appealing. Miss Trevor was like a female version of Cedric. And Cedric got into trouble as often as he managed to get out of it.

'So you think you can open the safe?' Michael asked curtly, forcing himself back into the moment.

'Yes. I would need a glass, preferably crystal. Would you like me to try?'

He smiled slightly at her defiant confidence. And at the fact that he believed her. He doubted she would promise what she didn't feel she could deliver.

'Not at the moment. Deakins for one will be delighted to meet you.'

'Who is Deakins?'

'He's one of the instructors here. He specialises in all sorts of less-than-legal skills. In fact, I think the two of you will deal admirably.'

Anderson shot him a quelling glance, but Michael ignored him.

'Perhaps we should tell you what you will be doing over the next few months. Before you become an operative agent, you will undergo a schedule of training, including a physical regimen, politics and a variety of other topics. If you complete your training to our satisfaction, you will join the others on whatever mission is assigned. Are you still interested?'

Sari nodded, trying and failing to keep her mouth prim. She didn't even trust herself to speak yet, she was so excited.

'Good. Anderson will take you around to meet the instructors. And I believe I mentioned that you should find accommodation not too far from the Institute,' Michael added practically. 'Penrose can help.'

'Thank you, I will keep that in mind, Lord Crayle, but George knows London quite well.'

'Will you come with us?' Anderson asked him as they stood up.

'No, I have some matters to attend to. I just received the latest reports from Denby and I want to review them. Come by when you're done, Anderson. Enjoy your tour, Miss Trevor.'

She nodded hesitantly as he walked out. She was almost relieved he wasn't coming with them. It was hard to be natural under the scrutiny of his cold grey eyes. Or rather, it was hard to be unnatural. She wanted so much to present herself as competent and worthy, but somehow she felt too…exposed when he was watching her. It would be easier to concentrate with just Anderson there.

An hour later Anderson entered Michael's office, and Michael glanced up from the documents he was inspecting.

'Well?' he asked, taking in his friend's relaxed smile.

'Well, you were right and I was wrong. I think she'll do just fine. I'll work on a schedule for her as of next week. Give them time to find accommodation and settle in the area first. What an extraordinary young woman…' He trailed off.

'A nonpareil,' Michael said drily after a moment. 'So, what training are you considering?'

'Well, given our experience in the Varenne case, I thought she should brush up on her social skills. She's not completely green—she spent three years in country society out near Oxford, but she was never in London society, so the finer points of Almack's are lost on her. Albermarle will be happy to have someone to train aside from the usual roster of ruffians as he calls them. Paretski on politics and Antonelli will start her on a physical regimen including fencing. And Deakins, of course.'

'Of course. Sabotage.'

'All right, Michael, what's wrong?' Anderson asked with uncharacteristic bluntness. 'This was your idea, but you're about as enthusiastic as mud.'

Michael considered his words carefully.

'I'm not sure we can trust her.'

'If you don't trust her, then why the devil did you recruit her?'

'That is different. I trust her to carry out whatever mission you impose in full faithfulness to you and King. I do not trust her...motivations.'

That was not quite the word he was looking for. In fact, now that he thought of it, he could not completely pin down where his feeling of unease stemmed from. Perhaps it was the undefinable quality of his discomfort that bothered him most about her. He preferred to know where the threat was coming from.

'I think you're just miffed she almost put a bullet through you.' Anderson snorted.

'You're probably right,' Michael conceded with a self-deprecating smile. 'What a blow to my self-esteem!'

'She's meeting Antonelli at ten o'clock next Monday morning,' Anderson said after a moment. 'You should come by and have a look.'

Michael felt a surge of affection for his gentle, always-conciliating friend. It was a constant wonder to him that someone so averse to discord could derive such pleasure from managing a band of spies.

'I will be there.'

Chapter Six

The following Monday morning Michael closed the door of the *salle d'escrime* quietly behind him. Both Antonelli and Sari were completely concentrated on each other and the clash of their foils. Antonelli was clearly a master fencer, guiding and correcting without a word or a discordant gesture. What surprised Michael was that the young woman was good, if unorthodox in her style.

She wielded her foil like a sabre, with long smooth strokes, coming in from irregular angles and forcing Antonelli to adjust in ways Michael knew must feel unnatural for him. What was most surprising was that the old master had not pinned her down, disarmed her and given her an earful for not respecting tradition. He had certainly done so to Michael during their first encounter some twenty years ago. Where the devil had she learned this?

Finally, Antonelli took the full offensive, drove her back off the strip and flipped her foil out of her grip with a powerful lunge.

'*Touché, et bien touché.*' She saluted with a breathless laugh, her cheeks flushed.

Antonelli gave a slight bow, his greying hair still almost perfectly coifed. Only the faintest sheen on his face denoted he had exerted himself at all.

'*Et bien joué,*' he returned. 'But you need a firmer grip, *signorina.* And there is too much swing in your arcs. Each should be an inch shorter; do not waste energy slicing the air. *Fluide, mais courte.*'

She stood to attention as Antonelli rattled off his criticism, fully focused, her hand unconsciously responding to his comments. Michael smiled. So far it seemed the only person who brought out her prickliness was himself. He took a couple of steps forward away from the door and they both looked up in surprise.

'Michael!' Antonelli exclaimed, using the Italian pronunciation, *Mee-ka-el.* 'But how wonderful! You are neglecting me, my friend.'

'Not intentionally, Marco. I have been busy up north.' He took Antonelli's hand warmly.

'Always busy. It is not good for the soul, young man.'

Michael smiled at Antonelli's mode of address. He had never stopped calling him *young* and he wondered what it would take for him to change.

'Well, I'm willing to make amends, if you have the time. And if Miss Trevor hasn't worn you out, *old man.*'

Sari was startled into an involuntary gurgle of laughter at the mock concern in the earl's tone.

'I tried. Desperately,' she said. 'I think Signor Antonelli could have disarmed me in his sleep.'

'I sympathise,' Michael replied. 'For the first year I trained with this taskmaster I don't think he looked up once from the book he was reading except to tell me the session was over.'

Sari laughed and Antonelli shook his head, smiling indulgently at them.

'It was surely a very enthralling book…' she offered as palliative, but Michael shook his head.

'I appreciate the attempt at redemption, but it was no such thing. I didn't even rank above Reverend Trull's *Sermons on the Decay of Modern Morals*.'

The absurdity of Antonelli being engrossed by such a book was clearly too much for Sari, and she burst out laughing. Antonelli chuckled.

'Enough of that, you two. Now, *signorina*, you had better run and change if you are not to be late for Mr Deakins, he of the gunpowder and smoke. It would not do to upset him.'

Sari was reluctant to leave, but she smiled at the two men and left the *salle*. She was intrigued by the change in Lord Crayle from her previous encounters. It was hard to reconcile his light hearted self-deprecation with the tight control or the watchful disdain that had characterised their previous meetings. She wondered which of these personas reflected the real man.

Certainly she knew he was anything but inept at fencing. Anderson had casually mentioned that Lord Crayle was one of the country's finest fencers. She had the instinctive feeling that although he might laugh at himself, it was because he could afford to. He might not be as forgiving towards himself if he were to fail in earnest. She would do well to remember that under his unexpected and disquieting charm was the cold and ruthless focus she had witnessed back on the Heath.

She shook her head, as if to free it of these thoughts. This was her first day at the Institute and she needed to be focused. She had to keep reminding herself this was real. From the moment she had returned to tell George and Mina that she had indeed secured employment, everything had been a slightly unreal whirl of activity. George had done them proud by using his contacts at the hostelry to find a lovely little house for rent in Pimlico with one room for her, one for George and Mina and another for Charlie when he would come to London for the holidays. The sorry sum of their belongings had not taken up half a cart, but Mina had inspected their new rooms with a sweeping martial gaze. When she was armed with a fistful of coins, Sari had full faith it would not take Mina long to turn the modest furnished house into a warm home.

But perhaps the most rewarding moment had been sending off the letter to Charlie's headmaster, including the arrears in fees, and another to Charlie himself telling him of their new direction. She had never told him how low they had sunk and she was not going to tell him how they were now evading debtors' prison. She wanted him happy and safe and unworried. For the first time in years she felt a return of optimism.

Back in the *salle*, Antonelli stood by as Michael prepared for their practice.

'Strange things wash up on your shores, young Michael,' he observed after a moment. Michael looked up from the foils he was inspecting. *Strange* was one way of putting it. The way Sari swung between that impulsive, uncalculated charm and a mix of hauteur and bravado was disconcerting.

'Stranger than even I thought. What did you learn about her?'

'She said a Sicilian had taught her to fence many years ago. Along with a few other tricks, I would hazard, knowing Sicilians. She has grace and daring, but not much method. It will be a challenge to discipline her.'

Michael wondered if her good behaviour would survive the test of time once the word *discipline* was mentioned.

'Good luck. She may be more intractable than first impressions indicate.'

Antonelli dipped his head to one side, considering. 'Perhaps, and yet I think she will meet me on this. It will be interesting to see what differences there are between men and women...' He paused as Michael faintly quirked a brow in amusement.

'Now, now, none of that nonsense,' Antonelli admonished. 'However, my friend, I am also wondering what will happen when the men notice a young and most attractive female is wandering the corridors?'

Michael frowned. 'I hadn't considered that. Perhaps we should keep her schedule different from the others. All these young fools need is an object on which to focus their bravado and easy infatuations and we will have mayhem on our hands.'

'I seem to remember a time when you, too, were young, my friend,' the older man pointed out mildly.

'A long time ago. Still, that is why I know the danger we may be stirring by dropping an unsuspecting female into the middle of this pack of wolves. And I have a feeling she is definitely unsuspecting.'

Michael picked up one of the foils absently, weighing it in his hands. The more he learned about this woman, the less comfortable he became. When he had thought she was clearly a criminal of sorts, making use of her seemed acceptable. Now that it was becoming clear she was just a young woman forced to desperate measures by circumstance, the thought of placing her in compromising or dangerous situations was less palatable. He was surprised that strait-laced Anderson, of all people, wasn't objecting on the same grounds.

'I hear she might be a good shot,' Antonelli said, interrupting his thoughts. 'Will O'Brien be training her in the gallery or will you?' he continued as they took their places on the strip.

Michael glanced up with some surprise. He hadn't considered the possibility. O'Brien usually trained the men when they first arrived in the rudiments of shooting while Michael did training outdoors with the most promising of the lot. Still, if she was as good as her shots on the Heath had indicated...

'I don't know yet,' he answered evasively. 'We'll see. *En garde.*'

Antonelli echoed his salute and Michael cleared his mind of anything but the other man's sword.

Chapter Seven

Stepping out of Deakins's class on the fourth day of her training, Sari was forced to admit the earl had been right about her and Deakins. He was her favourite instructor thus far, only after Antonelli. She loved his lab of chemicals, lock picks and trunks of disguises. There must be more of the lawbreaker in her than she cared to admit. She headed towards the clerk's office, wondering what other training had been assigned for her that day.

Penrose glanced up as she entered his small room by the main door.

'Ah, miss, follow me, if you please,' he said pleasantly.

Sari followed. She knew part of her role in the Institute included not asking where she was being taken or what she was expected to do, but as Penrose led her through a door and down a set of winding stairs, she began to feel slightly uneasy. They descended farther and farther, and she had the slightly hysterical thought that perhaps they were going to dispose of her in some underground dungeon.

'Almost there, miss,' Penrose said as the stairs ended and they proceeded along a narrow corridor. Rather than echoing, his voice became peculiarly muted. Finally, they reached a broad door and he motioned her ahead of him.

She entered and her mouth opened in awe as she realised she was in an underground shooting gallery. Three
long lanes stretched some thirty yards up to a well-lit wall
where life-size dummies were propped up on posts.

'Thank you, Penrose; you can return upstairs now.'

She whirled around in surprise. She hadn't noticed before, but at the back of the room there were several tall cab-
inets, and Lord Crayle stood beside one, pulling a wooden
case from one of the shelves.

Alone with the earl, Sari stood waiting uncertainly. He
didn't address her, just placed the case he held on a long
table by the wall and opened it. Inside was small elegant
pistol in dark wood and brass.

'This was designed for the Cavalry, so it is light, easy
to reload and not likely to go off if it's jarred. Here, it's
loaded and cocked. Just try not to shoot at me this time,'
he added with a sardonic half smile as he handed it to her.

She took the pistol gingerly. She felt unusually nervous
holding it. Perhaps it was because she had never been to a
shooting gallery before. With Cavalcatti they had always
practised outdoors. More likely it was because she suddenly felt painfully nervous around the earl without someone's mediating presence. Their light-hearted interchange
in the *salle* seemed very far away, almost as if it had taken
place with someone else, and now here again was the same
man who had faced her across the desk in his study. Hard
and watchful and knowing.

She tried to ignore his presence at her back and concentrated on the pistol. It was light and smooth and the brass
moulding on the handle was cold. She raised it and sighted
the dummy at the end of the lane where she stood. Then
she took a deep breath and let it out slowly as she aimed,
just milking the trigger the way Cavalcatti had taught her.

She took her shot. There was a muted explosion and the dummy jerked with a disconcertingly lifelike movement.

'I thought it would be louder,' she said, lowering the pistol.

The earl was looking towards the dummy with a slight smile.

'Deakins designed special walls to absorb the noise. Right in the chest. Not bad for a new gun. So you did miss me on purpose that night; I was wondering.'

'That was the first time I actually shot at someone,' she said.

'Lucky you. I hope you never have to do so again,' he said lightly, but there was something in his voice that made her look up sharply.

'Shall I clean and reload it?' she asked to break the silence.

He nodded and watched as she skilfully cleaned and reloaded the pistol. Her next practice was speed-shooting at a target marked with various coloured circles. After each reload he stated a colour and she took her shot as quickly as possible. Lord Crayle watched without comment. Then, after five circles he took the pistol from her and handed her a different one.

'Here, try this on the dummy. This is one of Joe Manton's finest. It's weighted at the tip so there is less recoil.'

'Is this a duelling pistol?' she asked, forgetting her nervousness slightly. He smiled, amused by her patent awe.

'Similar. I'm sorry to disappoint you, but there aren't many duels nowadays. Mostly it is just shooting at wafers.'

'I'm not disappointed,' she replied, returning his smile. She took the pistol from him. The barrel was longer and she could tell it was built for accuracy. 'I never understood why men would consider honour worth risking their lives for. Shooting at wafers makes much more sense.'

She aimed at the centre of the dummy's head and took her shot.

'I like this one better,' she said as she lowered the pistol.

'It obviously likes you just as much,' he responded, his eyes narrowing as he took in the damage to the dummy's head. 'I was intrigued to see just how good you were after your performance on the Heath.'

'And...?' she asked, raising her chin slightly. At least in this arena she knew her worth.

'Passable.' He shrugged.

'Passable!' she exclaimed, offended and annoyed, and he laughed, his face lightening.

'You're an excellent shot and you know it. You don't need me to tell you that.'

She flushed in pleasure at the compliment.

'May I try another?' she asked diffidently. She did not want this particular session to end quite yet.

He hesitated, then shrugged.

'Fine. But we need to correct your stance. You may not approve of duelling, but whoever taught you clearly did; that's a duelling stance. Standing sideways makes you a smaller target, but it's not always as effective for aiming, especially for long-distance shooting. Here, take this and come over here.'

Sari took the pistol he handed her and followed him to the second lane.

'Now aim as usual.'

She raised the pistol and waited, trying to stay calm. She felt the warmth of his body behind her and flinched slightly when his hands grasped her shoulders, moving her so that her body faced more squarely down the lane.

'I know this will feel strange to you,' he said calmly. He was so close she could feel his breath warm against her nape. His hand moved to her upper arm, closing on it gently, urging it back.

'Move your right foot forward just a bit and lean your shoulder back. Your arm should be at an angle to your body, like this.'

She obeyed, but she could feel her arm starting to shake, and she took a deep breath, trying to focus on nothing but the pistol.

'Relax.' His voice was soft and low, soothing. 'Remember, this is easy for you.' His hand moved down her arm slightly, steadying it. His hand felt warm through the thin fabric of her dress. He was mere inches behind her now and the contrast between the coolness of the underground cavern and the warmth radiating from his body was disorienting.

'Breathe and take your shot.'

She closed her eyes briefly, trying to clear her mind. Then she sighted and shot. She wasn't used to the stance and didn't hold her ground as well as usual when the recoil propelled her back. She came up hard against the earl's body and he steadied her, one hand on her waist and the other on her outstretched arm.

'He only lost some hair,' he said with a low laugh that flowed over her, mixing with her thudding pulse. 'It will be easier next time. You need more weight on your lead foot.'

Sari didn't respond and didn't move. She knew she should say something. Or step away. Anything. She wet her lips and waited.

The silence stretched on for a moment, then his hand slid down her arm, brushing over her hand as he grasped the pistol and pulled it away. Then he stood back and turned away.

'That should be enough for today. Do you remember how to get back upstairs?'

She nodded.

'Thank you,' she forced herself to say.

'There is no need to thank me. Practise that stance until it feels natural.'

She nodded again and turned, heading for the stairs. She needed air.

Michael took out the gun-cleaning kit absently and began cleaning the pistols with the ease of many years of practice. At least he now had an answer of sorts to Antonelli's questions. Training women was distinctly different to training men.

If he had needed any further proof of her lack of experience, he had found it in the unconscious way she had accepted his touch. A more experienced female would either have made a show of modestly demurring or made the most of the situation. He almost wished she had done one or the other.

In some respects, training her had been easier than he would have thought. As she had been with Antonelli, she had been attentive and immediately responsive to his corrections. It wasn't until the recoil had knocked her back against him that he had realised he had been far too comfortable touching her.

With his hand on the warm curve of her waist there had been a moment when it had seemed natural to pull her back against him, lean in and follow the faint, exotic scent of jasmine he could detect beneath the acrid smell of gunpowder. It had only been for a moment, but long enough to convince him he had been right—she was trouble. The fact that she was innocent trouble only made it worse.

Chapter Eight

Towards the end of Sari's second week at the Institute her muscles were protesting after the unaccustomed exercise of daily fencing practice and her mind was crammed with assorted chemical formulas, social dictums and political doctrines. But she didn't regret a second of it. For the first time in her life she felt a real sense of purpose. She told herself it was ridiculous to feel as if she truly belonged in this strange environment after little more than a week, but she just did.

She could hardly believe that a few weeks ago she had been drowning in fear and poverty and now her life had taken on a whole new glow of hope and purpose. Every evening she, Mina and George would sit in the small parlour of their new lodgings off Wilton Street in Pimlico, revelling in its cosy warmth. She had even allowed herself to buy two new books. She loved seeing the pleasure Mina derived from her new sewing basket and the relaxed smile on George's face as he watched his wife stitching, his newspaper in hand. She only wished Charlie could be there with them, but at least when the school holidays arrived they would have a safe, warm home waiting for him. Every now and again the amazed realisation would bubble up in her—for now her family was safe and cosy and content. She was so happy it was almost suspect.

The only faint cloud on her sunny horizon was one she would hardly allow herself to consider. Every day as she entered the Institute and reported to Penrose for her daily schedule, she indulged in the guilty hope of another summons to the shooting gallery. When none came she told herself firmly that it was better that way. She needed to be focused and confident, and as much as she enjoyed the shooting range, there was something about the earl that left her raw.

Other than that, she was increasingly comfortable with her instructors and their strange whims, but Antonelli and Deakins were still her clear favourites. Between her other assignments she spent every moment she could in the *salle* or in Deakins's lab. Therefore in the break between her classes that Thursday she entered the *salle* as usual to see what Antonelli was doing. She almost withdrew when she realised Lord Crayle was fencing with O'Brien, one of the senior agents, while Antonelli and another agent, Morton, watched. The two men fencing didn't notice her as she entered, but Antonelli smiled and motioned her to silence as she leaned back against the wall to watch.

They were both skilled, but Crayle was clearly a fencer of a higher order. His moves were economical but powerful and within the first few minutes it was clear O'Brien would lose the encounter. Antonelli kept well back, not making his usual comments.

Sari was enthralled by the grace of the game. It was obvious Crayle could end it when he wished, but he withdrew from each potential hit, allowing O'Brien to recover. His skill matched even Antonelli's, who had been fencing for over thirty years. And yet there was something more dangerous in his swordplay, a contained force that threatened to break through with each riposte, all the more formidable for being held in check.

Their shirtsleeves were rolled up and Sari could clearly see the muscles of the earl's forearm tense and flex with each strike and parry. From watching the foil she found herself drawn to the dance of shadows along his arm. It glistened with perspiration, its firm lines cording as he drove his opponent back. It was as if she had never seen a man's arm before, had never realised it must have a unique texture with the unyielding muscle, the smooth glide of warm skin and silky dark hair.

A peculiar heat rose in her, just skimming the inside of her skin and leaving her strangely cold outside. Her gaze was glued to the fluid, brutal moves as O'Brien was consistently destroyed, stroke by methodical stroke. She held her breath as Lord Crayle pushed O'Brien back almost to the edge of the strip. Then suddenly, with a slight flick of the earl's wrist, O'Brien's foil went flying and landed with a clatter at Antonelli's feet.

O'Brien leaned over, resting his hands on his knees as he drew breath.

'Damn you for a pitiless bastard, Major.' He chuckled breathlessly as he straightened, pushing back a damp lock of hair from his forehead.

'You asked for the meet, O'Brien,' the earl pointed out with a smile, leaning the tip of his foil on the strip and flexing it.

'So I did. Never did have an ounce of sense in this Irish brain of mine,' O'Brien returned good-humouredly as he bent to pick up his foil. 'Here, Jack, care to try your luck?'

'No, thank you,' Morton answered with a slow smile. 'I'd rather go and swim in a peat bog.'

The two men had turned to Morton and noticed Sari.

'What are you doing here?' the earl asked, clearly sur-

prised by her unexpected appearance, and Sari pushed
herself away from the wall nervously.

'Nothing. Just watching.'

'Shouldn't you be in some lesson or another?' he asked,
slipping his foil back into the rack.

'I am between lessons, my lord,' she answered, somewhat offended by his indifferent tones. 'I am not playing
truant if that is what concerns you.'

'I see no harm in the *signorina* observing, Michael,'
Antonelli interjected mildly.

'There is harm in her wandering around the Institute
at will,' Michael replied, a hint of impatience entering his
voice. Sari felt strangely hurt.

'I was not *wandering* around,' she replied. 'Signor Antonelli said I could watch the other men fence if I wished.
There is nothing wrong with that.'

He didn't even turn to acknowledge her comment, but
continued to address Antonelli. 'You shouldn't encourage
her to come in here at any time other than for her lessons.
For her own protection.'

Sari felt a humiliated blush wash over her and tried to
salvage some dignity.

'If you have issue with anything I do, you may direct
it to me, my lord.'

Michael turned to survey her.

'May I, now?' he asked with deceptive smoothness.
'Very well, Miss Trevor. I have issue with you entering the
salle at any time other than for your lessons. Or frankly
going anywhere in the Institute except where you are ex-
pressly directed to go.'

Sari knew she should not react. The three other men
were watching the exchange with interest and her sensible
side told her the best thing to do would be to accept his rebuke and leave. But the gap between his behaviour towards

her in the shooting gallery the previous week and his current dismissal hurt more than she could understand. Perversely, a wave of angry resentment bubbled up inside her.

'I hadn't realised I posed such a threat to the Institute's well-being. Should I be flattered?'

She almost quailed under the sudden blast of anger that appeared in his eyes as he moved towards her but she stood her ground. As he drew closer she could see how his damp shirt adhered to the muscles of his broad shoulders. The same peculiar feeling licked at the edges of her stomach again. She really was not comfortable with him being this close.

'I am not sure you quite understand the terms of your employment here, Miss Trevor,' he said silkily as he stopped a mere couple of feet from her, forcing her to tilt her head back to meet his eyes. 'I distinctly remember saying that you are here to follow whatever directives your superiors give you. That means when you are told to decamp, you decamp. Is that sufficiently clear?'

Sari squared her shoulders.

'Quite clear, my lord. However, you did not tell me to decamp.'

'Did I not? I would have thought the sentiment expressed with sufficient force. However, since you seem to require it made explicit, I am telling you to do so now.'

Sari raised her hand in mock salute.

'Right, Major. One decampment coming up.'

She turned on her heel and made sure she closed the door very quietly behind her, despite the urge to slam it.

Michael turned back to the room and the three other men pulled back their grins.

'You were trifle harsh on the *signorina*, Michael,' Antonelli expostulated.

'She can take it,' Michael replied.

'Sure and she can.' O'Brien chuckled. 'There must be some Irish blood in the lass. She gives as good as she gets, that one.'

'You must be more forgiving with her, Michael. It takes time to adjust to this place,' Antonelli said.

'I make no demands on her above what any one of us would make for any other recruit,' Michael retorted curtly, pulling another foil from the rack. 'Antonelli?'

The old master shrugged and took his place on the strip opposite him.

'As I understand it, the purpose of the Institute is to train our agents to be as effective as possible. I do not personally believe the best way of achieving that is browbeating a young woman into obedience.'

Michael flicked his foil through the air angrily. She had them all wrapped around her little finger. And in a mere couple of weeks. Why the hell was he the only one who realised this was a problem?

'She is miles away from obedience, Antonelli. And without a more serious measure of it she will be of no use to us at all. *En garde.*'

Fencing with Antonelli always required all his attention and the session helped to clear Michael's mind and focus it back on the most important matter facing the Institute at the moment. Their contacts at the ports had reported that both Frey and Junger had been sighted arriving in London, but discussions with the Foreign Office had yielded no more intelligence about the reason for the presence of the two Austrian mercenaries on English soil. There was some conjecture that they had been hired to protect the personal interests of an Austrian banker based in London, but Michael was unconvinced. He knew they had to intensify their efforts to find out what the two were doing in the city.

* * *

After the fencing match he went in search of Anderson and tracked him down outside Deakins's office.

'I want to update you on our two Austrians. Is Deakins in there?'

'I... Uh, no... I just saw him upstairs with Morton. Why?'

'Inside.'

Anderson followed him inside Deakins's office and closed the door, his brows raised.

'I met with Castlereagh and Wellington last night to discuss the business we just concluded up in Birmingham and we touched on Junger and Frey. They aren't convinced the two are here for political purposes, but they agreed we should investigate them in case Metternich is using that Austrian bank business as a cover. I asked O'Brien to investigate and he tracked Frey to lodgings above the Black Dog in Southwark last night, but he couldn't find Junger. I have put Morton on to tail Frey tonight while O'Brien goes down to the docks to dig for Junger. We need to know where he is and what he's doing.'

Anderson nodded. 'Fine. Let's hope they're right and this isn't political. From what you told me about Paris, I'd rather their business isn't ours.'

Sari stood silently by the closed door of Deakins's laboratory. After her encounter with the earl she had retreated to her other safe haven at the Institute, well ahead of her lesson with Deakins. She had not meant to eavesdrop on their conversation, but once she had recognised their voices on the other side of the laboratory door, she hadn't had the nerve to call attention to herself.

In fact, within minutes of her defiant retreat from the *salle* she had been swamped by a familiar rise of panic.

The Institute was becoming more than a means to an end, a source of the salary that kept Charlie in school and might even allow George and Mina to start the family she knew they wanted. This was something she wanted for herself. She had never felt such a sense of…rightness in her life. She knew the earl had his doubts about her and her behaviour back in Antonelli's *salle* had probably only added to his reservations. She had to prove herself, and quickly, or they might decide she was more trouble than she was worth.

Perhaps if she could help find this Junger, they might keep her, she thought. Whatever the case, she had best do something soon. She moved to inspect Deakins's closets of disguises. She would need to be inconspicuous and she would need to protect herself. She pulled out the streetboy's coat Deakins had shown her, with its cleverly concealed pockets hiding lock picks and a thin, deadly dagger. It was so much easier being a boy…

Chapter Nine

That evening Sari did not head back to Pimlico. She gave
a coin to a link boy to take a note to George and Mina telling them that she must stay late at the Institute and they
were not to worry. They would, of course, but she knew
George trusted her enough to calm Mina's worst fears.
Then she headed out to Westminster Bridge, calculating
that Morton would most likely cross there on his way to
Southwark. Dressed as a street boy, with a wool cap pulled
low over her face, she was as invisible as the moon on this
overcast night. It was a tedious wait, but at around eight
o'clock she saw the slight, unremarkable figure of the agent
heading south over the other side of the bridge.

She followed at a distance as Morton headed into the
alleyways off Lambeth Road. He finally stopped and settled onto a bench next to a couple of sailors playing back-
gammon outside the Black Dog. Sari crept by and slipped
into the recessed basement entrance of a cobbler's store
and waited. It was cold and damp and she pulled her coat
more tightly around her, comforted by the firm line of the
dagger in her pocket.

Eventually a man in a grey cap and dark coat stepped
out of an unlit doorway by the tavern, heading swiftly

southwards. After a moment Morton followed and Sari eased her way out as well. In Tooley Street, Frey and Morton were swallowed in a large crowd of men weaving down the road in a cacophony of drunken song. Sari hesitated, afraid to be caught up in the knot of drunken men, pushing and shoving. By the time they had moved on, neither Frey nor Morton were anywhere to be seen. Cursing her luck, she turned and headed back towards the bridge. But just as she reached New Cut Road she saw a familiar grey cap moving northwards towards the river. She glanced around the rough crowd which filled the street, but could not see Morton. After a moment she took a deep breath and hurried after the Austrian.

The heavy, rotten smell signalled they were close to the river. The narrow, depressing lanes gave way to dark warehouses and beyond them she saw the first of the unlit piers jutting into the Thames, like black fingers on the dark water. Across the river, the lights of the city glinted murkily and she wished she were there. But she had come too far to stop now.

Eventually even the gas lamps spaced out and then finally disappeared. Occasionally a light spilled out from a warehouse, but then the night closed in again, a palpable presence. Here sight was replaced with the vividness of smells—tar and rotting fish and the cool musty scent of the wooden piers above the brackish odour of the Thames. Rats scraped past her, their slick, naked tails twitching.

She almost faltered, but the man suddenly turned down an empty pier stretching out onto water so dark it might as well have been hanging from a cliff. Through the gloom Sari could just make out the shape of another man seated on a crate at the end of the structure, almost shimmering in the faint damp mist rising off the sluggishly moving water. She sucked in her breath, swallowing a frustrated oath; they were too far away for her to hear anything.

She moved behind a stack of barrels smelling strongly of wood tar and inspected the pier ahead of her. It had recently been widened and raised to accommodate the larger ships coming up the Thames, but the older pier beneath had not been demolished—it lay a few feet beneath the newer structure, narrow, neglected and invisible from the pier above. She inched closer carefully and climbed down beneath the new pylons, onto the older structure. The wood felt firm under her hands and she crawled cautiously towards the men. Below her the dark water swirled and eddied around the wooden beams. To her, with her tautly strung nerves, it almost looked as if it was laughing at her, waiting to pull her into its undulating dance. When she was finally within several feet of the two men she stopped, focusing on the conversation in German above the thumping of blood in her head and the gentle splashing of water.

'…meeting…did you arrange it?'

'Yes. The damn fool won't meet direct. He's sending some lackey. Amateur. If they weren't paying us so well…'

'But they are. Where is the meeting?'

'Nine at the Eagle and Crown.'

'Filthy hole. You always choose filthy holes, Jurgen. I'm getting too old for this business. Idiot English. Very well, let's get this over with. But next time I want see the man himself. I'm damned if we will take directions on the actual deed from a pawn. We need to make sure we can trust him to get us out of here once it's done. That's the only thing that matters.'

'We'll pass the message along tonight. Cheer up, Joachim, after this you will be able to retire.'

'If this damn English weather doesn't kill me first. Very well, I will see you there.'

Sari held her breath as the two men started back towards the shore. Their footfalls creaked overhead and Sari closed her eyes and waited.

When their footsteps finally receded she began to realise how foolhardy she had been. If they had found her, she would now be simply another corpse floating down the Thames with all the other refuse. Even her body might never have been found. Charlie might never have known what had happened to her. Her body started shaking convulsively, but she forced herself to move, keeping to the shadows until she reached the bridge.

She had to tell someone what she had learned. There would be no one at the Institute at this hour, but she had to contact Anderson, or Lord Crayle, as soon as possible if they were to reach the rendezvous on time. Since she had no idea where Anderson lived, she headed towards Grosvenor Square.

Once there, another fact became apparent—she could hardly knock on the front door and asked to see his lordship, dressed as she was. She hurried round to the mews and stared in some dismay at the tall ivy-covered wall that protected his house. With a sigh, she grabbed a fistful of the plant and hauled herself over the wall as quickly as possible. She was definitely earning her keep tonight.

She approached the dim light coming through a pair of long French windows which led into a sitting room. She could see no one there and after a moment's hesitation she selected one of Deakins's hooks and bent down to spring the lock. To her surprise it did not give in to her first attempt and she silently cursed the earl for having to make things especially difficult. He must have had these locks custom made. She took a deep breath, selected another, finer hook and tried again. It took her several long minutes to disengage the lock and, because she was annoyed and tired and the news she had to deliver was burning in her mind, Sari slipped into the room with less caution than was advisable when breaking into someone's home.

Without warning she was half raised off her feet and shoved back against the wall. She gave a shocked yelp and found herself staring up at the earl, whose eyes glinted with the same silvery grey as the sharp letter opener pressed to her neck.

'It's me!' she croaked, tugging off her wool cap with one hand, whilst her other pulled at the arm which pressed her back against the wall.

The dangerous look on his face was replaced by stark incredulity as he lowered the letter opener.

'What the…?' Words failed him for a moment. 'Where the devil did you come from?'

Then he saw the open windows and if anything the look on his face became even more dangerous than when he had first grabbed her. She realised suddenly that he was dressed only in a shirt, with his sleeves rolled up, and one arm was still pressing her against the wall. She knew she should remove her hand from his arm, but she didn't. It was warm and hard under her palm; she could feel the tension in his muscles and she remembered the image of him towering over her in the *salle*, his shirt clinging damply to his shoulders. She shivered even as a flush of heat rose through her.

Michael stared at her flushed face, the tumbled hair and the patched coat she wore. He had been working in the study when he'd heard someone working the lock. The fact that the burglar had succeeded in opening the lock Deakins himself had promised him would withstand even skilled thieves had prepared him for a professional criminal. The last person on earth he had expected was her. He shoved down his shock and focused on one thing. She had broken into his home. She had better have a good excuse, even though he could not imagine any excuse good enough to placate him at the moment.

'Well?' he prompted, biting out the word as if that was all he was capable of enunciating.

Sari wet her lower lip nervously, and decided to get straight to the point.

'I followed Frey. He met Junger and they are going to meet someone at the Eagle and Crown tonight, at nine. It's just a lackey this time, they said. They also said they would demand to meet with the man in charge before they went ahead and carried out whatever it is they are being paid for…'

She felt some relief as she saw she had at least succeeded in distracting the earl from her transgression for the moment. He still had not released her and she tried not to think about the heat of his arm as it pressed against her chest.

'What the devil were you doing following either of them? And how did you hear this? I cannot imagine them standing around in the middle of Piccadilly discussing it. Where was Morton?'

'He gave Morton the slip. They were on a pier in Southwark. I climbed on the pylons underneath it. They didn't see me.' She felt very warm suddenly.

'He gave Morton the slip and you were on the pylons under a pier,' he repeated slowly, and she nodded warily.

He was looking at her very strangely and for once she had no idea where she stood. He shook his head suddenly and as if he had only just realised he was still holding her against the wall, he stood back abruptly.

'We will discuss later both the reasons why you were

following Frey and your method of bringing this piece of information to me. Right now, I want you to sit here quietly and wait for me. Do you understand me?'

'I am not completely brainless,' she retorted, annoyed at his tone.

'Pretty damn close,' he replied curtly and left the room, closing the door behind him.

Released from his presence, Sari felt a wave of exhaustion wash over her. Next time she would go through the front door, or better yet, stay at home and do as she was told, she resolved unhappily. She sat down on a sofa and rested her head on the plush cushions. Just for a moment.

When Michael returned to the drawing room some minutes later, dressed in simple labourer's clothing, he thought for a moment that she had run away. Surely he had not scared her that much. She should not be out on her own at this hour. He scanned the darkened room and his gaze settled on the shadowy lump on the sofa.

She had fallen asleep. He almost laughed at how ludicrous the situation was. She had tracked two highly trained killers to Southwark where one of their best men had failed, climbed under a pier to eavesdrop on their conversation, broken into his home and now she had just fallen asleep as if it was all a bad play.

He walked quietly over to the sofa, debating what to do with her. If it weren't for the obvious impropriety, he would be tempted to leave her there to sleep. Her face was cradled on her arm and the unrelenting blue-green eyes were veiled, the long sweep of her lashes like fans above her cheek.

She looked different in repose, softer. His gaze moved to her mouth. A flash of memory ran through him, a brief picture of the way she had nervously wet her lips before answering him earlier. This was followed by another flash, this time a physical one that ran from his chest to his groin. It was so unequivocal and overwhelming that he leaned forward with rather more brusqueness than necessary, shaking her awake. She almost leapt up as her eyes opened, unfocused.

'I'm ready!' she gasped.

'For what?' he asked drily, and she blinked at him in confusion.

'Come, I will see you home.'

That woke her.

'There isn't time. We have to leave now or we will miss them!'

'*We* are not going anywhere... *You* are going home.'

'No, I'm not. You can't go there on your own! It's not safe.'

He looked down at her defiant face; he had heard the same determined tone in her voice when she had refused to abandon George that night on the Heath. The absurdity of presuming she provided adequate protection against two practised killers had obviously not occurred to her. He felt suddenly unequal to dealing with her. She was right; there wasn't time to take her to Pimlico first and however little she seemed to care for her safety, he didn't want her out at night on her own in such a neighbourhood. The thought of having her await his return here did have a certain appeal, but one which he quashed. He cursed his mind for sending up such uncomfortable ideas and his body for reacting so hotly to them.

'Very well, but you stay beside me and follow my instructions to the letter. Is that clear?'

She nodded without protest, and he pointedly closed and relocked the garden doors.

'Put your cap back on. The servants' exit will be more comfortable.'

* * *

The Eagle and Crown was an unsavoury public house on the border between Spitalfields and Whitechapel, a haven to the dregs of London and not someplace to be wandering around in the dark without a very good reason and even better defences. The streets were narrow and stank of refuse, human and otherwise. During the day the area was crowded with tradesmen, shopkeepers and beggars, but at night it was taken over by whores, sailors, thieves and drunkards. Even the hardiest of Bow Street Runners preferred not to venture there after dusk.

Michael strode through the stench, still annoyed that he had allowed her to join him. This was no place for a young woman, ex-highway robber or not. Although she showed no signs of flagging, he could only imagine she was tired. He himself was glad for the exercise. He needed to rid himself of this nervous energy and focus his mind on the problem of Junger and Frey and their contact.

They finally reached the Eagle and Crown, with its half-broken sign that showed only the Eagle. It was common lore that a thief had stolen the 'crown'. He pulled his worn grey-serge coat closer about him and tugged his cap lower over his eyes, then turned to inspect his companion. She had tucked her hair back under the wool cap and as long as she kept her face out of sight she looked a decent boy. Still, even in the sickly light spilling out from the Eagle's open door, her dramatic eyes drew attention.

Michael sighed. 'Keep your eyes down, understand?' Then he turned on his heel and mounted the warped steps.

Inside the taproom, the stench of refuse was replaced by that of old ale and urine. The smell and press of unwashed bodies was enough to make anyone ill, and Michael doubted that for all her bravado and travels she had experienced this particular brand of poverty, so specific to the seamy centres of large European cities. He felt her grasp timidly at the back of his coat as he wove his way through the noisy crowd and stifled a twinge of concern. Served her right for insisting upon tagging along.

Luckily, he found part of a bench by a long wooden table with a decent view of the taproom and of the stairs leading up to further drinking rooms off an open balcony above them. They had fifteen minutes to wait, and Michael called for two home-brewed beers. One of the most surprising facts about the Eagle and Crown was that it had good home brew.

'Drink slowly,' he murmured as he continued to scan the room over his tankard. 'The last thing I need is for you to get foxed.'

He heard a faint snort of derision from under her cap and smiled grimly.

She was really a glutton for punishment, Sari told herself angrily. She could have been safely at home in bed instead of squeezed onto a warped bench and enveloped in the smell of stale spirits and dirty bodies. She had reacted without thinking, unable to accept the thought of him going alone to track those killers. What on earth had she thought she would be able to do? Now all she had succeeded in doing was alienating him further.

She tried to inspect the room without exposing her face. She felt the moment Crayle noticed Frey by the subtle shift in his body beside her. She inspected the Austrian across the room clouded with smoke from cheap cheroots and pipes. He was unmistakably Teutonic, with sharp cut features and shortly cropped pale hair under his cap. He moved to the other side of the room towards the stairs leading up to the private drinking rooms.

She wondered whether they would follow, but they

merely remained seated for another twenty minutes, watching as quite a few people went up and down those same stairs, none of whom she recognised. Finally, Crayle motioned to her to stand up. She followed him back through the crowd to the door and out into the street. She wondered if perhaps he knew another way up to the rooms. But to her surprise he headed back towards Whitechapel Road. She hurried after him through the rough crowd, wondering what would happen next.

'What happened?' she whispered.

'I saw what I needed to see,' he replied without slowing down.

'What? I only saw Frey.'

'I saw Frey and Junger and their...friend.'

'Who? Someone you know?' she asked, tamping down her excitement.

He did not answer immediately.

'Yes, someone I know; a small fish but an interesting one. I am not quite sure...'

His voice trailed off, and Sari knew that would be the extent of his confidences. He made his way almost absently through the crowd, obviously caught up in his own thoughts. The men and women moved out of his way instinctively, but Sari wasn't so lucky and, trying to catch up with the earl, she bumped into a burly man just stepping out of a tavern.

'Here, you clumsy oaf!' he roared at her, grabbing her and giving her a rough shake. 'Out of my way, boy!' He shoved her towards the street, but she only landed against another man whose arms closed around her, enveloping her in his stench.

'Boy? This ain't no boy, Murphy!' he chuckled hoarsely. 'Here, feel this!'

It had happened so quickly she hadn't even realised

the danger until she saw the sudden intent look on the other man's face. She took a deep breath and brought her heel down as hard as she could onto the man's foot and he gave a wounded yelp, his hold slackening. She pulled away, but the other man she had bumped into grabbed her arm with a beefy hand, grinning down at her from bulbous brown eyes.

'Well, well, we've caught ourselves a little tigress! Now we'll have some sport.'

Before she could act another arm slid around her waist, drawing her back. Instinctively, she knew it was Lord Crayle and she gave a little gasp of relief as he pulled her against him comfortingly.

'Not tonight, I'm afraid, I've already paid for her and I don't share,' he said to the burly man who still held on to her arm. His tones were light, but the menace was there. The look on the man's face turned distinctly ugly. He dropped her arm, but only to draw out what looked like a whaling knife from a sheath inside his coat.

'Finders keepers, toff. Don't make me dirty my knife on you.'

He raised the knife menacingly and Sari's fear lurched into a kind of desperate fury at the thought that he might try to hurt Michael. Without thinking she reached into her coat pocket and pulled out her short dagger. The burly man blinked in surprise, but then burst out laughing.

'Mine's bigger than yours, tigress!'

Before she could react Michael grasped her wrist with a grip of steel, bearing it downwards.

'Give me the knife, sweetheart. What did Madame Bella tell you about cutting people? It's not good for business.'

His voice was still calm, almost comforting, and he pulled her back more fully against him. She could feel the heat of his body and the warmth of his breath as he dipped his head above her to repeat his command, his voice low and firm.

'Give me the knife, Sari.'

Surprised by his familiar address, she forced herself to relax her hold and he slipped the dagger out of her grasp.

'She's one of Bella's? In those clothes?' the burly man asked belligerently, his knife still extended towards them, but with obvious respect. Clearly Madame Bella was a force to be reckoned with in Whitechapel.

'There's no accounting for taste, is there?' Michael said drily as he slipped the dagger into his coat pocket. 'Now if you don't mind, we're running late. Tell these nice men you're sorry you bumped into them, sweetheart.'

She shrugged, slipping into a replica of Mina's heavy cockney accent.

'I didn't mean nothing by it, did I?'

'That's a good girl. Good evening, gentlemen.'

To her relief the burly man gave a snort and stood back. The interested crowd that had gathered to watch the show shifted and dispersed, disappointed.

'Mind your step next time, tigress!' the burly man yelled after them as they moved away.

They walked swiftly and in silence until they reached the traffic of Whitechapel Road. Michael hailed an empty hackney and gave the driver her address in Pimlico. It was only when they had sat down and the horses began the trip westward that Sari realised she was shaking. When the earl spoke it took her a moment to focus on his words.

'What the hell were you planning on doing with that knife?'

He had seemed so casual in the middle of the encounter that Sari was shocked to hear his voice tight, vibrating with anger. She closed her eyes briefly.

'I thought he was going to attack you...' She trailed off, realising how foolish she must sound.

'God help me,' he bit out, pressing the heels of his hands to his eyes. He took a deep breath before he continued. 'Do you realise what would have happened if you had tried to stab him? You wouldn't have lived long enough to be raped! What is wrong with you?'

Sari pressed her shaking hands together. She had ruined everything. She had obviously only succeeded in proving that she was a hopeless case, a mistake. She knew she had no one to blame but herself. In her pride she had sought to prove that she could be as good as any of the Institute's agents. She could hardly believe her stupidity. Now she had lost whatever respect she had gained. This loss affected her more deeply than she could have imagined. She could have no future at the Institute after this escapade. It was over.

The hackney stopped suddenly and he jumped out almost as if he couldn't stand being next to her for a moment longer. She followed, trying desperately to think of something that might stave off the inevitable dismissal.

The narrow streets in the residential area were empty at this hour, with only the flickering light of a gas lamp illuminating them. She started to move towards her house.

'Just a moment,' he said ominously, his hand closing on her arm, pulling her ungently into the small alleyway that lined the back of the houses. She followed, steeling herself.

'You are not to mention anything of what happened tonight to anyone, is that understood?'

She nodded stiffly, not meeting his eyes. His voice was calmer, but she did not delude herself that she was forgiven.

'I want to make it extremely clear that what you did today is not only against everything you were supposed to be learning at the Institute, but that you endangered an important mission.' Even as he spoke she could hear the forced calm give way to anger once more. The next words burst from him, his voice tight and low.

'What were you thinking? Do you think this is a game? Did you really think you could take on two practised assassins or a crowd of drunken brawlers? What fantasy world are you living in? Answer me, damn it!'

His anger and contempt were more painful than the fear of the past hours. She knew it was over, but against all reason she dragged up some anger, determined to find anything to shield her from his scathing dismissal.

'I can take care of myself,' she retorted stiffly.

Michael felt something give way in him at her response. Calm spread through him like the warm seep of blood. It was incomprehensible to him that she could not understand the extent of the danger she had been in tonight. Firstly, she had been within a whisper of having her throat slit by two of Europe's most vicious mercenaries and then of being raped and killed by a couple of East London thugs.

'Can you, now. Can you really.'

It was not a question. He had gone beyond questions. Beyond explanations.

'Show me precisely how,' he invited as he pinned her to the wall. He held both her wrists in one hand above her head, his knee pressed high between her legs so that she was forced onto the tips of her feet. His eyes blazed down into hers.

'I am waiting,' he gritted out.

Sari looked up at him. He was well and truly furious. She had never seen him like this before. He'd been annoyed, dismissive and cynical, but not furious. He was too controlled a person to show fury. And though she hated to admit it, he was right. There was nothing she could do.

'Let me go,' she hissed.

'So soon? I think not. Show me what is up your sleeve. Show me you can damned well take care of yourself!'

His voice was steel sharp and cold and it slashed through her as uncompromisingly as when his foil had disarmed O'Brien in the *salle*.

The best she could do was squirm, but he merely pressed her farther against the wall, sliding his knee down and replacing the pressure with his whole body, half raising her off the ground as his head descended towards hers.

Even if he had given her an opening then, Sari would have missed it in her total shock. She expected an assault, but the moment his lips brushed over hers, the pressure of his body against hers changed. He just held her there for a moment as if waiting for a wave of pain or dizziness to pass, his lips just brushing hers. She was no longer sure what she was supposed to be fighting. Then his mouth moved over hers with a gentleness that was all the more devastating in contrast with the steely grip that held her.

Sari abandoned her struggle, drowning in the heat of his hard body pressed to the length of hers, in the drugging warmth of his mouth as her lips parted beneath it and in the mounting tension that was spiralling from her, responding to every inch of contact between their bodies. When his mouth moved to taste the soft flesh of her neck, her body involuntarily surged against his. Oh, this was what she had wanted, what she had been waiting for.

Somewhere, in a small corner of common sense in his mind, a voice was yelling at Michael to stop. He had made his point in spades. She could no more fight him than push over a brick wall. And she knew it. He should let her go. But with that little mudslide that had propelled him to make his point so physically, he had surrendered his usual control.

He had just meant to demonstrate to her how horrible it was to be incapable of fighting back. That it was no game. But even as he made his point, his body betrayed him. There was no escaping the feel of her body pressed to his, the contour of her breasts rising and falling swiftly, the faint light of the street lamp gilding her lower lip, the sweet softness of her neck and the incredible taste and smell of her. He told himself it was just part of the demonstration, but he knew he was lying. From the moment he had tasted her mouth he knew his agenda had changed. Or rather, perhaps this had been the agenda all along. His body was throbbing with fire, screaming the lie at him, focused only on the tremors running through her he knew had nothing to do with fear. He coaxed her lips to answer him, a groan escaping him as she suddenly gave in, her mouth opening to meet his, letting him taste her fully.

Need burst through him at her surrender and his mind searched feverishly for a solution to the need for immediate privacy. As desperate as he was, he could not take her here in the middle of a cold night on a public street. He released her wrists, sliding his hands under her coat, his fingers brushing the swell of her breasts on their descent to cradle her thighs, pulling her tightly against him.

A shudder racked him at the thought of pulling off her clothes, sliding his hands over her warm skin. His erection pressed painfully against some hard object hidden in Deakins's infernal jacket, only that pain keeping him in a semblance of sanity. He buried his face in her neck again, trying to pull back and regain control, but her body suddenly moved against him as she turned her mouth to brush his neck, sending a dual shock through his body that collided explosively in his chest. He wanted her. He wanted her naked beneath him; he wanted her tasting him beyond that tentative caress… He felt the sound burst from his chest, somewhere between desperation and surrender. And with it came sudden, sobering panic. What the hell was he doing?

Sari's body bucked with response to the sudden, almost primeval growl that burst from his throat and her released arms rose to move about his neck. But then suddenly she was free, her arms sliding weakly to her sides as she leaned back against the wall. He had turned away and his whole body was rigid, one outstretched arm grasping a nearby iron railing with a force that made his knuckles gleam white.

Perhaps it was the memory of the violence from earlier that night that brought her back to sanity. Or perhaps it was just the incredibly foreign sensations that were crashing through her, almost unbearable in their intensity. So she shut them out and took a step away from the wall. He turned to her with an abrupt movement. His eyes met hers for a blazing second before he turned to look away down the street.

'Go inside,' he bit out.

For the first time since she had met him, she did as she was told without comment or delay, leaving him standing by the railing.

Michael detached his hand stiffly and set off towards Grosvenor Square. He had no intention of thinking. None whatsoever.

Back at his house, he opened a bottle of port. He would regret this in the morning, he was sure, but right now he wanted oblivion.

Chapter Ten

He did regret it. The morning light slammed into him when he opened his eyes before his brain succeeded in warning him that doing so was a very bad idea. His mind was a jumble of strange images, leftovers of dreams of trying hopelessly to push his way through a crowd of drunken brawlers as Junger stood above them on a balcony, slowly and methodically throttling a young woman with long honey-coloured hair. With a groan, he turned over onto his stomach, praying for a return to oblivion.

When he next opened his eyes the light streaming into the room was slightly less vicious. He forced himself to sit up and glanced at the clock. It was past nine o'clock. He had to talk with Anderson as soon as possible. And he had agreed to meet Antonelli at eleven. He considered sending a message with his apologies, but then pushed the tempting thought aside. He deserved to be thoroughly thrashed for his stupidity. He might as well let Antonelli do the honours.

An hour later Michael walked into Anderson's office and pulled the blinds shut, to the latter's surprise.

'What...? Michael, what's going on?'

He sat down heavily in the chair across the desk and closed his eyes.

'Keep your voice down, Sinjun, please. My head is splitting.'

Michael sat there for a moment, savouring the silence. His trip to the Institute, short though it was, had reminded him just why he abhorred heavy drinking. Still, he was almost grateful for the drum in his head since it effectively silenced most of his thinking faculties. He concentrated on the problem at hand.

'I saw Junger and Frey meet with Elliot Hamlin yesterday night,' he said at last.

'Hamlin? What would they want with him?' Anderson asked, bemused.

'I have no idea. It makes no sense for them to involve an immature rakehell unless someone is using him as a go-between. But he's a gambler and an unlucky one and he might be in hock to someone who is using this hold to have him run errands. Not the best choice, if you ask me, but perhaps our man has little choice but to use what he has to hand.'

'How on earth did you come across them? Morton reported he lost Frey somewhere near Lambeth Road.'

Michael knew he had to make a decision. It was in his power not merely to expose Sari's reckless behaviour, but also to press Anderson to get rid of her. While his friend was definitely more forgiving than he was, he might be convinced to remove her for her own protection.

'A contact of mine,' he said finally. He would save this decision for later.

'Very well, what do we do from here?'

'Hamlin might be the weak link in this chain. Ask Thompson to find out to whom he owes money and whether he has been receiving funds from anyone. If I think of anything else once my brain starts functioning again, I'll let you know.'

He left Anderson and went in search of Antonelli.

* * *

Antonelli raised an eyebrow as he slipped past Michael's guard after ten minutes of hard fencing. He made his hit and stood back, positioning himself for the next round.

'You are not with me, Michael. I cannot remember the last time you conceded a point so easily.'

Michael smiled grimly. He must be getting old. It would have taken more in the past for him to feel so worn.

'My apologies for being such sad fare, Antonelli.'

'Apologies are not in order. Concentration is. I do not know where your mind is, but it will undoubtedly benefit if you clear it for the duration of our hour.'

Michael's smile changed. Bless Antonelli for his common sense. He saluted his old teacher and made sure he presented a more challenging opponent for the remainder of their encounter. In fact, Antonelli's stricture proved true. At the end of the hour he felt refreshed and the drum in his head had gone silent.

He also knew he had to take the bull by the horns. He had left Sari to stew under the sword of Damocles long enough.

Sari received the summons to Lord Crayle's office just as she was leaving her lesson with Mr Albermarle. A cold wave rushed down to her toes, leaving her feeling slightly ill, but she squared her shoulders and went upstairs. Michael was seated behind his desk and did not rise as she entered. Sari faced him as rigidly as if he was her executioner.

'Sit down, Miss Trevor.'

She obeyed, trying to gauge his tone or his expression, but both were alarmingly neutral.

'You are part of an organisation, Miss Trevor. You accepted that when you accepted our money and our training. Although it obviously does not come naturally to you, you committed to carrying out orders, and by inference never to act without consultation. You are not an agent and you could have seriously endangered the business of the Institute. Do you understand this?'

Sari nodded once. Her muscles were so tight even that small motion hurt.

'Good. I am sure this will never occur again. You had best return to your classes.'

Sari remained seated, too stunned to move. She was sure she had misheard, that she had somehow imagined his last sentence. She was afraid to leave without being certain.

'My lord?' To her shame her voice was merely a whisper.

Michael watched the shock cut through the control that had held her rigid. She had indeed expected to be dismissed. He felt a surge of guilt. He had not realised how important this position was to her, but of course he should have. In all likelihood, that was exactly what had driven her to such reckless action yesterday. She had probably wanted to prove her value. Little fool. His anger melted at her naked fear.

'We have already invested a great deal of time and effort in you and I have no intention of getting rid of you merely because you made one mistake, albeit a serious one. I am sure this won't recur.'

'No, my lord. I…I assure you, my lord.'

He watched intense relief replace her shock. He could only imagine what this was costing someone as proud as her. It had been too long since he had been subject to such a humiliation. She stood up to leave.

'Just one moment, Miss Trevor.'

She paused and looked back, her hand on the doorknob.

'I owe you an apology. What you did was no justification for my actions.' There, it was out. He could see by the sudden return of colour to her pale face that she knew precisely what he was referring to.

'That is all,' he said firmly. 'You may go now.'

To his relief she turned and left without a word. As the door closed behind her he sat back, releasing a slow breath. Surprisingly, he felt better for having apologised. It had made the encounter an issue of little import, an afterthought. Yes, that was the best way to have dealt with it. It would make it easier to forget. Now he had only to determine what to do with her.

Chapter Eleven

Lady Montvale had already rounded off her at-home hour when Michael arrived that afternoon. She gave him her trademark Mona Lisa smile and extended one surprisingly youthful hand that belied her fifty-odd years.

'My dear boy, but how delightful of you to visit. Allie has just left for a ride in the park with the Bennetts, but since you are unforgivably tardy I conclude this is not a social call?'

Michael smiled fondly at the woman who had once been his mother's closest friend and was now overseeing his sister Alicia's début in society. Her knowledge of both polite and political circles had made her an invaluable ally since the establishment of the Institute and he trusted her judgement implicitly. Although both her father and husband had been the staunchest of conservative Tories, Lady Montvale had always had a mind of her own, although she had kept it to herself and to those people who mattered.

'It is business, I'm afraid,' he said apologetically, knowing she preferred honesty. 'I need your perspective on a... problem we have at the Institute.'

'Splendid, I have been pining for something to do. The Season has only started and already I am dreading it. I dearly love your sister, Michael, but playing chaperon is not the height of excitement. So, tell me.'

Michael tried to keep his version of Sari's introduction to the Institute as brief and as neutral as possible. Still, he was not surprised to see the gleam of interest in the lady's eyes.

'Splendid,' she said again as he finished his tale. 'My dear boy, how splendid. A gently born highway-robbing female. And she almost shot you? But how delightful! I must meet her.'

'I would be grateful if you did. I have been trying to think what precisely to do with her. The instructors are all very enthusiastic, possibly too enthusiastic. I need some-one who can give an unbiased opinion and be a…source of influence for her.' He hesitated, wondering how much of his dilemma to disclose. 'She and I don't always agree.'

'I see,' Lady Montvale said slowly, her dark eyes watch-ful. 'Well, first you must bring her to see me. Tomorrow morning if you can. And quite frankly, if she is present-able, then you should present her. I have told you time and again that you need more eyes and ears inside the *ton*, someone who can blend in and pose a threat to no one. What better than a little miss in her London début? Are her looks passable?'

'She is pretty enough,' Michael answered stiffly.

'Good, you know how loose men let their tongues run around a pretty face. If she passes muster, we'll make her a respectable heiress, nothing too extravagant, but enough to rouse interest…'

Michael tried to ease the tension from his shoulders. Having Lady Montvale assume responsibility for Sari and help position her as an agent from within the *ton* might be a perfect solution for all parties. That way she could still be useful while staying out of harm's way. And out of *his* way. Right now it was imperative that he and Anderson focus on Junger and Frey.

'Very well, I will discuss it with Anderson and bring her by tomorrow.'

'Brilliant! Why didn't I think of that?' Anderson exclaimed when Michael presented Lady Montvale's idea the following morning. 'I won't deny it has been bothering me. I know she has all the skills necessary to be a good agent and you will probably think me sadly old fashioned, but I just can't seem to get my mind around the fact that she is gently born. Have you told her?'

Michael shrugged non-committally.

'I was thinking you might. You will explain it better than I could. I need to get something from my office. I've told Penrose to summon a hackney in fifteen minutes. Tell her to meet me downstairs.'

Anderson stared after him with a faint frown, but went to locate Sari and inform her of the new development.

Fifteen minutes later, Michael found her standing by the Institute's front door. He had known any encounter between them would be strained, but she looked as stricken as if she was entering a tumbril on her way to the guillotine, rather than a hackney on her way to one of the leading ladies of the *ton*. She sat rigidly on the edge of the seat with her hands clasped together tensely. He inspected her with a frown, resisting the urge to lean forward and pry them apart. Surely he wasn't the reason she looked so pale and drawn.

'You had better sit back. You'll fall off at the first bump that way,' he said mildly after a moment.

Sari looked up with a startled gurgle of laughter, then took a breath and settled back farther on the seat. He realised with some surprise that her unease wasn't a result of what had happened between them.

'Why are you so nervous?' he asked bluntly.

'Shouldn't I be?'

'Perhaps you should, but you seem much more nervous about this meeting than about the rest your encounters at the Institute.'

'This is different,' she replied.

'How so?'

Sari hesitated, touched by the concern in his voice, but she could hardly tell him the truth. When Anderson had informed her of the change in her status at the Institute her immediate reaction had been one of cold fear. It had taken her a moment to realise that Anderson was presenting this opportunity as a testament to her success rather than a punishment for failure. He had spoken very fondly of Lady Montvale, highlighting her leading role in society. As far as he was concerned, if Lady Montvale took Sari under her wing, she would be placed in the best possible position to be of use to them in the future.

But Sari knew what this meant. She had been right that her hopes of becoming an agent just like all the others at the Institute were at an end. Luckily she was not to be dismissed, but though she should be thankful that a niche was being carved out for her, as far as Sari was concerned, they could hardly have found a worse role for her had they searched the nine rings of Purgatory. Her memories of Abingdon society were mostly of the petty but persistent malice of Mrs Ruscombe and her cronies along with the deepening disappointment of her father, which had been crowned by Hector's betrayal when his betrothal to Miss Ruscombe had been announced.

She felt slightly ill at the thought that this society lady would have a say in her future. She glanced down at her clasped hands, realising with some shock that she was more frightened now than she had been that night on the Heath. The absurdity of fearing humiliation more than arrest and hanging was so extreme that she gritted her teeth in self-disgust. She had survived everything life had thrown at her so far; she would be damned if she was going to let some idle, censorious, parasitical woman decide her fate. If this was what was required in order for her to keep her place at the Institute until they realised she could be as good an agent as anyone, then so be it. She would show them.

'Mr Anderson said it is important to make a good impression. I don't want to disappoint him,' she replied briefly, hoping that would suffice as an answer.

Michael turned away to look out of the window.

'I see.' His voice was flat, almost uninterested, but Sari felt she had somehow misstepped. She tried to think of something to say to break the silence, but the carriage stopped and the moment was over.

Her determination wavered as the butler, Henries, showed them into Lady Montvale's spacious, elegant drawing room. The pale blue-and-gold walls were a perfect foil for the tall, still raven-haired woman who stood up as they entered. She moved towards them, offering her cheek at Michael's affectionate salute, but her eyes were on Sari, bright and probing. She inspected her as she might a statue, or worse, a horse, and Sari struggled as the familiar inner shakiness threatened to vanquish her resolve. She pressed her lips together tightly. She was *not* going to think of that again. She was finished with being intimidated, manipulated, humiliated...

'Not bad,' Lady Montvale remarked as she grasped Sari's chin, turning her head from side to side. 'Not quite a beauty, but interesting nonetheless. We should focus on bringing out her eyes; they are by far her best feature. We must do something about her hair, though. It is completely unfashionable.' She paused, inspecting the colour that was blooming in Sari's cheeks.

'Oh, dear, you are not a blusher, are you, Miss Trevor?'

Sari took a deep breath, willing her temper to stay under control, but Michael spoke before she could respond.

'I think that is the colour of temper, Margaret, not embarrassment,' he murmured.

'Ah,' said Lady Montvale, releasing Sari's chin and taking a step back. 'Temper. Not an attribute of a lady.'

'Neither is being ill mannered,' Sari bit out before she could stop herself.

The older lady's brows arched upwards. Sari squared her shoulders, cursing herself inwardly, awaiting her dismissal. But Lady Montvale merely returned to her seat and steepled her fingers.

'Dear me, child, I believe you are right. However, next time you wish to make such an observation, you should try to couch it in more...ambiguous terms. Lord Crayle, here, is a master of the art of subtle annihilation. You should take a leaf from his book.'

'You are too kind, Margaret,' Michael conceded, and Sari's antagonism rose a notch.

'I would not presume. Even emulating a master is still counterfeit,' she replied sweetly and was surprised when Lady Montvale laughed appreciatively.

'Oh, but that is perfect. Michael, you terrible boy, why did you not tell me she was intelligent?'

'I believe we just walked in the door. Hardly time to lay out Miss Trevor's many...talents.'

'Nonsense. Now I am beginning to get a better picture of what we have to work with.' She looked again at Sari's drab dress and shuddered delicately.

'Michael, do run along and leave her to me. Stop by with Anderson this evening on your way to the Belmonts, before we pick up Lady Alicia.'

Michael hesitated, then he bowed dutifully over Lady Montvale's outstretched hand and gave Sari an almost commiserating smile.

As much as he unsettled her, when he had left Sari immediately wished he had stayed. She had no idea what this imposing woman had in store for her and she longed to go back to relative safety and comfort of the Institute.

They waited silently as Lady Montvale sent for her personal maid.

'Heloise, I want this young woman transformed. I place my faith in you,' the older woman said grandly.

'And our objective?' asked Heloise.

'The very best, my dear. I think…the orphaned daughter of my wealthy friends from the country here to make her début. How old are you, child?'

'Twenty-three,' Sari answered resignedly.

'Twenty-three? That old? My goodness. Well, my dear, never mind,' she replied generously. 'Heloise, if possible, let us see if we can effect this transformation by this evening. I have an idea.'

Heloise allowed herself a small, tight smile. 'Very well, my lady. Come with me if you please, Miss Trevor.'

Between the attentions of Heloise, along with an assortment of maids, and occasional visits from Lady Montvale, who bombarded her with question after question, Sari did not have a moment to herself. For the rest of that long, long day she was bathed, measured, coiffed, dressed, measured again, undressed, fed, covered with various balms and lotions, dressed again, recoiffed and applied with delicate paints.

When they all finally stood back and settled into silence, she could only stare back at them half-dizzy. It looked as if the whole household barring Lady Montvale herself stood about her in a half-circle. Afraid to move lest she set off another attack of dressing and undressing, Sari just stood there, enjoying the silence.

'We take her down now to Lady Montvale and the gentlemen, no?' Heloise said finally. The group parted as Sari moved towards the door, rather like children before a hunchback. Sari suddenly realised that in all the commotion she had not even seen herself in the mirror and resisted the urge to turn back. Heloise led her downstairs, opened the door of the drawing room and stood back, motioning her to enter. Sari raised her chin a notch and walked in.

The three people in the room turned as she entered. Lord Crayle and Anderson were dressed in stark black evening dress, the darkness alleviated only by snowy shirts and beautifully arranged cravats. Anderson had a gold pin in his and the earl's showed the faint glimmer of a diamond that made his eyes glint an icier grey than usual. They both looked ridiculously handsome. A nervous flush tingled in her cheeks and fingers and she turned instead to Lady Montvale, who looked lovely in deep-purple satin with fine black lace at her throat and wrists.

It took her a moment to realise they were all staring at her with something akin to bafflement. A wave of apprehension washed over her. Then a movement behind her broke the spell as Heloise stepped into the room.

'*Madame?*' she asked with a touch of archness to her voice.

'Heloise, I commend you. I asked for a transformation and you have delivered. *Brava*.'

Lady Montvale moved forward, circling Sari, one hand

fluttering out to touch the arranged curls and the shoulder of her low-cut gown.

Sari ducked her head, but the lady tapped her arm impatiently.

'Chin up, child. You are lovely and you know it. Always look the world in the eye.'

Sari, confused, looked up at her, but Lady Montvale had already turned to the two men.

'Well, gentlemen? Have we done you proud?'

Anderson gave a short, almost embarrassed laugh.

'As you said, a transformation. I hardly recognised her.'

Sari frowned and moved to the gilt-framed mirror over the mantelpiece. Her mind told her it must be a trick mirror. Where she had expected to see herself stood an aloof young woman dressed in a pale sea-green satin gown cut low across a bosom that was distinctly larger than she had imagined hers could ever be.

The bodice shimmered with seed pearls, like phosphorescence on waves. And yet it was a simple dress, free of the usual lace and trimmings Sari had seen even on walking attire on the streets of London. Her only adornments were a creamy pearl choker that looked incredibly expensive and pearl-and-diamond teardrop earrings. Her hair was piled high in silky waves and woven through with green satin ribbons matching her dress and the occasional sheen of a carefully placed pearl. The subtlest of colour had added warmth to her lips and cheeks and emphasised her eyes, which gleamed back at her with an intensity that almost made her uncomfortable. She had a sudden urge to laugh.

Anderson moved into view in the mirror beside her.

'Well? What do you think?' he asked with a slight smile, meeting her eyes in the reflection.

'I think... I look very strange.' She smiled and turned,

meeting Michael's gaze, realising he was the only one who had not said a word since her arrival. His previous look of surprise had been replaced with his more habitual shuttered expression. He turned towards Lady Montvale.

'We should be off.'

'Off? Where?' Sari asked, bemused.

'To the Belmonts', my dear,' supplied Lady Montvale.

Sari relaxed. Thank heavens, now she could finally go home.

'I think it is a perfect venue for introducing my wealthy young protégée from the country,' Lady Montvale continued, turning to the two men once more. 'Do you not think so, Michael?'

'That is somewhat premature,' Michael said carefully.

'Not at all,' interjected Anderson with sudden enthusiasm. 'The Belmonts' place is always crowded to overflowing. An excellent opportunity to observe the *ton* without becoming a focus of attention. We will all stay close and make sure she knows what to do. It is a pity to waste such a spectacular get up.'

'I say it is risky to expose her before she is ready,' Michael insisted, his tone hardening.

'And I say she is quite ready. Albermarle gives her top marks for deportment.'

'Her calling Lady Montvale ill mannered to her face rather undermines my confidence in Albermarle's judgement,' Michael said, but he was interrupted by the lady herself.

'Nonsense, Michael. I don't know why you are being so contrary. This was your idea to begin with and you know perfectly well that I would not suggest such a venture if I did not think she was able to assume the role. You have been lucky enough to find someone as lovely and as capable as Miss Trevor…' She turned to Sari. 'Do cover your ears, my dear; it won't do for you to become conceited.' She spun back to Michael and continued as if no interruption had occurred. '...and what must you do but turn all missish on us? Unless you have a concrete objection? No? Lovely, then we should be on our way. Remember we have to stop in Grosvenor Square to pick up Alicia on the way.'

Anderson cleared his throat nervously and Sari was distracted from her own thoughts for a moment by his suddenly conscious expression. Clearly Anderson was not immune to the earl's sister.

When they stopped at Grosvenor Square and Michael stepped down to help Alicia enter the carriage, it was equally obvious that Lady Alicia, lovely in a dark cape just showing a pale-yellow dress underneath, regarded Anderson as no more than a favoured friend of the family. All of her significant enthusiasm was focused on the prospect of dancing the night away with her various beaus, and Sari felt quite sorry for her sweet benefactor. She met Anderson's uncomfortable gaze with a slight encouraging smile, and he relaxed a touch, returning her smile.

When Lady Montvale introduced the two young women, Alicia responded with haughty disinterest just bordering on rudeness.

'Trevor? Of the Bedfordshire Trevors?' she asked in a tone aimed at depressing pretentions. She looked so lovely and poised that Sari once again felt herself thrown back to those horrible days in the Abingdon assembly rooms. Then the image of that woman in the mirror came back to her and she reminded herself that right here, right now, she was Lady Montvale's heiress.

'No. Of the Somerset Trevors,' she replied with the cool dismissiveness a more experienced young woman might employ with a girl some years her junior. Lady Alicia

flushed slightly, chastened, and her haughtiness subsided.
Lady Montvale gave Michael a faint, complacent smile.

Michael turned to look out of the carriage window as
they made their through Mayfair traffic towards the Belmonts'. His mind struggled to reconcile the headstrong girl
he had recruited with the striking, poised young woman
whom Lady Montvale had produced.

He had been somewhat surprised when he had arrived
with Anderson to find the older woman looking relaxed
and smug. She had evaded his questions, engaging Anderson in light conversation as they had waited for Sari to
come down. The few remarks he had managed to extract
had not prepared him in the least for her transformation.

He had known she could be pretty and that there was
a tidy body beneath her practical dresses. That much had
been inescapably obvious in the *salle* and the shooting gallery. But he had somehow managed to convince himself
she was just an inexperienced girl, under his protection
and therefore out of bounds. But when she had walked into
the room that evening it had been obvious that although
she might be inexperienced, she was definitely a woman.

His discomfort had taken on a sharper edge when he
had seen the shine of pride in Anderson's eyes as he had
stood beside her at the mirror. They had looked ridiculously well matched, side by side. Both fair haired and blue
eyed—Anderson's conventional good looks a foil for Sari's
newly revealed sensuality. He remembered what she had
said in the carriage on the way to Lady Montvale's. She
did not want to disappoint Anderson. And the comfortable,
almost complicit smile they had exchanged just a moment
ago had intensified Michael's vague unease into a sharp,
bitter sting. The thought that this tense burning might be
jealousy, and of his closest friend, was unthinkable.

He was struck by a sudden memory, the image of his father standing rigid and furious in the hall after his mother had escaped upstairs to her room following one of his father's jealousy-fuelled tirades. Michael had never fully understood how his dour father allowed himself to be so weak and pathetic. And blind. Michael had always thought his mother was too sweet and timid to be unfaithful, but he knew she would not show that face to them. After his mother had died of a fever ten years ago he had asked Lady Montvale whether there had been any grounds to his father's jealousy. She had smiled rather sadly and shaken her head.

'She was completely in love with him when they married. He wore the love out of her, poor dear, but she was never unfaithful to him. Frankly, she hadn't either the courage or the inclination. Sometimes I wish she had. Perhaps if she had lived longer after his death she might have found someone…kinder, more forgiving. She kept thinking she could fix him. She couldn't, of course. Your grandmother did as much damage to your poor father as any mother could to her son. You don't remember her, but she was a cruel, bitter woman and she poisoned your father against your mother until the blessed day she died. Your poor mother's love was too little too late. He loved all of you, but he never trusted himself to show it. And least of all to her. She knew how horrible it was for you all to see what went on between them, especially for you, Michael. Your father was even jealous of her attention towards all of you. The only one he seemed to trust was Lizzie and when Lizzie died… Anyway, that was why she kept him so much in London when you were all down from school. It wasn't that she didn't want to be with you. She told me once that you were doing a better job of raising the children than she and your father could ever do. That you were better off without them.'

That sad portrait of his parents had tempered some of Michael's youthful antagonism towards them, but had strengthened his resolve never to be like either of them. He had never allowed jealousy to force his hand, not even in the throes of whatever early infatuations he had gone through like the rest of his friends at school. By the time he had reached the army, he had learned how to get what he wanted from women with sufficient ease and how to move on without acrimony when he didn't.

The pointless agony his parents had experienced at each other's hands only seemed more ridiculous and avoidable as time went by. There was no way in hell he was going down that path. He was not going to allow this foolish attraction to Sari affect his behaviour. It had caught him off guard; that was all. Right now he had to focus on getting her safely through the treacherous shoals of the London *ton*. Everything else was irrelevant.

Within five minutes of reaching the Belmonts', Sari understood why Anderson and Lady Montvale had been so unconcerned. It had taken them twenty minutes to make their way up Mayfair to the Belmonts' mansion. The receiving line itself moved only marginally faster than the traffic of carriages and much socialising was carried out as they advanced, with people milling about in the hallway, magically appearing with glasses of iced champagne and other beverages. Lady Alicia quickly attached herself to a group of young women who sank into accustomed gossip and giggles behind their fans. Lady Montvale happily introduced Sari to all and sundry as the daughter of her dear friends. Between smiles and curtsies she could see the curious looks gliding across her face and dress, assessing the value of the pearls that lay coolly against her throat.

'Such a charming gown, my dear. French, is it not?' asked an alarming matron with a martial gleam in her eye, and Sari almost sighed in relief when they finally entered the ballroom. But here, too, there was hardly room to breathe and she wondered how all the people still waiting in the line would fit.

'My God, Crayle! What the devil are you doing here and at this hour?' drawled a stylishly dressed man with carefully arranged auburn curls who inspected them through his looking glass. Beside him stood a taller, well-groomed man, in his early forties perhaps, whose light blue eyes settled on Sari with a serious intentness that made her wish she could hide behind Lady Montvale's stately form.

'Family duties, Gerry. I could ask the same of you,' the earl responded briefly and turned to address the other man. 'Good evening, Edgerton.'

'Of course,' the first man said, noting the members of the party and bowing elegantly. 'Lady Montvale, Lady Alicia, Anderson. I, dear chap...' He paused, noticing Sari with a slight lift to his brows. His eyes skimmed her body, settling briefly on the pearl choker at her throat. 'I came to meet this most exquisite young woman. Introduce us.'

There was a moment of silence into which Lady Montvale sailed with the grace and presence of a first-rate ship of the line.

'Gerald, behave yourself, do. Miss Trevor, may I introduce Sir Gerald Aitken and Lord Edgerton. Sir Gerald, Lord Edgerton, Miss Sari Trevor.'

Sari curtsied demurely, hoping she was doing Mr Albermarle proud. Sir Gerald, employing the opportunity to get a better view of her *décolletage*, and never daunted by formality, reached across to raise her gloved hand to his lips, sending her an audacious smile. Sari, realising one area that had been sorely neglected in her education had been the art of flirtation, had no idea what to do at this point and therefore succeeded in doing precisely the right thing, looking flustered. The prospect of unspoiled goods quickened Sir Gerald's interest, and his smile deepened, and his expression took on a lascivious look.

Michael watched the exchange with ill-concealed disgust.

'She is new in town, Gerry. No need to stampede her in the first five minutes on the scene.'

'Nonsense, old chap. All the more reason to secure my interest before the rest of the fellows catch sight of her. My dear Miss Trevor, may I request a dance? Pray tell me you are not already spoken for.'

The *double entendre* of his question was blatant, and Sari glanced at Lady Montvale questioningly. The latter was holding back a sly smile and nodded briefly.

'I believe you have the quadrille free, Miss Trevor.'

'I would be honoured to secure a dance as well, Miss Trevor,' Lord Edgerton interposed with significantly more propriety and Lady Montvale's brows rose slightly, but she assented, taking control of Sari's dance card like a general disposing troops.

'The quadrille, then,' exclaimed Sir Gerald with another flamboyant bow and, with a last sweeping glance at his new prey, he linked his arm with Lord Edgerton and wandered off.

With some surprise Sari realised she had not spoken a word during the whole exchange. No doubt they thought her some simpering country miss. Fine. That made her job much easier.

'My God, are they all going to be like that?' she asked under her breath.

'Womanising rattles? Quite a few, Miss Trevor,' Michael replied abruptly before turning to Lady Montvale. 'The pearls may not have been the best idea,' he said quietly, making sure that Alicia did not overhear.

'Nonsense, Michael. Remember the image we are trying to cultivate. She must attract enough attention to be effective, and the pearls hint at "heiress". I think we are already showing great success. Everybody saw Gerald fawn over her. And Edgerton! My dear, I couldn't have hoped for better! I cannot remember the last time he took an interest in a young woman of marriageable age, let alone danced with one. You take the first dance, Anderson, and you the one after the quadrille, Michael,' she commanded grandly. 'Between Gerald, Edgerton, yourself and Anderson she will be swamped with dance offers, mark my words. Dear me, the third dance is a waltz. Never mind, I shall have a quick word with Sally Jersey and Lady Lieven and see what we can do. I think that was perfect, Sari. Just the right mix of shyness and reserve.'

Sari refrained from pointing out that she was hardly acting and thankfully allowed a grinning Anderson to guide her towards the dance floor, her hand tucked securely about his arm. As they left the group, she was surprised to see a rather annoyed look cross Lady Alicia's face as her eyes followed them from where she stood with her friends and she wondered whether the pert young woman was perhaps not completely indifferent to Anderson after all.

When the country dance ended Anderson handed her over to Sir Gerald with a sympathetic squeeze to her hand. To her astonishment she swiftly accustomed herself to the role they had set out for her. She assumed a slightly shy demeanour but with a touch of the 'farouche' as Lady Montvale called her natural eagerness. Countrified innocence was a useful excuse for wilfully misunderstanding

Sir Gerald's innuendos. Still, she was relieved when the quadrille wound down, even though it meant she now had to dance with Michael.

Since this was a waltz, Sari had learned enough from Mr Albemarle to expect Lady Montvale to tell her to sit it out until she was formally introduced at Almack's. However, she had reckoned without Lady Montvale's social standing and excellent relations with the Ladies Sefton and Jersey. Apparently, she had argued that at Sari's advanced age, awaiting formal introduction like a débutante was unnecessary. With permission granted, Lady Montvale handed her to Lord Crayle with a smug smile of victory.

After everything they had been through, Sari almost wished Lady Montvale had not been successful. She almost stumbled when they reached the dance floor and his hand moved to her waist, whilst his other hand clasped hers. When he pulled her slightly closer as he turned in the dance she watched her skirts swirl out, sliding against his legs before falling back, and wondered what it would be like to close the small gap between them. It was impossible not to remember what it had felt like to be pressed between his body and the wall, to be kissed, touched... A hot ache tightened her body, and she drew a deep breath. She must think only of the music, of how much she loved to dance. Dancing had been the one area where her Abingdon nemeses had not managed to ruin her enjoyment of social gatherings. And waltzes were her favourite.

'You can look up now. Or do you need to count your steps?' he asked above her. There was a smile in his voice, and as she looked up she saw the severity that had dismayed her earlier was gone. She should have known that whatever his reservations, once a decision had been taken he would do whatever necessary to ensure she succeeded in her role. She gave a quick smile of relief and some of the tension that had held her faded.

'Don't tell poor Mr Albermarie. He will be so disappointed.'

'Hardly. "Poor" Mr Albermarle will be living vicariously through your début and will be delighted to hear that at least your dancing does you credit.'

Sari felt herself flush. It was nice to receive a compliment for something other than her shooting skills.

'If you had omitted the "at least" that might actually sound like a compliment. As it is, I find your comment somewhat ambiguous.'

'What a suspicious little mind you have. If this is how you react to all of your compliments, I am surprised you receive any.'

'Most are delivered with rather more gallantry, my lord.'

'I know. I am a sad hand at these things. I never could turn a neat phrase to save my life.'

Sari shot him a sardonic look at this blatant untruth.

'I am sure Gerald was free with his compliments,' he continued. 'He's a hard act to follow.'

'Sir Gerald was free with more than his compliments. Thank goodness one has to wear gloves at balls. The way he kept pressing my hands in the quadrille I was sure he would leave a mark.'

'Shall I scare him off?'

She felt a flush of pleasure at this offer. Not that she particularly wanted to be treated the way he might Alicia, but at least he didn't seem so distant any more.

'I think I already have. I stepped on him. Twice,' she admitted mischievously.

Michael burst out laughing.

'I'm beginning to feel sorry for him instead.'

'Don't be, he got his own back. He took advantage to

steady me by moving his hands to areas not strictly required for the quadrille…'

Her breath caught as Michael's grasp tightened and something dark glinted in his eyes. Then the moment was gone and he turned her again in the dance.

'I shall definitely have to scare him off. It won't do to have you do violence to your dancing skills simply to keep Gerry at bay.'

Sari smiled gratefully, but shook her head. She didn't want him to think her helpless.

'I am fine. Really. I can take care of myself.' She flushed slightly as she remembered the last time she had employed that phrase, but he did not seem to notice and merely gave her a slightly quizzical look.

'The point is that you don't have to. Being part of an organisation means you have people who can help you if you are in need. Remember that.'

She was shocked at how much this simple, almost prosaic statement affected her. She lowered her eyes to her feet again to hide the sudden burn of tears. She still found it hard to think of the Institute as a place where she belonged. The thought of belonging anywhere at all was still too foreign…too dangerous to trust.

She realised in dismay that the music was winding down. She didn't want the dance to be over yet, but already she saw Lord Edgerton moving towards her and she smiled up at him as he took her hand to lead her towards their place on the floor.

'You dance very well, Miss Trevor,' he said formally as they came together in the dance. Sari remembered what Lady Montvale had said about his aloofness. He did seem rather uncomfortable. In other circumstances she might have been intimidated by his rather dour demeanour, but she was still caught up in the pleasure of dancing and she

felt surprisingly more comfortable with him than the flir-
tatious Sir Gerald.

'I enjoy it,' she replied simply. 'But please don't tell
anyone I said so. Lady Montvale said one must not show
enthusiasm too explicitly in London for fear of being
branded countrified. Which I am, I suppose. I dare say
I will learn.'

He blinked in surprise at her unfashionable, self-
deprecating candour and seemed to struggle for a suitable response.

'It is an ill society that condemns enthusiasm. It would
be a pity if you were to change to suit this place.'

They moved apart again in the dance and when they
came together he spoke to her with far greater ease. When
he discovered her appreciation of Byzantine antiquities
they spent the rest of the dance in comfortable discussion
of the recent archaeological finds at Mystras in Greece.
Here Sari didn't have to feign any interest and it was with
real enthusiasm that she questioned him about his reading
on a topic so dear to her.

Lady Montvale's prediction of the interest in her bore
out as the evening progressed and she never lacked for
dance partners. Still, she was relieved when the older
woman finally announced they would be departing, extracting Lady Alicia from her circle of admirers. Hopefully
George and Mina weren't waiting up for her, she thought
with a pang of guilt. As if reading her mind, Lady Montvale glanced across at her once the two of them eventually
arrived back at Montvale House.

'It really will not do, dashing back and forth between
Mayfair and Pimlico every time you are to make an ap-
pearance. If we are to proceed, you had best remove to
Montvale House for the Season.'

Sari regarded her in dismay. She didn't want to leave her

safe haven with George and Mina, but she had resolved to do whatever the older woman asked of her.

'I would not like to impose—' she stammered, but she was interrupted with a laugh.

'My dear child, you are not imposing. I am enjoying this immensely. Never mind, we will discuss this tomorrow with Michael and Anderson. Right now Heloise will help you change and the carriage will take you back. Tomorrow I shall send for you and we will go for a turn in the park. From now on you must be seen everywhere that is fashionable.'

Chapter Twelve

Lady Montvale had reason to be smug about her decision to take Sari for a ride in the park in her elegant barouche the following afternoon. They were not five minutes into the park when they were hailed by Lord Edgerton, seated astride a handsome bay mare. Lady Montvale smiled serenely and motioned for her driver to stop.

'Good day, Lady Montvale, Miss Trevor.' Edgerton smiled pleasantly at Sari. 'Did you enjoy your first London ball, Miss Trevor?'

Sari remembered her role and smiled warmly at him. She was beginning to get his measure.

'Very much!' She glanced mischievously at her companion. 'Lady Montvale assures me I shall soon become jaded, but I do hope not. Like Johnson I am coming to believe that when one is tired of London one would as well be tired of life.'

He laughed, but his eyes gleamed in interest at the literary allusion just as she had hoped.

'I, too, agree with Johnson that living in a large place enlarges the mind. Your fervour does you no discredit, believe me. I am glad our paths have crossed, as I was wondering if you might join me some morning for a visit to the museum to see the new Byzantine exhibit. I believe it will please you, if you are interested.'

Sari dipped her eyes modestly.

'May I?'

Lady Montvale nodded her assent serenely and they had just agreed on the time when they noticed a young man on horseback coming down the path. He was attractive, but had a downward, petulant pull to his mouth, and Sari recognised him immediately. Edgerton's eyes narrowed and the young man hesitated, pulling back slightly on the reins, but Lady Montvale had already seen him and nodded.

'Good day, Mr Hamlin. Have you met my dear friend and protégée, Miss Trevor?'

Hamlin's eyes moved away from Edgerton and focused on Sari. Although she recognised him clearly from that night at the Eagle and Crown, she had no fear he would recognise her. In the intensity of his gaze she read only calculation as he realised she was Lady Montvale's wealthy protégée. The intent look soon melted into a disarming smile and Sari echoed it shyly as he bowed. Edgerton's hands tightened on the reins, causing his horse to fidget.

Once they parted from the two men Lady Montvale gave Sari's hands a contented pat.

'That was nicely done, my dear. And it never hurts to make a man a little jealous. Not too much, mind you. Edgerton can pick and choose. He has been widowed for more than a dozen years and no one has succeeded in attaching him yet. Don't waste your time on Hamlin, though. He's nothing but a young wastrel intent on gambling his inheritance away. He's definitely interested in you for the money... Dear me, I forget we aren't after a husband.'

Sari laughed, struck by the absurdity of the situation.

'Thank goodness. But politically they are both interesting, aren't they? Edgerton is quite a conservative zealot from what I understand, though he does seem so very mild in person. And isn't Hamlin in the Young Conservative Club? They can be quite extreme.'

'Indeed, though I frankly cannot see Edgerton engaging in intrigue. A very punctilious man, Lord Edgerton. Still, it can only help your standing if you are lucky enough to hold his interest. It won't be easy—the heiress card won't play with him,' she added.

Sari shrugged, surprised that she didn't find Lady Montvale's statement insulting. There was something so comfortingly businesslike about her approach to society that robbed it of its power to unsettle her. The more she moved into her role, the more she wondered how she had given Mrs Ruscombe and her cronies such power over her.

Sari turned her thoughts to Hamlin. It had probably been him whom Michael had seen and called a 'small fish'. It was very strange that someone such as he was involved with the likes of two practised mercenaries, but she sincerely doubted his presence in the Eagle and Crown had been a coincidence. Finally, here was a way she could prove her usefulness. If Hamlin was in need of money, attracting him should be easy.

In fact, at a soirée that evening Hamlin proved even easier a catch than Sari had hoped. After only a few minutes in his company, his preference for shy, silly and adoring little misses became obvious and though it went sorely against the grain Sari did her best to play along. Her act, coupled with Lady Montvale's allusions to her inheritance, had him well on the way to being snared. She was only disappointed she hadn't succeeded in learning anything substantial regarding his political beliefs. He seemed no more or less zealous than most young men. Before she could probe further they were interrupted by Lord Edgerton, who came to claim his dance.

Once again she noticed Hamlin's strange behaviour in Edgerton's presence. They exchanged no more than civilities, but to Sari it seemed there was an undercurrent of tension between them. Whether it was jealousy or something more sinister, she reasoned that anything about Hamlin was of interest to her at the moment.

She smiled encouragingly at Lord Edgerton as he led her towards the dance floor, resolving to charm him as best she could. Thankfully, of all the men she had met in London outside of the Institute, he was the one who most appealed to her. Expending time and effort trying to charm him would not be a hardship.

Chapter Thirteen

'You will finally have some time to yourselves,' Sari said lightly as George and Mina helped her pack a small trunk for her removal to Montvale House. There wasn't much to pack, mostly her books. Sari glanced around her narrow but comfortable room and felt a rush of fear. It would be so strange not to have George and Mina waiting for her at the end of each day. She hadn't realised how much she had come to depend on their solid presence in her life.

Mina stopped in the middle of folding a simple muslin dress and raised her apron to cover her eyes for a moment.

'Stay out of trouble, do, miss. Don't make me come scolding!'

'Ay, you'll not want that, miss. A fair terror she can be when the wind's at her back,' George said jokingly, but he enveloped his small wife in a comforting hug. Sari smiled lovingly at them and closed the lid of her trunk.

'I'll do my best, Mina dear. But there's not much trouble I can get into now, I'm afraid. It's all parties and balls and foolishness. I'm in no danger at all.'

She thought again of those words as she arranged her meagre belongings among the increasingly impressive array of clothes and accessories which filled her new room at Montvale House. It had been a blatant lie, for although she might not be in physical danger in her new role as social débutante, emotionally she was in greater danger than she had ever been in her life. Every time the memory of that night in Pimlico resurfaced it would strip her raw. She might be able to control her behaviour around Michael, but not what was going on inside her.

She was almost thankful that as her social commitments increased, she had less time to spend at the Institute. Somehow it was easier to maintain the proper distance when she met the earl in social settings. Perversely at the Institute she felt more exposed.

It was therefore with some consternation that she entered the *salle* dressed for her scheduled fencing session the morning after her removal to Montvale House and saw him with Antonelli on the strip. She was about to withdraw when Antonelli called her over.

'Come in, come in. We were just finishing, *signorina*. I fear we have taken more than our hour here.'

Sari shook her head, but stepped into the room nonetheless. A retreat now would only call attention to her uneasy relations with the earl. Sari tugged her protective gloves nervously between her hands.

'I am sorry, perhaps I should come back later,' she said warily and Michael glanced over at her, his impersonal and distant scrutiny only making her more uncomfortable.

'Antonelli said we are done, did he not?'

Sari nodded nervously. Obviously she couldn't say anything right. 'I merely meant… I could return later…'

Michael paused as he was about to return his foil. He told himself he should be grateful she was finally learning compliance, but only succeeded in feeling guilty at having reduced her to this uncharacteristic meekness. It did not suit her.

'It is convenient that you do as Antonelli says,' he replied and watched with some relief as his response drew some life back into her, even if it was in the form of annoyance.

'I was trying to be polite, my lord,' she said.

Michael noticed her hands clench and tried for a lighter vein.

'Is it to be fisticuffs, then? We have already tried pistols at dawn. Or perhaps you would rather try your hand at running me through this time?'

Antonelli's eyes gleamed with sudden interest.

'An excellent idea. You two fence; I watch.'

Both of them stared at Antonelli in dismay——the prospect of actually having to follow through on their verbal fencing held no appeal for either of them. But the fencing master brushed aside their denials.

'I have softened him up for you, *signorina*,' he joked. 'You see how he is, in fencing as in life. He waits for you to come to him, then cuts you down. And he is at his most brutal when he is bored.'

Sari could not hold back an apprehensive smile at the parallel. She forced herself to relax. It was hard enough to avoid the earl's verbal barbs. She had no wish to face him on the strip and Michael appeared to share her reluctance.

'For heaven's sake, Antonelli. She is almost a foot shorter than me, not to mention the difference in weight.'

'Precisely. She is a great deal lighter than you, but I am sure you can compensate for that.'

'Antonelli…'

'Michael? You will have me thinking you are afraid to meet the *signorina*. This is good training for her——to experience styles other than my own.'

'You fence every style in the book… Hell, all right, let's get this over with.'

With that inauspicious comment he raised his foil in salute, and Sari echoed his *en garde*.

It began strangely. Michael was uncharacteristically diffident, not following through with ripostes as he had with Antonelli and as the tutor did with her. Sari's initial fear was soon overtaken by frustration. He fenced with her as she might have expected Anderson to, as if she were made of bone china.

She began making more offensive moves, more subtle feints, but he merely raised the level of his parrying, his movements economical, deflecting her increasingly aggressive attacks with a mere twist of his wrist. At this rate, Sari thought, they would be here all day, or rather until she ran out of strength. She kept thinking Antonelli would intervene, but he remained silent.

Then she remembered a tactic Cavalcatti had taught her. Sometimes sacrificing a battle was necessary in order to win the war, he had said. She thought for a moment and then came forward in a demanding lunge which forced him to parry more aggressively, causing his foil to run up the length of hers. Normally she would have withdrawn in a recovery to escape his approaching blade, but this time she took another step in, disengaging and allowing the tip of his foil to come within an inch of her jacket. She saw the flash of concern in his eyes as he swiftly corrected to prevent himself from striking her, pulling back his foil as he quickly sidestepped to the right, and leaving Sari with her opening.

She never quite made it. Michael realised the trick and parried at the last moment, but this time without his usual finesse. The force twisted the foil out of her hand and sent it clattering to the floor.

Well, she thought, with the force of his blow still singing up her arm, at least it was over.

'What the hell were you trying to do?' Michael demanded angrily.

She wiped the perspiration from her brow with the back of her hand, wondering much the same thing. It was as if she had had to prove to him she was not as powerless as she had seemed that one night.

'She was trying to use your weakness against you, Michael. I think that a very good tactic,' Antonelli interjected calmly.

'Curse it, Antonelli. I almost cut her.' Michael rounded on the Italian.

'But you didn't. And I think Sari knew perfectly well that you would not, did you not, *signorina*?'

'Perhaps not perfectly well, but I was rather hoping you would not,' she said as calmly as possible. 'I didn't mean to scare you,' she added with an apologetic smile.

Michael wished he could wipe that smile from her pretty mouth. Scare him? His pulse was still fast and hard. He had been an inch away from cutting her. Fear had ripped through him as his foil had slid towards her chest, followed by a wave of heat as he had realised he had been tricked. He had a wild urge to pin her against the wall as he had in Pimlico, to scold her for frightening him.

He had been shocked by the calm, watchful look on her face as she had stepped towards his foil, her eyes on his own rather than on his sword. What if he had not caught himself in time? His sword, with its protected tip or not, might have sliced through the jacket and to her ribs beyond. It wouldn't have caused a fatal wound, but a wound nonetheless. And the reckless little fool had been willing to risk that simply to trick him into giving her an opening.

He returned his sword to the rack. He had no one to

blame but himself. He had been foolish to try and bring them back to a more normal *modus vivendi*. He had no one to blame but himself, he repeated grimly, and without another word he turned and left the *salle*.

They stood looking after him for a moment, then Antonelli turned back to her.

'Do not mind him, *bella*, he does not like to be scared. He will get over it.'

'Well, I doubt he can mistrust me any more than he does already,' she replied, keeping her tones as light as possible in sharp contrast to the ache in her chest. Antonelli's brows shot up, creating a field of furrows on his forehead.

'Mistrust you? Nonsense, *bella*. Believe me, you would not be here if he did. It is simply that he cannot control you that makes it difficult for him. Remember he has been in command of his family and troops since before he was even fully grown. He has lost many friends and men who were his responsibility to protect. You do not come out of such experiences as you went in. He has become very good at what he does, but the price was very high.'

Sari fingered her sword gingerly. She tried to imagine what it had been like for him. He had been her age when he had gone to war. And then spent years of fighting the French inch by bloody inch across Portugal and Spain and France. She could hardly imagine what that would do to a person.

She was only now beginning to realise the magnitude of her mistake that night. She knew that as hard as it might be to face him, she owed him an apology. She smiled at Antonelli and replaced her foil. It did not take her long to change and she headed upstairs, not certain if she wished he were in his office or not.

'Come in,' Michael's voice called out abruptly as she knocked on his door. She drew a deep breath and entered his office resolutely. He glanced up from the sheaf of papers he held and his mouth tightened.

'Lord Crayle, I was wondering if I might have a brief word with you?' she asked quietly.

By the stony look on his face it appeared he was none too delighted at the prospect, but he waved her towards the chair facing him and waited.

Sari was becoming accustomed to facing him across desks and usually at a serious disadvantage.

'My lord, I wanted to apologise for what I did in the *salle*. You have given me an opportunity to escape a very unpleasant fate and I have been repaying this. .godsend with the presumption that I might be as good as anyone at the Institute, which I realise now is a degree of hubris I never thought I was capable of. I am not sure I deserve the second chance I have received, but from now on I intend to do nothing more than what is required of me. That is all.'

She stood up.

'Sit down,' he said, and she sat down again with a thump, her gaze losing its resolution.

Once again Michael could see the fear there, just under the surface of her bravado. What on earth was he going to do with her? Every time he thought he had her firmly in place on the board she rearranged the pieces.

He sighed. 'I want to add something to your list of intentions.'

Sari straightened. 'Yes?'

'Stop trying so hard.'

Sari blinked in surprise. 'What?'

'We brought you in because you have potential, but potential takes time to realise. At the moment we are asking you to learn, not to prove anything. The men who are currently on assignments have not only each received over a year of training, but also mostly come from military backgrounds or have other experience. This is not a short-term endeavour. I know you realise you are an experiment, but that does not mean you have to regard yourself as under some form of constant examination. Frankly, every time you have tried to prove your worth you have gone too far and put yourself at risk. Right now all you have to do is let Lady Montvale guide you and pay attention to your surroundings. That is all. Stop trying to grab the reins.'

Sari lowered her head, biting down hard on a sudden urge to cry. The invitation to relax her vigilance was so seductive, but part of her bridled with mistrust. She knew her biggest test would be to subdue that part of her that couldn't believe she might be worthy just as she was. But he was right. Every time she had tried to prove her worth, she had gone too far. Desperation coupled with pride was a dangerous mix.

She took a deep breath and stood up. 'You are right. I promise not to step outside my bounds again,' she stated somewhat formally and then added in a rush, 'I really am very grateful—'

Michael stood up as well, cutting her off.

'Just go easy. Agreed?' he said lightly, and she nodded, suddenly swamped by a wave of relief and joy she had no idea what to do with. She tried and failed to subdue her smile.

'Agreed.'

Michael remained standing as the door closed behind her. She never stopped surprising him. He had seen the sheen of tears as she had lowered her head and he'd had to hold himself back from reaching out to comfort her. He was struck again by her lack of artifice. Many women would have made good use of that threat of tears, but it hadn't even seemed to occur to her to capitalise on them.

He knew she would make every effort to do precisely what she had promised. But he was not so certain that she would succeed. It was not that she had no respect for boundaries, she just sometimes didn't seem to comprehend that they existed, and existed for good reason.

And her best characteristics might also be her most dangerous. The loyalty that had made her fight for George's safety—even the way she had drawn her dagger when that Whitechapel thug had threatened him with a knife—there was something both touching and ludicrous about it, but above all it was dangerous. Gestures like that just made it clear that she was the antithesis of everything he had so carefully built and he didn't know if she could be trusted to keep herself safe.

He sat down again. He told himself that at least with Lady Montvale she was out of harm's way. But somehow he couldn't subdue his fear.

Chapter Fourteen

Standing in Penrose's little office the next morning, Sari glanced at her training schedule for the day and her heart raced uncomfortably.

'Oh, dear,' she blurted out before she could stop herself.

'Something wrong, miss?' Penrose asked, surprised.

'No, no... I just forgot something. Never mind. Thank you, Penrose.'

She hurried out and headed towards the stairs leading down to the shooting gallery. Her conversation with the earl the previous day had left her feeling both lighter and more confident than she had in a long time, but it had also made it clear she was on very dangerous ground. She didn't fully understand what was happening to her, but every time she was around him it was like going aboard a ship in rough weather—even standing in place became a conscious effort.

Her reaction to Michael was so different from the mild affection she had felt for Hector that it was hard to believe she had ever considered marrying that earnest young man. Hector had held the promise of stability after a lifetime of wandering and an escape from her family's descent into painful poverty, but his kisses had never evoked in her a fraction of what she felt even when Michael was doing no more than correcting her shooting stance.

When she entered the gallery, Michael was just laying down a long, elegant-looking rifle on the table and her heart, which had already been thumping wildly, picked up yet more speed.

'I've been practising my stance,' she said to fill the silence as he laid out the guns.

'Good. Come and help me load.' He did not look up, but his voice was easy, casual, and she relaxed slightly.

She stood next to him, her hands moving swiftly to measure and load.

'Here, try Manton's again. You liked that.'

She took the gun and, forcing herself into the still-foreign stance, aimed and fired. This time she stood her ground and the dummy gained a third eye.

He shook his head.

'This is too easy for you.' He turned to her with that lazy, almost wicked smile that made her want to do something very foolish. 'If you're good and behave, I'll take you to the outdoor range in Barnes... No.' He frowned suddenly, reaching out to just touch the tip of his finger to her shoulder. 'You're bound to get bruises until you're used to it and Margaret would have my head if you showed up in a ball gown with a bruised shoulder.'

Sari was tempted to tell him she didn't care, but nodded. She wondered how she had ever thought he was cold or dispassionate. It was true that he was guarded, but it was also obvious there was a great deal going on behind his impassive expression.

'Is that the Baker rifle?' She indicated the rifle he had laid down as she had entered, seeking an opening.

He hesitated and then picked it up with the same ease with which someone might pick up a walking stick, but his mouth had thinned. She was beginning to recognise his moods. In the past she might have thought he was angry, but now she could see something else was going on. Like a drawbridge being pulled up, his defences had been mounted.

'Yes. It's very accurate, but harder to reload than the standard-issue Brown Bess,' he said at last, his tones flat and clinical. 'It's good at long ranges. A very efficient killer.'

There was something ambiguous about his last statement. She knew enough about the war to know that the Ninety-Fifth Rifles where he had served had been an elite unit specialising in sharpshooting and skirmishes. Unlike many soldiers who had just shot into the mass of opposing soldiers, the Ninety-Fifths had chosen their targets and had shot to kill. She wondered what that did to a man. What that had done to him.

'Had you always wanted to join the army?' she asked tentatively.

He laughed briefly, but without mirth. 'Ever since I was a boy. We were army mad at school and not much better at university. We followed everything that happened in the wars with France; I remember how disappointed we were when they signed the Peace at Amiens. It's amazing to think how naïve we were.'

'You were young.'

'I suppose. I was the eldest son so I wasn't meant for the army, but I joined up anyway. I signed up with the Ninety-Fifths because I was a good shot and because I didn't have to buy a commission since I knew my father would never agree.'

He stopped. He was tracing the elaborate curve of the trigger guard with his fingers.

'Did he agree in the end?'

He shrugged, and at first she thought he wouldn't answer. He raised the rifle to his shoulder almost absently, sighting down the lane. When he spoke again she started slightly.

'It was ironic—he was the one who demanded that I excel at shooting and fencing in the first place. He had a very...rigid image of what it meant to be a gentleman. When I told him I wanted to join up and follow Wellington to Portugal he was more furious than I thought even he could be, which is saying quite a lot. That was the first time any of us had dared defy him. He gave me an ultimatum, so of course I left.'

He lowered the rifle, replacing it in the gun cabinet. Sari held herself still. She knew instinctively that if she said anything at this point, he would shut down.

'The day after our argument he had a heart attack while he was driving with Lizzie, my older sister. The curricle overturned and she broke her back. It took her a whole month to die. He told me it wouldn't have happened if I had accepted my responsibilities. We both knew he couldn't stand me being there after... So I went. I thought if I could at least be of use during the war... He was right about that, too. I was an immature, romantic fool—there was nothing heroic about the war. Every mistake I made cost men's lives—men whom it was my responsibility to defend. And every success was about killing men you didn't even know. You get better just so you can minimise death. War is the least romantic thing imaginable.'

Sari's whole body ached with a pain as intense as that which she had felt when she had realised her mother was well and truly dead. She wasn't misled by the curtness of his voice. She tried to imagine Michael before that fateful accident, before the rejection and accusations of his father, and before the persistent scarring of the war. She wondered if anything was left of the boy. Obviously there was, but shoved as deeply underground as they were now. She was almost overpowered by a need to hold him, to offer something… She didn't even know what.

'I was twenty-two.' He shot a glance at her. 'About your age. I thought I knew what was right. I didn't. I still don't, but at least now I know that.'

She shook her head, and Michael realised with some surprise that she was trying not to cry.

'I'm sorry for him, but your father was a fool. Just because *he* felt guilty…to blame his own son! How *dared* he do that to you?' The words burst from her, her voice husky and unsteady. 'It was not your fault. How can you even think that—?' She cut herself off and turned away slightly, brushing her hands across her eyes.

Shaken, he reached over to touch her shoulder lightly. He had no idea why he had told her about Lizzie. About any of it. Only Anderson and his sister Letty knew parts of the story, not even the whole of it. He had just wanted to explain how important it was to be careful. To not get caught up in some false romantic notion about what they were doing at the Institute at the expense of caution.

He had expected her to either resent the lecture, or perhaps be embarrassed by it. The last thing he had expected was tears.

'I'm sorry; I didn't mean to upset you.'

'I'm not upset… Yes, I *am* upset, but not… It's not fair,' she ended lamely. 'If someone had said such things to Charlie, I don't know what I would have done.'

He shifted away slightly. He didn't want to be categorised with her brother.

'Never mind. Here. I've set up wafers for you so you can see how they do it at Manton's.'

Sari took a deep breath, suddenly embarrassed, and

grateful he had been so tolerant of her emotional outburst. It amazed her anew that he could be so empathic. It was a testament to his nature that neither his father's emotional cruelty nor the depredations of the war had managed to destroy that side of him. She only wished it wouldn't affect her so deeply. After a moment she picked up the pistol he indicated and followed him to the last lane.

Chapter Fifteen

Sari adhered strictly to her good resolutions. That week she spent most mornings at the Institute and then slipped on her ingénue's mask, flirting and cajoling and admiring and entrenching herself firmly into the insular world of the *ton* under Lady Montvale's approving gaze. The only hitch was caused, perversely, by her improved relations with the earl. She encountered him almost daily and every encounter only confirmed that she had gone too far down a rather hopeless path.

At a ball celebrating the début of one of Alicia's friends, Sari found herself standing by two giggling young maidens who were cataloguing the various pros and cons of the attending gentlemen behind the cover of their fans. One, a pretty redhead, spoke of Lord Crayle with patent adoration.

'He has the most meltingly beautiful smile,' she said dreamily.

Sari grimaced, as much at the swooning tones as at her own stupidity as the memory of his smile came to her mind unbidden. He did indeed have a magnificent smile, warm and teasing, all the more potent for being rare. Whenever he directed it at her she found herself foolishly wishing he would touch her again. She was far from forgetting the explosive encounter between them on that otherwise dreadful night. When he was not looking she would allow herself to glance at him and torture herself with the inexorable heat that rose at the memory.

But she was still level-headed enough to realise the futility of her feelings. She was no better than these two silly misses, she told herself brutally. No, she was worse. At least they had a chance. They were properly raised and perfect fodder for matrimony. She never forgot for a moment that whatever her role, the truth was that she had not even been good enough for the son of a country squire. And although she might be moderately pretty, she had heard enough of the gossip to know Michael's mistresses had been beautiful, mature women. On no front could she deceive herself into believing she had any chance of capturing his attention outside of his concern for her as part of the Institute. This thought left her so morose she did not even notice when someone came to stand behind her.

'Wool-gathering, Miss Trevor? That is unlike you.'

Sari started and whirled around as the object of her thoughts glanced quizzically down at her.

'I...I was distracted,' she replied falteringly, praying the heat rising from her chest wouldn't bloom into a blush.

Michael watched the faint flush spread across her cheeks, and glanced around, wondering what had thrown her off kilter. He could only imagine it was the strain involved in maintaining her persona as Lady Montvale's country-bred protégée. He had been wrong about her lack of finesse. His initial suspicion that she was an accomplished little actress had been borne out by the ease with which she had slipped into her new role. But he knew there was so much more to her than that. It had to be hard to keep so firmly within the lines of her performance at all times.

'Are you tired?' he asked. 'Do you wish to retire? I could find Lady Montvale for you.'

Sari shook her head.

'No, I am fine. I merely realised I am promised for a dance with Mr Morgan and would rather avoid that particular torture. I don't think I can bear another lecture on the proper methods of storing snuff.'

Michael held out his arm.

'Then by all means, let us avoid him. Come, I will find you some refreshment. You look as if you could use the rest.'

'And I was just about to thank you for your gallant gesture, my lord, but hinting that a young woman looks hagridden is not calculated to restore her spirits!'

Michael smiled and tucked her hand more firmly around his arm. There was something infectiously appealing about the way she tried to hold back a smile, he thought, as he watched her dimples flash and disappear.

He had felt peculiarly privileged watching her performance over this past week. As if he were the only one who knew the real purpose of the play, while the audience remained in sublime ignorance. Sometimes her eyes would meet his in the middle of one of her flirtations and the amusement in them would shimmer and deepen and he would not be able to hold back an answering smile.

He was also surprised how remarkably easy it was to talk to her. She was so different from the usual London misses that he found it almost inconceivable that she managed to play that role so well with some of her beaus.

He picked up a glass of champagne from a tray and handed it to her. He watched her take a dainty sip and then unconsciously run her tongue across her lower lip. He breathed in slowly, wishing his own code of honour didn't prevent him from doing some of the things he was

contemplating at the moment. His gaze skimmed over the
line of her shoulder down the embroidered blush silk that
clung lovingly to her breasts. As it had back in the shooting gallery it seemed it would be the most natural thing
in the world to reach out and pull her to him.

He looked away, taking in the noisy crowd around them.
Whatever society might say about her if it knew of her
role at the Institute, as far as he was concerned she was
no different than any young woman in this room. And that
meant that whatever his body was signalling, she was not
mistress material.

The fleeting thought that he might be willing to consider breaking his iron rule and wedding her in order to bed
her, assuming she was even interested, just convinced him
that he had to be more careful. Lust was a damn poor reason for tying himself for life to anyone, let alone someone
as impulsive and uncontrollable as Sari. She might keep
herself on the side of caution by sheer force, but he knew
instinctively she would always be in danger of breaking
through whatever boundaries surrounded her. Especially
if someone else was at risk. She was constitutionally incapable of being detached.

The point was that she was firmly out of bounds, he
told himself rigidly. The sooner his body caught up with
his mind on that issue, the better. He was almost glad
when he saw Hamlin approaching them. He wished he'd
had time to tell her to take special care around him. He
would have to tell her later that Hamlin was of particular
interest to them.

'Ah, Miss Trevor, it is my dance next, I believe?'

Michael watched as Sari transformed once again, smiling shyly and dropping her eyes modestly under Hamlin's
avid gaze as he led her towards the dance floor. She was
far too good at this.

* * *

Sari almost wished Hamlin wasn't so easy to snare. It was no challenge convincing him to take her for a turn in the garden after the dance. She suspected he had been drinking more than usual, which served her purposes well—he might reveal more under the influence of spirits. The garden was well lit and there were other people wandering about. Lady Montvale herself had assured her that such *sorties*, if brief, were considered acceptable.

'Vulgar din that French music they were just playing, don't you think?' he began inauspiciously once they were on the balcony. 'Give me good English church music any day to soothe the soul, eh?'

Sari smiled demurely and edged away as he pressed her arm meaningfully, wishing she could push him into the ornamental fish pond.

'Oh, I'm sure I don't know, Mr Hamlin. We did not have such music in Somerset. You do not like the French, then?'

'Crawling with liberal lunatics if you ask me. Nothing they'd like better than to force their fancy Frenchie sauces on to every English table.'

This ridiculous assertion in a city that probably had as many French cooks as English chimney sweeps almost made her laugh out loud.

'Oh, but surely now that the war is over there is nothing to fear, is there, Mr Hamlin?' she asked breathlessly.

'Nothing to fear? There dam…dashed well is a great deal to fear. But rest assured there are those of us who are not waiting on fate. We'll not let this government drag us any further down the path to ruin. You can put your faith in us, Miss Trevor.' He accompanied this portentous statement with an attempt to slide his arm around her waist, and she slipped lightly away, flicking open her fan and wishing she could blush on command. He was clearly too tipsy to be cautious, but she had no intention of courting scandal, no matter how tempted she was to press him further. She would just have to continue her inquest on safer ground.

'Oh, I do have complete faith in you, Mr Hamlin. Now we really should go back inside or Lady Montvale will be ever so cross with me.'

Hamlin conceded with another fatuous smile and led her back into the house, obviously satisfied with his night's hunting.

Sari was no less satisfied with hers and was hoping to find Michael to tell him about her conversation when a firm hand grasped her elbow. She glanced up at the earl himself, but to her surprise he was looking rather grim and her heart sank.

'You look rather heated, Miss Trevor, perhaps you need to retire for a moment?'

He led her past the entrance to the main drawing room and into the corridor beyond, beckoning to Anderson to join them as they passed. The three of them found an empty room and entered, Anderson closing the door behind them with an enquiring look.

'"I am sure you are right, Mr Hamlin..." "Of course, Mr Hamlin."' Michael mimicked the missish tones she had adopted in the garden. 'What the devil do you know about him?' he asked pointedly, keeping his voice low with apparent effort.

Sari squared her shoulders, shooting him a warning glance. 'We were just talking.'

'You were doing a great deal more, and you know it. Why didn't you tell me you knew it was he at the Eagle and Crown that night?' he asked accusingly.

'That night? What does Sari know about that night?' asked Anderson, bemused.

Michael turned to him, suddenly realising his slip. Sari jumped in, thinking fast.

'Oh, the devil. I am sorry, Anderson, but you might as well know the truth. I was changing for fencing in the *salle* when you and Lord Crayle discussed that meeting. I was only half-dressed so I could not very well come charging out and warn you I was there, could I? I did not intend to eavesdrop.'

She watched the ruddy wave of colour spread across poor Anderson's cheeks at the image. He was such a lamb, she thought, so easy to distract from the fact that as far as she knew, no such conversation had taken place. She was about to hurry on before he overcame his embarrassment, but just at that moment, the door opened and Alicia swept in.

'There you are!' She glared accusingly at Sari. 'Emily Brigham said she saw you and Mr Anderson sneaking off together…' She stopped as she stepped further into the room and noticed her brother.

'Go back to Lady Montvale, Allie, this does not concern you,' he said briefly.

'What does not concern me?' she insisted mulishly.

'This is no time for tantrums, Allie, we're busy.'

'Really, Michael,' Anderson interrupted. 'There is no need to take that tone with her. We can talk with Sari later.'

Alicia, caught between shock at the familiar address Anderson had used with Sari and annoyance at her brother's dismissal, fell back on tried-and-proven methods. Her lower lip trembled ominously.

'I want to know what is going on!'

'What your brother said is true, Lady Alicia, this is none of your concern,' Anderson said calmly. 'Come, I will take you back to Lady Montvale.'

Despite a flicker of surprise at his uncharacteristic firmness, she moved away from him.

'No. You are all being cruel to me! Why do you always take Chris and Letty seriously and yet forever treat me like a child?' Alicia accused Michael, her voice rising dangerously.

'It is a bit difficult to treat you like an adult if you won't behave like one,' he replied in exasperation.

Sari watched anger and a sad neediness do battle in Alicia's eyes and took pity on her. She hooked her arm through the younger woman's.

'Come, let us see if we cannot find some iced champagne.'

To her surprise Alicia's shoulders sagged and she gave in without resistance, but Michael's voice stopped them.

'We are not done here yet, Miss Trevor.'

Sari took a deep breath. She was determined to do whatever it took to succeed at the Institute, but there were limits. Without releasing her light hold on Alicia's arm, she turned to Michael.

'Lord Crayle, I realise you have some issues you wish to discuss with me and I will be glad to address them. However, this is neither the time nor the place. You may seek me out tomorrow and we will discuss them then. Goodnight, gentlemen.'

She guided her companion out gently but firmly, trying not to smile at the look on the two men's faces.

For a moment Michael just continued to stare at the closed door. But then he turned towards Anderson who stood there, grinning.

'Don't take it so badly, Michael. If this were a fencing match you would have conceded the point gracefully. Instead, you are putting me forcibly in mind of one of Allie's sulks. Why are you so annoyed? If she was getting information out of Hamlin, it sounds like she was doing just what we asked of her, no?'

He felt a wave of self-disgust as he realised just how he had reacted. Anderson was right. She was just doing what she was commissioned to do. And she had been right, too. This was neither the time nor the place to question her about it.

He never should have followed her in the first place, but when he had seen Hamlin guiding her towards the balcony he had acted without thinking. He had not even been thinking primarily about Hamlin's role in this case. He just had not been too happy about the thought of her alone in the gardens at night with that fool. He had skulked after her like an antiquated chaperon, or worse, like a jealous lover. Even as he had processed what the man was saying he had become even angrier, to the point where he had not been thinking rationally when he had pulled her into this room. He never should have motioned to Anderson to join them. But no, then it would have been worse. Perhaps that was why he had wanted his friend there, to keep him under control.

Was this what it had been like for his father? This mindless pull that made him act against his character, against all better judgement. When she had looked at him with that mischievous smile he had the urge to pull her out of whatever room they were in and continue where they had left off in the deserted alley in Pimlico. Watching Hamlin put his hands on her had been almost more than he could stand and he hated it. Even as a boy he had felt contempt for his father's jealous sulks. The thought that he was heading down the same path was unbearable.

He shook his head and put down his glass, moving towards the door. The worst thing to do was to dwell on it.

'You're right,' he told Anderson as they left the room. 'She's just doing as we asked.'

Chapter Sixteen

'Lord Crayle would like to see you in his office, Miss Trevor,' Penrose announced, peeking into Deakins's laboratory the next morning. Sari started and almost dropped the beaker she was holding and Deakins took it from her cautiously.

'Better run along then, Miss Sari. Not a man to keep waiting, eh?'

Sari wished she could disagree. She rubbed her hands apprehensively on her simple poplin skirt and went upstairs.

He was standing by the window, his hands clasped behind his back. With the light behind him she could not make out his expression so she waited for his opening, her own hands clasped before her, her chin raised bravely.

'I owe you an apology,' he said finally.

Sari's jaw slackened in surprise. One corner of his mouth rose in a faint, self-deprecating manner.

'Well, at least you seem to realise the novelty of it,' he said mildly after a while. 'This is the second time, too. It is becoming quite a habit.'

'Just so I am clear; what precisely are you apologising for?'

'Damned if I know. My general behaviour. I have a suspicion I have been unfairly harsh on you.'

Sari had an incredible urge to grin. She had to make
him ruin a perfectly good apology by asking, didn't she?
She ducked her head, holding it in.

'Well?' he demanded suddenly as she remained silent.

'Well what?'

'I am not very practised in these matters, but I assume
at this point you indicate whether or not you accept the
apology.'

Sari could not hold it in any longer and the smile peeked
through. For an intelligent man he could be quite spectac-
ularly witless sometime.

'You would like me to forgive your general behaviour?
Very well, then. I absolve you,' she offered grandly.

Sari watched as an answering smile came reluctantly
to his lips.

'You'll burn in hell, Sari Trevor.'

'I will save you a seat.'

He merely shook his head and stood there hesitantly,
leaving Sari wondering what was coming next.

'Allie apologised to me,' he said finally.

Sari raised her eyebrows in surprise. 'It is becoming
quite an epidemic.'

'So it seems. I dare say I have you to thank for that as
well?'

'Not really. Anderson, I believe. I think she would not
mind gaining his respect.'

'She already holds hostage whatever common sense he
ever possessed.' Michael sighed.

'I am not sure she sees it that way and I think it would
be best to let her go about it in her own way. It appears to
be doing her some good.'

She paused. He was looking at her inscrutably.

'Do you mind… I mean, that Anderson…' He trailed off.

Sari's puzzlement gave way to dismay. Had this been part of the problem all along? Had he been worried that unsuitable little highway-robbing Sari Trevor would try to entrap his friend?

'No, I don't fancy him, if that is what you mean.' She crossed her arms defensively, her eyes suddenly hot with the sting of tears. She had thought he was at last beginning to trust her.

Michael noted the belligerent stance and wondered whether she was telling the truth or simply protecting herself. The increasingly familiar curl of jealousy, hot and bitter, tightened in his stomach and he was about to continue his prodding when his censorious side came to his rescue, reminding him it was none of his business. And speaking of business…

'You still owe me an explanation about Hamlin.'

She nodded. 'I recognised him from the Eagle and Crown when we were introduced in the park last week. All I did was act the wide-eyed widgeon and he delivered the goods himself. That was the first time I had heard him mention anything of even the vaguest interest and I was going to inform you.'

Michael glanced out of the window.

'We have been watching Hamlin, but there is nothing unusual about his activities so far,' he said at last.

Sari stared at him in surprise. Clearly the last thing she had expected was a confidence.

'Do you believe he was just used once?' she asked tentatively.

'Perhaps. But judging from what he said to you, he still believes himself very much involved. Or perhaps that was pure bravado.'

'He was somewhat…inebriated.'

'So I noticed.'

'Were you spying on me?' She grinned.

'I was keeping an eye on him. I did not think you knew who he was.'

'That was kind of you,' she said demurely.

He smiled reluctantly. 'Doing it a bit too brown, Miss Trevor. Do not fall too deeply into your persona of a pea goose, it does not suit you.'

'Really? I thought I was rather good at it.'

'Let us put it this way, it is not convincing to anyone who knows your real nature.' He changed tack. 'As for Hamlin, he should make an appearance at the Flannerys' tonight. We should be there. Lady Montvale already knows.'

'What should I do?'

'Continue in the same vein, but stay low.'

Staying low was easier said than done. Since her appearance in society, Sari had, somewhat to her surprise, developed a following. The most obvious of her beaus were Sir Gerald and Mr Hamlin, but the most pleasing was Lord Edgerton. Despite her antipathy for his politics, she enjoyed his company and found it was no hardship to keep him close. It was especially gratifying since she knew his interest in her wasn't driven by the rumours of her fortune. He treated her with respect and without the fervour and cockiness typical of the young dandies, and she reasoned that his prominent position amongst the more conservative of the Tories could prove valuable.

Lady Montvale was delighted with his growing *tendre* for Sari and practically crowed every time Sari received a gift from him. Side by side with the flowers and sweetmeats of her other beaus, his presents stood out as well. He sent books and once he had even sent a print of the Dorset coast. Lady Montvale said she had never heard of him bestowing similar gifts on anyone in the past.

When he came to claim her for a country dance at the Flannerys' soirée Sari began by thanking him for the print.

'Have you ever been to Dorset?' he asked, his eyes settling on her with a warmth she rarely saw him exhibit elsewhere.

'No, never. It seems lovely, though.'

'It is indeed. I hope that you will one day enjoy a visit there. It would be a fine setting for your loveliness.'

Sari blushed. This was the first time he had made an overt reference to his appreciation of her looks and she found she did not know how to respond. The fact that she knew his family seat was in Dorset only made it more significant. He recollected himself and continued in more casual tones.

'You are happy with Lady Montvale?'

Sari, thankful for the change of subject, smiled.

'Oh, indeed. She is very kind.'

'Both her father and husband were outstanding Englishmen. They knew what was important for our country. Unfortunately, fewer and fewer of our young people are aware of what makes this country great.'

'Surely that is just a symptom of youth, Lord Edgerton? As people mature they become more responsible.'

'Perhaps. Unfortunately Britain may be changed beyond recognition by the time they come to their senses. And our government has lost its role as society's guide. These are dangerous times indeed.'

'Isn't *dangerous* rather a strong word, my lord?'

'Not at all. We are perhaps in greater danger today than when we were at war. At least then we were all aligned against a single enemy and our position against liberal reform was crystal clear. Now this so-called peace

is opening us to the real revolutionary threat. Napoleon
may have failed to destroy the England we love, but that
knave Castlereagh is succeeding in doing just that, and in
a much more insidious manner. Masquerading as an arch-
conservative, through his foreign policies he is in fact
opening England to precisely those ideals he professes to
abhor. The most insidious threats are often from within…'
He seemed to remember himself and gave an uncharacteristically self-deprecating laugh. 'You are too good a
listener, Miss Trevor. I should not bore you with such matters.'

To Sari's dismay the dance was winding to a close. Her
time on the floor with Mr Hamlin that evening was significantly less enjoyable. He could not be derailed from
discussing his new horse. The best she could achieve was
an invitation to go riding two days hence in Hyde Park.
She thought of reporting her conversation with Edgerton
to Anderson or Lord Crayle, but felt that his comment, although interesting, was hardly conclusive of anything but
factional disagreements within the Tory party. If it had
not been for the peculiar tension between him and Hamlin that persisted, she would not have thought much of it.
As it was, she felt it best to wait until she had something
more to offer. Perhaps having Hamlin to herself during
their ride she might finally uncover something of value.

Chapter Seventeen

The following day she had no chance to pursue her questioning as neither Lord Edgerton nor Hamlin were planning to attend one of the highlights of the Season, a masked ball at the Scunthorpes' residence in Richmond. Seated in the carriage with Alicia, who was bubbling with uninhibited enthusiasm and very prettily dressed as a shepherdess, Sari admitted she was also excited at the prospect of masked anonymity. She would love to forget herself for a few hours and Lady Montvale had provided her with the perfect costume for this purpose. It was an exotic Venetian dress of rich brocaded royal-blue velvet and silver lace, complete with a brunette wig and, instead of the traditional domino mask, a Venetian masque which fully covered her face.

The ball was in full swing when they arrived and Sari was soon enjoying herself immensely, inventing various identities as she passed from dance partner to partner. With a rather rotund Roman centurion she adopted a French accent and amused them both with tales of a daring escape from Napoleon's armies. Once the dance ended he led her towards the refreshment tables just as a tall figure in a black domino entered the room. The centurion surveyed him, laughing.

'By Gad, Crayle, you don't even make an attempt at a costume, you dog!'

'I am sorry to disappoint you, Ponsonby. I'm afraid I don't have your skill for concealment,' Michael retorted satirically. Ponsonby chuckled, unruffled.

'Devil take you, man. I protest,' he expostulated, turning to appeal to Sari. '*Mademoiselle*, have you ever met a crueller fellow?'

'Since I have not been introduced to your friend I cannot presume to say I have met him, *n'est ce pas*? And so I must answer that, indeed, I have met crueller.'

She wondered if her French accent and her low tones would be sufficient to fool Michael. She could detect nothing but amusement in the faint smile that touched his lips as he turned to her.

'That is an omission then that must be rectified, *mademoiselle*. Ponsonby, make yourself useful and introduce us.'

'Faith, I would if I could, but Mademoiselle la Mysterieuse is as cruel as you and denies me. Add your entreaties to mine, Crayle.'

'Then I would be cruel indeed, to force *mademoiselle* to do anything that does not please her.'

'You are very gallant, *monsieur*, to take my wishes to heart,' she responded, enjoying herself.

'Then I hope you take my wishes to heart and allow me this dance?'

'Now see here, old chap,' Ponsonby exclaimed. 'I was just going to procure *mademoiselle* some refreshment.'

'Very kind of you, Ponsonby. Don't let me stop you. *Mademoiselle?*'

He held out his hand to her and with a laugh she placed hers in it as she thanked the poor spluttering Ponsonby and allowed Michael to lead her back to the dance floor.

'Perhaps you were a little cruel to Monsieur Ponsonby, no?' she said as they took their place in the set.

'My only cruelty was in depriving him of your company, *mademoiselle*. No doubt I will find his second calling on me tomorrow for the offence,' he replied, switching to French now that they were alone. He spoke fluently and without a betraying accent, and she wondered if he had always had this ability or if this, too, was something he had picked up during those years of war with France.

'His second? Oh, you mean a duel. You are laughing at me, no?'

'Do you mind?' he asked as they turned in the dance.

'Not at all. I prefer humour to compliments.'

She saw his smile take on a quizzical cast and hoped he would not identify her too soon. It was freeing to be able to flirt with him anonymously. She knew it would be over with the dance, but for the moment…

'Do you? You are quite unique, then. Not many women share your preference.'

She gave a Gallic shrug. 'That is only because they convince themselves the flattery is sincere. I think it is much more enjoyable to laugh with someone than listen to contrived compliments about one's eyebrows.'

Michael laughed.

'Though I have not had the felicity of inspecting said eyebrows I rather doubt much strain is involved in flattering them. Still, I imagine if you are of a practical mindset, such flattery doesn't appeal.'

'I am afraid that I am terribly practical. It is very sad.'

'For your *beaux*, perhaps. To be confronted with practicality when one is straining to find an original compliment can be quite disconcerting, *mademoiselle*,' he said, still with the same amused and relaxed smile. She was so caught up in the pleasure of having his attention fo-

cused on her so gently that she did not think before she
corrected him.

'It is *madame*, not *mademoiselle*.'

He bowed slightly, a touch sardonically, and she realised that a married woman who admitted openly to a
multitude of beaus and an intimate acquaintance with flirtation was clearly sending signals that had nothing to do
with propriety.

'I apologise, *madame*. Have you been long in England?
Are you here with your family?'

Here was her chance to redeem herself. She knew him
well enough to know that all she had to do was mention
the presence of her fictitious husband and she would be
categorised firmly as off-limits. She also knew it would
bring an end to the flirtation.

'No, my husband returned to France, but I did not wish
to go.'

There, she had stamped herself quite unequivocally.
She felt a mixture of shame and breathless excitement at
her daring.

'I find it hard to believe any man could be so blind as
to leave you behind. I gather he is not the most astute of
men?'

She shrugged again, wondering how a woman would
react in such a situation.

'I was married very young and we do not suit, you see.'
She paused, wondering if that was perhaps too much. 'You
must forgive me, *monsieur*, for becoming serious; you are
so easy to talk to that I fear I must bore you.'

'No, you do not bore me. But our dance is ending and
you must allow me to make up for my earlier cruelty in
denying you refreshment by procuring you some now.'

She nodded, dismayed that it was already over. In her
inattention she almost stumbled on a loose carpet as they

made their way down the corridor to the refreshment room. His hand clasped hers where it rested on his arm as he steadied her.

'Are you all right?'

'I am perhaps a little tired, the dancing, you see...' She trailed off, breathless, and to her consternation he turned and steered her into a side corridor.

'Of course. There is a quiet room here where you can rest for a moment,' he said politely as he led her into a small sitting room which looked onto the gardens and where two armchairs were placed at a comfortable distance from the lit fireplace. Sari sat down tensely on the edge of one of the chairs, wondering what she should do. She knew it was folly, but she did not want to unmask herself, not quite yet. In the sudden silence of the room the promise of some more time alone with him was so seductive she felt it would take much more willpower than she currently had to call a halt to this. She searched desperately for an opening as the silence stretched on.

Michael inspected her. Her mask, with its silvery tear, was a very effective cover. The mouth was rosebud perfect, raised slightly at the edges in a secretive smile. A mask that laughed silently at its own misfortune. She seemed tense, but he could hardly reassure her he had no intention of pouncing on her without adding to her confusion, if that was indeed what had her sitting rigid in her chair.

'Are you warm enough?' he asked finally, hoping to relax her with an innocuous opening. Her shoulders sagged slightly and she laughed.

'Yes, thank you. Your terrible weather has not vanquished me yet.'

'You are a brave woman then. It has defeated many valiant souls.'

'It is a formidable opponent. Do you not mind it?'

'Oh, I'll escape it one day soon,' he said lightly.

She started, one hand rising slightly in her lap.

'You would travel then? Somewhere warm?'

'It is only a vague dream,' he said dismissively.

'A dream…' She sighed. 'Tell me where you would go.'

It was a peculiar command. The wistful echo in her voice removed the sting of its directness. He looked away, into the flickering gold-and-orange flames. It brought to mind desert colours. Sand and heat.

'Egypt,' he said impulsively. 'I would find a horse and guide and ride along the cliffs by the Nile to the Valley of the Kings. Sleep under the stars and watch the sun rise over the temples in Luxor.'

His voice was matter of fact, as if he were discussing the rethatching of a tenant's roof. But it did not obscure the thirst in his voice. It was all the more potent an image for the force with which it was reined in.

'Why not go, then? The war is over and the world is open. What stops you?' she prompted tentatively.

'Responsibilities,' he replied non-committally, surprised by the seductiveness of the image which he had conjured up.

'Are you afraid?' she asked after a moment.

He started at that.

'Afraid? Of what?'

'I do not know. Perhaps that reality will fall short of the dream. Realising dreams often leads to disappointment.'

He smiled. Perhaps there was a grain of truth in that.

'And you. What are your dreams?' he deflected.

'I wish I were free to do as I choose, to go where I choose. Sometimes I think I should have been born a man,' she answered without hesitation and there was a hint of both anger and desperation in her voice.

'That would have been a great loss to men.'

'That is gallant, but hardly sincere. It would be no loss to the world and a very great freedom for me.'

'I understand, but I would argue against your accusation of insincerity. And this freedom, what would you do with it?'

'I would come with you to Egypt,' she said simply.

His body tightened at the thought. What would it be like to escape with her? Riding together through the scorched desert, trailing the fata morgana that wavered elusively on the horizon, taunting... There was a release in the charade of anonymity, in the fact that she obviously still thought he didn't know who she was. He knew he should call a halt to it, tell her he had known who she was most likely from the moment he had heard her voice, and certainly from the moment he had taken her hand to draw her into the dance. But he didn't want it to stop. Not yet.

Oh, to travel with her. To let himself be swept along by her energy and curiosity. To ally himself with her fiercely protective loyalty. And her passion. She might be inexperienced, but her response to him that night had been incredible. She had reacted with the same force and excitement as she grasped at life.

He reminded himself brutally there were other sides to her. Her headlong pursuit of her interests might not differ from his own in essence, but it definitely did in its reckless execution. He had had enough of that during the war. He had gone into that conflict already scarred by his family and his role in their tragedy and the war had only made it worse. An essential part of him had come out of those years paper thin. If he admitted that she was important, he risked shredding what was left when something happened to her. And it would. She seemed to have no restraints when she set her mind to something. He could not trust her. It would be setting himself up for destruction.

'Once you leave the protective cocoon of the British Empire it is not at all glamorous,' he said finally, as much to himself as to her. 'Dirt, flies, heat, sweat and bad food might dim your fantasies of self-reliance a little.'

She stiffened, her hands fisting in her lap. 'You think I'm a…a hothouse flower? That I cannot cope with such an environment because I am a woman?'

He relented; he did not want to abandon the fantasy yet. He picked up one of her gloved hands and gently eased it open before he even realised what he was doing. He knew he should let it go, but he did not want to.

'Not because you are a woman. I think women are hardier than men as a rule. But you are no farm woman working the fields. In a way we are all hothouse flowers. I would lay money on the fact you would manage better than any woman at this ball, but that is no yardstick by which to measure your ability to control such an environment. It is dangerous to delude yourself that you can.'

'I see you took my "no compliments" directive to heart,' she replied slowly after a moment. 'You are quite unstintingly direct.'

'You can always repay in kind,' he said almost playfully, but there was a challenge there.

'Very well.' She considered in silence for a moment, then straightened slightly, but she didn't withdraw her hand from his light clasp. 'You seem to believe you can only trust what you can control. That is a very limiting approach to life, and to yourself. Standing very still on a rope bridge may stop it from swaying, but it is hardly a good way to get across.'

His grip tightened, his eyes narrowing. Who did she think she was with her facile analysis? He kept his hands rigid around hers to prevent himself from pulling away her mask. For a second he saw the image of the mask snapping

off and revealing…nothing, an empty shell of clothing that
sighed into a heap on the armchair. He drew a deep breath
and relaxed his hands. Overreacting again. He closed his
eyes briefly and laughed.

'Close enough, *chérie*. But not very flattering, you will
admit,' he said wryly.

'I do not agree. I think you underestimate yourself and
others. I would wager there is more than enough strength
in you to keep safe even without all that control.'

He laughed again, somewhat embarrassed and flattered
despite himself.

'Thank you, I think. But you should practise what you
preach. It seems to me you believe you can create a better façade of yourself than the person you really are.' He
leaned forward and ran one finger gently over the cheek
of the ivory mask. 'You should have more faith in what
lies beneath.'

The masked face dipped and again he resisted the urge
to remove it. Instead, he leaned back, forcing himself to
release her hand.

'What about Italy?' he asked suddenly, and she laughed,
accepting the olive branch.

'What, now it is Italy?'

'Why not? Less exotic, but more manageable. We can
sail along the coast…do you like to sail?'

'I love it. Not a big boat, though…just two wanderers.'

'Two travelling minstrels.'

She tilted her head, again giving the mask a quizzical
air. 'You can sing?'

'As fine as any dog.'

Her laughter broke free once more, incongruous against
the mask's circumspect smile. The longing to remove it
gripped him again, more powerfully this time. It was ridiculous to continue the charade.

'Take off your mask,' he said abruptly.

'No!' Her hands flew to her face as if to secure it by force if need be.

'Then how am I to kiss you with the mask on?'

'You wish to kiss me?'

'Yes,' he answered tensely, throwing caution to the wind.

She hesitated, her hands still hovering near her face.

'In the dark, then.'

'Why?'

'Because I wish it. You wish to kiss me; I wish it to be in the dark.'

Despite himself, he smiled at her stubborn tone.

'Very well, in the dark. Into the garden, then?'

He led her out to the balcony and down the marble steps into the shrubbery. The night was overcast and the narrow paths between the high-trimmed yew trees were a thick, pitch black. They groped their way along, stumbling and laughing until Michael finally gave up trying to find his way to an open space and turned and fumbled for the strings of her mask.

'I'll be lucky to find you in this, let alone kiss you,' he whispered.

She gave a breathless laugh. 'If you miss, I will tell you.'

'I never miss.' He slid his hands up her neck to her face. It was warm and soft, firm where his fingers grazed her cheekbones. He gave himself over to the sensation of mapping her face with his fingers and palms. He had wanted to touch her for so long.

He felt her breaths quicken in the feather-soft exhalations against his fingers as they brushed her mouth. The heavy smells of the garden overlay the gentle scent that emanated from her, but he could almost taste it, exotic, welcoming, haunting. He gave in at last and bent to find her lips with his. As he stood in that pocket of inky night, utterly lost in her taste and feel and smell, there were no thoughts but the most primitive. Just lust, sheer glorious lust.

Then she broke away. He heard her gasp and then she was nothing but the swish of her skirts against the bushes.

He didn't follow, merely fumbled in the darkness for the mask she had dropped. Her words came back to him. She had read him with devastating accuracy. He did fear abandoning control, letting go… Dangerous. Every time he let down his guard she provided more evidence of just how dangerous she was.

He turned the mask absently in his hands. As for her masquerade…he would leave it. She would certainly not mention it. No doubt she thought he had not pierced her disguise. He would leave before the unmasking and act as if nothing at all had happened that night. For a moment he contemplated tossing the mask into the darkness, but then he gave a short, harsh laugh. No, he should keep it to remind him of his folly. He had an unpleasant premonition he would need reminding.

Chapter Eighteen

The following afternoon, Sari tied on a chip bonnet with rather abrupt movements, preparing for her scheduled ride with Hamlin. She stared at her reflection in the mirror with something approaching despair. What had she gained in that flirtation with Michael? She had only lost herself a bit further for the price of a kiss in the dark while he…he added another innocuous dalliance to a long and no doubt only half-remembered list. She had no idea what she felt—restless, elated, depressed, confused… She knew she had to continue as though nothing at all had happened. And nothing had, she reminded herself sternly. She squared her shoulders and went downstairs to meet Hamlin.

After some twenty minutes of gentle riding in the park Sari's already tried nerves were on the verge of snapping as Hamlin disregarded another conversational gambit aimed at directing him to the topic of politics. He seemed nervous and distracted and she wondered why he had asked her to go on this ride. She didn't delude herself that he was really fond of her, but she thought him greedy enough to at least make an effort to charm her. Clearly, even the appeal of her wealth was paling and her only achievement that day was to secure a waltz with him at the Bennetts' ball due to take place outside London that evening.

To her surprise, he insisted they ride farther than usual, and she was just wondering whether to demand that they turn back when Hamlin reined in. He excused himself nervously and strode a few yards to where a man on horseback stood waiting. Sari stared after him in surprise and inspected the man. He was obviously not a dandy. He looked more like a bailiff, with neat but unostentatious clothing. The two men exchanged a few words, some of them appearing heated, as the stranger made an abrupt gesture in her direction. When the man had left, Hamlin returned to her side and appeared quite relieved when she suggested they head back.

'I say,' he burst out. 'I'm dreadfully sorry to cry off, but I won't be able to attend the Bennetts' ball in Richmond tonight after all. Things to take care of, don't you know,' he mumbled, obviously embarrassed.

Sari did not know, but she definitely had her suspicions. Clearly, something the stranger had mentioned to Hamlin had forced him to forgo this entertainment. Reanimated by a flush of excitement, she was as anxious to be rid of him as he clearly was of her.

Later, after changing out of her riding habit, she slipped out of Montvale House and took a hackney cab to the Institute.

'Is Mr Anderson in, Penrose?' she asked as she entered.

'No, miss, he is away until tomorrow. I believe Lord Crayle is in his office, though.'

Sari's heart gave an almost audible thump. She was not ready to see him, not so soon. But this could not wait. She nodded to Penrose and headed towards the stairs. When no one answered her knock on the door she was swamped by a mixture of relief and bitter disappointment. Perhaps if she just left a note…

'Miss Trevor? Is something wrong?'

She whirled around as the earl came down the corridor. As usual, she lost some assurance under the scrutiny of his grey eyes. She pressed the palms of her hands together and decided to present her facts as simply as possible.

'I was riding with Hamlin this afternoon in the park. He met someone suspicious. I think they are planning something tonight.'

Stated so bluntly it sounded flimsy. Perhaps she was just desperate to prove herself worthwhile. She clasped and unclasped her hands nervously, wishing he would say something. He motioned her into his office, and she entered, her nerves tightening as he closed the door behind them.

'The man. What did he look like?' he asked curtly.

She stared at the floor, concentrating. 'He was several inches shorter than Hamlin, perhaps five foot seven, clean shaven but with long side whiskers and dark-brown hair with a reddish tinge; he had slightly bulbous eyes and his nose looked as if it had been broken and set wrong. He wore a low-crowned hat and a simple worsted suit with a white shirt and dark cravat—no fobs or rings—just a silver chain, maybe a watch chain. And his boots looked more like Henries's than yours or Anderson's, sturdy but simple.'

'So you are saying he is a tradesman or a steward, perhaps?'

'Perhaps, I am not sure…' She faltered. 'His horse looked expensive, though, a very neat chestnut mare with four white socks.'

'That's a very detailed description.'

'I made sure I inspected him very carefully,' she said defensively.

Michael raised his arms before him in surrender.

'Calm down, I was not doubting your word. I was merely impressed.'

Sari relaxed somewhat. It was nice to be able to impress him.

Michael turned away from her shy smile and moved towards the window overlooking the sombre buildings outside. It was too damn soon to have to deal with her after last night and he could tell she was as uncomfortable as he was although it seemed she had no idea he had been aware of her masquerade. This only made it more clear that what he had done last night had been as irresponsible as anything she had ever done. For the second time in his life he had indulged lust over duty. Kissing an innocent young woman was a breach of society's rules and bad enough, but kissing a young woman who was effectively under his professional responsibility was a breach of his own code of honour. For the second time he had crossed a line he would condemn anyone else for crossing. It was both self-indulgent and hypocritical, two characteristics he despised.

He wished he could just terminate her role at the Institute, but he knew he could not do that to her. Being part of the Institute meant more to her than it ever had to him. For him it was a means to an end. For her it seemed to have become an essential part of her existence. Removing her simply so he could avoid temptation would add cruelty to his growing list of transgressions.

Not that she realised the effect she was having on him. In fact, aside from the night of the masquerade, this past week she had been treating him either with the same playful friendliness she bestowed so easily on Anderson and Antonelli, or worse, with that protective loyalty she reserved for her family.

He had never before allowed lust to dictate his behaviour and he had no intention of allowing it to do so now.

The only way he had survived those endless years of war, of chaos and tragedy and brutality, had been by establishing barriers and staying in control wherever possible. Relations with women were no different. He had gone from one carefully selected mistress to another, always receiving and providing pleasure, but never letting anything break the boundaries he set between the various compartments in his life.

He was a grown man, for heaven's sake, and he would just have to resign himself to the fact that he could not, in honour, act on this desire. Lust wore itself out—it was by its nature transient, moving from object to object. He would just have to wait this one out.

He fixed his mind on the information she had given him. It could be nothing, but at this point they had to explore every option. If there was any connection between this encounter and their case, they had best heighten the watch on Hamlin that night. And if it was nothing more than a secret gaming meet, well then, all their other leads had fallen through so far.

He turned back to her.

'Would you remember this man if you saw him, even dressed differently?'

'Yes,' she replied unhesitatingly.

Michael weighed his next words carefully. He knew he should not involve her further, but he couldn't afford to let this opportunity slip through his hands. It might all depend on her identifying the man. He decided to compromise.

'Would you mind having a headache tonight?' he asked.

She blinked at him in surprise.

'A headache?'

'I would like you to stay at Lady Montvale's tonight when she and Allie go to stay with the Bennetts in Richmond. Margaret will understand. We might need you, so wear something inconspicuous. I am warning you, however. You are to do nothing but what you are explicitly told to do, do you understand?'

A thrill of excitement ran through her and she nodded firmly, trying to subdue her smile.

Michael saw the light that entered her eyes and shook his head almost ruefully.

'You are an unnatural person, do you know that?'

'Why? What have I done now?' she asked, bemused.

'Most proper young ladies would prefer going to a ball rather than spending the evening cooped up waiting in a dark carriage.'

Sari coloured slightly but wrinkled her nose dismissively as she opened the door.

'You know perfectly well I am not at all a proper young lady and I would not serve your purposes if I were. I'll be ready.'

Chapter Nineteen

Sari was ready hours before the call finally came. The weather was unseasonably warm and under her cloak she wore a simple cotton shirt and trousers she had taken from Deakins's chest of disguises before returning to Lady Montvale's house. She ran down the steps and into the waiting unmarked carriage. Michael was already inside, dressed in equally plain clothes.

'O'Brien and Morton followed him towards Southwark. It looks like you were right and something is up after all. They'll leave directions on the way,' he said abruptly and then settled into silence.

Sari wanted to ask him a million questions, but knew better than to talk. They drove fast, with the blinds pulled down, leaving them almost in full darkness except for the periodic dull light of the gas street lamps. They stopped once and she heard a street boy's voice squeak something at their driver, who then whipped up the horses again. Then suddenly, the carriage took a sharp turn and sank into a rut in the road, lurching dangerously.

Sari grabbed for the strap, but missed as the carriage righted itself abruptly and she was flung backwards. Luckily Michael braced his leg on the seat in front of him and grabbed her before she slammed against the window. She landed against him, her head hitting the side of the carriage with a dull thud.

It was not a serious blow, but enough to daze her. Michael's hand tightened on her waist, his other going to her head.

'Are you all right?' he asked, his fingers running gently across her temple, searching for the bruise. He found it, just as his fingers slid into her hair, and she gave a slight yelp.

'Hold still,' he commanded, probing gently. 'The skin isn't broken,' he said finally, his voice husky.

But Sari was no longer paying attention to the bruise. The pain accentuated the feel of his fingers in her hair. They were warm and gentle and each time they moved against her scalp, they sent off a tingling that burned through her. She squirmed slightly, but that only made her realise she was sitting on his lap. A wave of heat rushed from her chest, settling between her thighs and she barely bit back a moan at the strange sensation.

'Hold still,' he said again, his voice rough. She knew she should get off him—they were steady now—but the blow seemed to have detached her mind from her body because she remained seated, her hand on his arm. One of his hands still clasped her waist and the other was threaded through her hair, cupping her head. She could almost feel his pulse through it, although perhaps it was just the pounding of the horses' hooves. She felt very strange.

'Are you all right?' he asked again, but his voice sounded hollow.

'Yes.' She heard herself breathe and nodded slightly, which only increased the friction of his hand against her scalp, sending another wave of wonderful sensations through her.

'Hold still,' Michael said for the third time, just managing to bite down a groan. The silk of her hair was warm against his hand and under his palm he could feel the swift pulse at her temple. It matched the harsh throb of his erection that had appeared swiftly after she had landed on him. What manner of fool had he been to think he could stand being alone with her in a carriage for what might be hours without touching her? Maybe he might have succeeded, but having her literally thrown at him was too much. Or perhaps he had just been waiting for an excuse...

She was so warm against him, with her bottom settled softly on his thighs. He wanted desperately to slide her closer, to feel her fully on him. He wanted to move his hand from her waist to her breast. She had left her cloak on the seat and was wearing only a dark cotton shirt that rose and fell with her short breaths. With each passing street light he could see her lips, half-parted. He waited for her to move, to pull away from him, to sit back in her corner and restore things to normal. But she just sat there, her hand braced gently on his arm, waiting.

He gave up with a curse, digging his hand deeper into her hair, pulling her to him. But there was no need for force; she slid towards him as naturally as she might have adjusted herself on a horse, letting him guide her mouth to his. He kissed her gently, trying to keep some distance, tasting her lips one by one, hoping this burning could still be brought under control. But she undid him, her mouth opening under his, inviting him in. Her hand moved to his shoulder, allowing their bodies to slide closer, her breasts just brushing against his chest.

He tightened his grip, pulling her flush against him so that her thigh pressed against his erection, dragging a moan from his throat that made her whole body shake in response. She whimpered against his mouth, trying to turn herself more completely against him. He touched his lips to her throat, finding that beautiful point below her ear that had made her cry out before. She did not disappoint him and her body bucked as she moaned, her hands threading through his hair. He moved his own hand, running it up the deep curve of her waist, his fingers tracing the swell of her breast before he cupped it and ran his thumb across her already taut nipple.

'Michael!'

Through the pounding of blood in his ears he heard her gasp his name as she twisted under the contact as if she had been struck. He could feel her ragged breaths against his throat and some part of him knew he must stop, but he ignored it, intoxicated by her need. She wanted him, thank the saints. He had her so close, he could feel her shaking, the way her legs parted involuntarily, one bracing on the floor as she tried to move even closer. He wanted to taste her again before he had to put a stop to this.

But before he could pull her back she turned her head and ran her lips up his throat, stopping his breath with the intensity of the sensation. He held himself as still as he could, letting her explore as she tasted the sensitised flesh below his ear just as he had done to her.

With each caress of her lips, blood pounded through him, driving with maddening insistence downwards. Her lips skimmed over his ear, the warmth of her breath caressing it as she moaned faintly, a faraway supplication that almost pushed him over the edge. With molten fire spilling through him he abandoned his passivity, his hips thrusting to increase the pressure against her as he dug his hands into her hair and captured her mouth almost savagely, his hand brushing down over her breasts to between her legs. She cried out, her body rising involuntarily against his hand, and he could feel her heat pressing against his fingers even through her trousers.

Any intention he had of stopping was burned in that heat. There was no question in his mind now that he would take her. Any thought of propriety, responsibility, the fact that they were in a carriage on their way to danger, none of that existed. Everything had boiled down to a very simple decision driven by the raging heat in his blood. It was very simple: he would take her, brand her, make her unequivocally his. His hand was already fumbling at the buttons of her shirt when the carriage suddenly slowed to a halt.

Chapter Twenty

Sari found herself dumped unceremoniously back in her corner of the carriage. Before she could even understand what had happened, the door swung open and Michael jumped out. The sudden wave of cold air it let in was a sharp contrast to her heated body and she hugged herself tightly, beginning to realise just what she had done. Another wave of heat washed through her, this time of sheer burning shame. Had she completely lost her senses? She had literally thrown herself at him.

She had heard enough about men on her travels to know that they were relatively easy with their bodies, so it was hardly surprising he had taken what she had so shamelessly offered, but she…she had had no more control over herself than the worst wanton. The deep throbbing pulse between her legs mocked her and she pressed her thighs tightly together with a moan, covering her face with shaking hands. She was mad.

Then the carriage moved forward gently and with sudden panic she thought he was sending her home. That he could not even face her after what she had done. But after a few moments of moving quietly it stopped again. She heard some whispered voices outside and sat up, bringing herself under control. When the door opened she was sitting rigidly upright. He did not look directly at her, but pulled out a spyglass and handed it to her.

'They are standing at a position of two o'clock from us; tell me if you can see the man from the park.'

She took the glass from him, willing her hands not to shake. It took her a moment to spot the group of men standing at the end of a dock some three hundred yards away past the warehouses shielding their view of the carriage. She saw Hamlin, standing slightly apart from the group. Frey was there, next to a shorter man who looked somewhat familiar, who must have been Junger, and across from them stood two other men. One of them was the man with the broken nose from the park, standing to the left of the taller stranger whose face was obscured by a scarf and low-brimmed hat.

'He is the one to the left, across from Frey. I don't recognise the tall man.' she replied, happy to note her voice did not shake.

'Are you sure?' he asked.

'Yes. Definitely.'

'Good. Wait here and don't move.'

He disappeared again, closing the door behind him quietly and leaving her in total darkness. She could smell rotting fish and tar and hear the faint snapping of ropes against masts, the creaking of old wood and beneath it the rush of water.

She pushed the blind back slightly and directed the spyglass towards the group of men, focusing on the tall stranger. There was something vaguely familiar... A movement in the corner of her line of vision attracted her attention and she shifted the glass to follow Junger as he detached himself from the group. He walked in a slow half circle towards a stack of crates, his head raised as if smelling the air, and she could see the dull flash of the large knife he held. Sari moved the glass to the crates and realised in shock that O'Brien was crouched there, watching the other men and unaware of the danger closing in on him.

She eased open the carriage door and hurried around the warehouse in the direction of the boats. She found a rusted crowbar lying on a pile of rope and threw it as far out onto the stone quay as she could. It hit the ground with an explosive clang. Then she ducked, lying flat behind the coil.

She saw Junger snap around and break into a run in the direction of the noise. Behind him all hell broke loose. Hamlin started to his feet and ran in the opposite direction, as did the masked man and the stranger from the park. Frey ducked low, but she could see the flash of a pistol as he swung around. Thankfully she saw O'Brien had taken advantage of the distraction to make a low dash towards the warehouses without being seen. She wondered if it would be safe to return to the alley when she realised Junger was more astute than she had bargained for and, having found nothing on the quay, had headed back in the opposite direction, directly towards her hiding place.

This was not something she had planned for. There was nowhere for her to go but the water. She crawled as silently as possible towards the edge of the quay, hearing his footsteps come closer and closer. She steeled herself and slid gently over the edge and into the water. It was so cold her breath caught painfully and she clung desperately to the algae-covered stones, hoping that even if he did look directly down, he might not see her in the dark.

She heard him stop and then he was joined by another set of footsteps.

'Silly cowards. A hundred boats out here and they run at the first sign of some drunken sailor tripping over his own feet. No one could have heard us that far away.' It was

Junger. He kicked something off the quay into the water and it fell in with a small splash.

'His lordship doesn't want to be seen, Joachim. It would ruin him, upright citizen that he is. You must be more civil with them, old friend.'

'Civil! An amateur playing grown-up games! All right, all right, as you said his motivations are none of our business, but I swear he is getting cold feet. And that young fool he has running errands for him is a loose screw in all this. He's not trustworthy. If your lordship doesn't find us our opening soon I'm leaving, gold or not.'

'Finding such an opening is not easy, even for someone in his position. We made it clear we cannot stay above the week, which will force his hand. Come, I need some food. If you can call what these island skunks eat food.'

Junger laughed at that and their footsteps receded down the quay.

Sari finally breathed again. The tide was either getting rougher, or her strength was ebbing, but she could no longer keep her purchase against the slippery stone wall and the cold water began to draw her out. She brushed against a rope hanging from one of the boats and clung to it convulsively.

Michael watched as the two men finally walked off, moving from the edge of the quay back towards the main road. He lowered his pistol. He had no idea where that sound had come from. Whatever it had been, they had lost their chance to follow the tall, shrouded man. O'Brien, Morton and Stack the coachman were beside him now, gathering quietly from their respective shadows.

'Did one of you do that?' Michael asked in a whisper.

They all shook their heads.

'No, but it sure as hell saved my life,' whispered

O'Brien. 'I hadn't realised he was almost on me and I had nowhere to go but at him. And I didn't fancy my odds. His knife is big enough to gut a whale.'

A sudden calm fell on Michael and he turned abruptly towards the carriage. The others, surprised, followed him as he ran back and tore open the door. They stared at the empty carriage. Michael rounded on Stack.

'Where is she?'

'I don't know. I was at the alley entrance like you told me, sir.'

Michael cursed, fighting a cold wave of dread.

'Sari?' asked O'Brien and Michael nodded.

In a split second they were all running in the direction of the quay.

'Spread out,' Michael commanded quietly and they split up.

The sound had come from farther up the quay, Michael thought desperately, but she could not have gone so far without being seen and she wouldn't have tried. She must have thrown something from a closer point. He had seen Junger and Frey walk towards the edge of the quay. What would she have done and why had she not come back once they had disappeared? He stared at the boats weaving in the tide. Surely she would not have been mad enough to…

He ran. He stopped at the edge of the water and, throwing caution to the winds, called out her name. Junger and Frey were likely long gone into the traffic of drunken sailors. And if they weren't he didn't give a damn anyway. He called her name again, his eyes scanning the dark desperately. He tried not to think of the cold black water below him. It had been minutes since Junger had stood on the edge of the quay. There were no rowboats he could see, nothing she could have climbed onto, just the large hulking forms of the docked schooners. He had an incredible urge just to jump in, but knew this was foolish, at least until he knew where she might be. She was strong, he told himself, trying to pull down the wave of panic in him that was fast spiralling out of control. She would hang on to something. He called her name again, more loudly.

Sari heard her name. At first she thought it was just some strange distortion of the creaking boards to her tired mind, but then it came again.

'Michael!' Her voice broke in the middle of his name. *Oh, God, Michael, please hear me.* She heard a splash somewhere and tried to call his name again. Then something was pulling at her.

'Let go of the rope, Sari. Here, I have you now, let it go.'

She was not even sure if it was him or some hallucination, but the hand that pulled hers from the slimy rope was strong and she let go.

'O'Brien, send a rope down!' he yelled and that woke her up a bit, enough to cling to him when he began swimming back, his arm crooked under her chin. Then suddenly a swell took them and she saw the looming hulk of a boat descending on them.

Michael tried to adjust without letting her go, twisting around to shield her. Sari heard the boat strike him with a sickening thud. His hold on her slackened and he went under, the black water closing over him. Sari grabbed his sleeve but he kept sinking, pulling her with him.

She held on desperately, tugging at his sinking weight, and finally his body surged upwards. He broke the surface, gasping and coughing. Another swell raised them, shoving them against a slimy wall and she heard shouts above them and a rope slapped into the water. Michael grasped it and together they managed to tie it under her arms. She held on, comforted by its rough surface as she was hauled on to the dock. A coat was thrown over her and she heard the men help Michael up. Someone was rubbing her hands and she looked up into O'Brien's smiling blue eyes.

'You're a brave madwoman is what you are. Thank you for taking that Prussy off m'back, but you are never to do it again, clear?'

Sari nodded dumbly and closed her eyes. She had almost forgotten how it had all started. Then somebody picked her up, coat and all. She knew instinctively it was Michael. She also knew there was something important to tell him. She remembered it when they reached the carriage and he sat her on the steps and took her cloak from the seat to wrap it around her.

'They didn't know they had been seen,' she managed to say, trying to subdue her chattering teeth. Michael ignored her and moved to pick her up again, but she stopped him.

'Wait! I heard them. Frey said it would ruin the man if he were seen since he was a…an upright citizen, a lord. But Junger said his lordship was an amateur playing grown-up games. They said he has to get them a…an opening and that it would have to be next week…'

She paused for breath, looking at the five faces standing around her. She realised with surprise that something dark was running down Michael's face.

'You're bleeding,' she said numbly.

Michael reached up instinctively to the gash above his temple where the boat had struck him, but then withdrew his hand and without another word lifted her again and put her into the carriage, handing her a flask of whisky someone had produced. She tried to tell him he needed something to stop the bleeding, but he just told her to be quiet and drink so she did, closing her eyes and letting the warmth fill and engulf her.

Chapter Twenty-One

She must have fallen asleep because when she next opened her eyes they were in a fully lit hall. She realised Michael was carrying her. She could feel his arms shivering convulsively as he held her. A young woman with startled violet eyes, guileless as a child's, stood at the foot of the stairs and she thought for one confused moment it was Alicia. Yet it was a slightly older face, not quite so pretty, a touch plumper, but very sweet.

'The poor, poor dear,' this woman was saying. 'Pottle, a hot toddy right away, and—oh, goodness…what else? Shall we call a doctor? A mustard bath? Michael, you must put her down, your face is covered with blood.'

'Calm down, Letty, it is merely a flesh wound. She needs a hot bath, a warm drink and sleep, in that order. No doctors or mustard plasters.'

'Mustard bath!' The woman's voice followed them up the stairs.

Sari wanted to tell him he had to put her down, but he was already going up the stairs. She closed her eyes again until he put her down on a sofa. She looked up, but he had already turned away towards the others who had followed him in.

'Meg, get her into the bath as quickly as possible. Letty, could you stay and keep an eye on her? Pottle, please send up something hot to drink. Watson, when you can could you bring some hot water to my room as well?'

The voices faded as the door closed behind him and the two menservants, leaving the two women with her. Sari assumed the violet-eyed one must be Letty, Michael's other sister. A housemaid was pouring a bucket of hot water into a tub. It smelled very nice as it soaked through the smell of the Thames which clung to her foggy brain. She wondered how they had prepared a bath so quickly and noticed the trunk on the floor, which was partially unpacked. She realised the bath must have been intended for Lady Letty after her journey. She turned to her with some chagrin.

'Your bath…' she started, but her teeth chattered despite the hot cocoon of the blankets, more from shock than the cold.

'Nonsense,' Letty admonished her with a sweet smile. 'You are in much greater need than I. Here, can you stand, do you think? We need to take these off.'

Sari, shivering as her warming blankets were peeled away, leaving her in her still sodden clothes, did not feel like arguing further. When she finally sank into the warm, scented water, it was so heavenly she actually started crying, so she sank her head under the surface for a moment until the burning in her throat eased.

Michael leaned back in his favourite chair in the drawing room, crossed his ankles on the footstool and closed his eyes. He had bathed and changed and tried to eat, but his appetite had failed him at the sight of food. Watson had placed a plaster over the ugly gash on his head where the ship had struck him and his whole head throbbed numbly.

The thought of trying to sleep had filled him with a peculiar terror and he had gone downstairs instead.

He felt as though he had just blown through a vicious storm. He had strong memories of this sensation from the war. At the point when it was finally clear a battle was theirs he would be swamped by an almost physical gratitude that it was over, his whole body slackening from a tension that had lasted days or weeks.

That was when he was at his weakest. When it was over and he realised he was still standing and that it was time to count those that weren't. The fact that he had a better record than most commanders was poor comfort when he thought of the men he had cared about who had died or been maimed. Because he hadn't been good enough, or fast enough or careful enough. He should have become inured to it by now. But it had just become harder. It was like Lizzie and his father again and again. None of his men had ever held those lost lives against him. Death had been an integral part of war. He knew they would have been shocked to find out just how brutally he was haunted by the ones who hadn't made it. Not just shocked, but distrustful. You couldn't trust a man who was certain that sooner or later he would fail again.

He should have realised that becoming involved at the Institute would bring him effectively back into active duty and make him responsible for other people's lives once again. But until now it hadn't affected him. But *her* life... She had almost died. And this time, this loss, would have changed everything. Though his rational side resisted this realisation, he knew that if she had not survived, the consequences would have been far worse than even Lizzie's or his father's death.

The thought that but for a stroke of luck he might now be standing in a world where she no longer existed...

There was no point in lying to himself. His whole life had wrapped itself around her existence. This wasn't just lust any more, if it ever had been just that. He had no idea how he would keep her safe, but he had to. After her behaviour in the carriage he knew she was attracted to him, but it might be no more than that. Perhaps her passion was just another aspect of the same recklessness that kept propelling her into danger. She kept throwing herself at life and it terrified him. He didn't want this. He wasn't strong enough. It would destroy him. But he didn't see how he could escape it any longer.

The memory of her response in the carriage still burned in him, underneath his fear. He had no idea what might have happened if the carriage had not stopped when it had. He had been so far gone he had completely forgotten where they were and where they were heading. All conscious, sensible thought had been burned away by the inexorable heat she had set ablaze with such innocent ease. His body tightened even now at the memory and he leaned his head into his hands.

He had always told himself he was nothing like his father, that he would never have so little pride as to put himself at the mercy of his feelings the way his father had. But he was already there. At this point, he wasn't sure whether the pain in his head was physical or mental. He wished there was something, anything he could do to just make it all go away.

Footfalls alerted Michael to someone's approach, and he opened his eyes and forced a smile as Letty walked in. He had been surprised to see her when he had returned that night, but whatever the reason for her appearance in London, he was glad she was here. Letty had always been a pillar of sanity and this way he did not have to worry about sending all the way to the Bennetts' house for Lady Montvale to play chaperon at this late hour.

'How is she?' he asked as impassively as possible as she sat down on the sofa across from him.

'Asleep. She will be fine. I think it is merely the cold water and sheer exhaustion. You said she fell in the Thames? What happened to your head?'

He sidestepped the question.

'Not that I am not glad to see you, but what are you doing in London?'

She smiled. 'After a year of haunting the nursery I found I needed some quiet. My formal excuse is that I came to shop and Andrew couldn't accompany me since we are now deep into some form of crop rotation. I would have written, but I decided to surprise you and Allie.' She paused.

'Well, at least I thought I would surprise you, but it is rather the other way around... I know it is none of my business, but I cannot help being curious.' She raised her eyebrows hopefully.

Michael knew he should not tell her anything, but suddenly he had an incredible urge to talk.

'I am not sure where to start,' he said slowly. 'Her name is Sari Trevor—' He broke off as Letty gasped in surprise.

'Miss Trevor? Why, Allie wrote to me all about her. She said she is Lady Montvale's cousin or something and that she is quite an heiress and she couldn't come down to London before because there had been an illness in the family. Is this true?'

Michael hesitated. Letty knew in vague terms about some of his activities and he knew he could trust her implicitly. He had done so in the past when the need had arisen to excuse his disappearances.

'Not quite.'

'Not quite,' Letty repeated. 'Very well, then I presume she is somehow mixed up in the affairs you and Anderson concoct. Does she work for you?'

Michael nodded.

'I see. Well, that explains her rather unusual mode of dress. And is her name really Trevor? Is she gently born? It seems so, even though she does appear somewhat... original.'

'Yes to both questions. Her father was an antiquarian and they travelled a great deal. That may explain her less conventional side.'

'And where did you find her?'

Michael laughed somewhat shakily.

'She found us. She and an accomplice tried to rob Allie and me.'

Letty's eyes widened.

'The female highway robber on the Heath! Oh, my goodness, Allie told me about it, but...my goodness!' she repeated.

Michael rubbed his forehead. The pain in his head was appearing and disappearing arbitrarily, like some malevolent devil circling him and swinging at him with a cricket bat.

'I'm tired,' he said abruptly.

Letty reached over and clasped his hand.

'You take too much on yourself. You always have, Michael.'

'I can't stop now, not yet.'

Letty's brow contracted with concern. The tightness in his chest eased somewhat at the sight. She was such a sweet soul. She never could stand anyone being upset. In the past this characteristic had aggravated him. He had thought it opened her to the importunities of others. Now he found it touching, if disconcerting. It was rarely directed at him.

He smiled at her reassuringly.

'I am fine. You should go to sleep, you must be tired. I will go up soon as well.'

She hesitated, but stood up.

'Don't stay downstairs long. You need to rest.'

He nodded, but in the end he sat there, too tired to move, long after she had gone and the house had descended into silence.

It was past one o'clock before he finally went upstairs. The deep cold that had held him since his plunge into the Thames had melted into a strange uncomfortable heat and he climbed the stairs heavily, listening to the comforting silence of his house.

The noise was so faint he hardly noticed it at first. Then he stopped, turning towards the door it was coming from. He hoped for a second Letty would hear, but her room was by the nursery at the other end of the corridor. He considered ignoring the sound, but he remained standing there on the landing.

Finally, with a muffled curse, he walked to the door and opened it quietly. Sari was obviously having a nightmare. She was curled up in the big bed, her face gilded by the still-glowing embers in the fireplace. She was shaking and he could hear her faint cries of denial. He closed the door gently behind him. The least he could do was wake her from it.

He bent over her and rested his hand gently on her shoulder.

'Sari,' he whispered. 'Wake up; you are having a bad dream.'

She woke immediately. Her eyes stared at him as if at a hellish apparition, and he sat down on the edge of the bed, tightening his hold on her arm.

'It's all right. It is only a bad dream,' he murmured again.

Her eyes fluttered and then closed briefly.

'It was so cold and I couldn't find up. Everything was dark and there was no up,' she whispered.

'I know, I know, but you are safe now.' He rubbed her arm gently.

She was wearing a plain cotton nightshift with laces at the neck that had come undone. She was very warm under his hand and he could clearly see the outline of her breasts under the shift. The warmth spread up his arm into his chest, and he closed his eyes in surrender as his body woke to her heat.

Everything that had happened since the carriage had stopped at the docks rolled back, and desire crashed through him. It was even stronger now, more desperate, and he did not even try to stop himself from pulling her fiercely into his arms.

Sari closed her mind to the sense of it all and pressed her cheek into his shoulder, feeling the warmth of his flesh beneath. His heartbeat was fast and sharp and his arms were crushing her, but she did not mind. She was alive and warm and he had saved her. She did not care if she was wanton. She wound her arms around him and held on as she had when he had pulled her from the water. She shuddered at the memory of the darkness and she pressed her temple to his collarbone, willing herself not to cry, but the tears came anyway. His grip slackened and he moved his hand to caress her hair.

'It's over, you're safe now. I have you. You're safe now,' he said softly, pressing his lips to her hair.

He withdrew slightly and brushed the tears from her cheek with his thumb and then he kissed her with a fire that would have been frightening if she had not felt it her-

self, if she had not opened to him, tilting her head back
to meet his mouth.

Her hands moved under his shirt, against the strong
muscles that were cording with tension across his back.
Everywhere they touched burned and she let him push
her back onto the bed, took his weight on her and almost
laughed when he kissed her eyes, her jaw, then her neck.

Michael knew he was almost crushing her, but he
wanted his weight imprinted on her, he wanted to feel her
length against him. He raised himself enough to pull the
covers off her so that he could feel her fully. He leaned
his head briefly to the valley between her breasts to quell
a burst of pain behind his eyes before he raised it again,
sliding one hand up to cup her breast as he lowered his
mouth to its peak.

She arched against him with a small cry as he gently
suckled through the thin cotton gown, drawing the fabric against her nipple with his tongue. Her body pressed
against him even with his weight on her, her hands tan-
gling in his hair, pressing him there. He obliged her, biting gently into the flesh and she cried out his name as she
had in the carriage, as she had in the water.

It was strange, that his name on her lips could excite him
more than anything. He wanted to hear it again, he wanted
her to cry it out as she climaxed. He slid his hand down,
pulling at her gown, drawing it up, taking just enough
weight off her so he could pull it about her hips. Then
he slid his hand between them, touching her as he had in
the carriage, but this time there were no barriers between
them and he had to stifle her cry with his mouth as his own
groan exploded in his chest. She was hot and wet and he
was burning to be inside her. Her nails dug into his shoulders and her knee, released from his weight, drew up the
length of his thigh.

'Say my name,' he whispered shakily against her neck, pulling her earlobe into his mouth and teasing it with his tongue even as his finger kept massaging her gently. She was whimpering now, her breath coming in short cries.

'My name,' he whispered again, more urgently, and her hips rose against his fingers.

'Michael,' she gasped. 'Oh, God, Michael, stop.'

He smiled fiercely. He had no intention of stopping. He increased the pressure and the speed and bent his head to her breast, matching the rhythm of his fingers with his tongue. Her hands anchored on his arms, as if trying to stop him, but her hips were moving with his rhythm now, rocking back and forth against his fingers, and his name spilled through her again and again with each shudder until she tensed on one last spasm and he caught his name against his mouth, muffling her cry, his hand capturing every last quiver as her body relaxed.

The easing of her tension only reminded him of his own and he held himself rigidly above her, trying to minimise the contact. But then she pressed against him, seeking his warmth. He knew he should leave now, but when her hands moved up to twine about his back he stayed there, his head bent, his eyes on the perspiration that glued her nightshift to her breasts.

He knew that unless she told him to leave, he would not. He knew it was madness. But he also knew that at this moment he could not think of anything he had ever wanted more in his life than to be inside her.

She shifted against him, sliding her body more deeply against his with a small sigh, and he gave up with a curse. Then he was raising her and pulling the shift over her head and pressing her breasts against him. He thought she might have laughed, but the pounding of blood in his head was too loud to know. He pulled off his shirt before reaching down to undo his trousers, sliding them off and kicking them away before he turned over, pulling her on top of him.

Her hair fell about them in shiny waves that caught the colour of the fire. His erection was between her legs and he pulled her mouth down to his, penetrating her there where he did not dare penetrate her elsewhere. Her thighs tightened about him and he groaned, moving against her. She was unbearably soft. He pushed himself up, sliding her so that she was positioned directly over his erection. He raised his knee to press her even closer. She was so hot it burned in his chest, and he bunched his fists in her hair, pressing against her arms, as if that could relieve his frustration.

Then she moved and gasped and he lost the last of his control. He did not care any more. He didn't care. He raised her hips and she held herself there, unsure. Then he reached down to touch her lightly and her body bucked, her head arching back at the sensation. He guided his erection to the centre of her heat and pressed her down slowly. She was so wet he slid in almost easily, stretching her as he went, swallowed by the incredible burning heat. When he reached the barrier he stopped, cool reality washing over him with stark suddenness, but it was separate from his body and when she suddenly rocked back he let go and felt it tear.

He heard the sudden cry of pain and the tension freeze her form and closed his eyes tightly. He could barely breathe she was so tight around him. He knew he should not move, but his body was trying to fight him. He knew his fingers were biting into her hips, but he could not relax them. He prayed she would not move, not speak.

The pain shocked Sari out of her heady stupor. She stayed there, trying to pull her senses together, knowing full well it was too late. His hands were biting into her and she dared to open her eyes, but his were closed and she was shocked by the tension she saw on his face. She knew enough to know he had had no pleasure yet in this encounter and was surprised as she felt a sudden wave of heat, a strange possessiveness.

Now that the pain was subsiding she could feel him inside her, and although it was not the almost maddeningly sweet pleasure he had given her earlier, it was a deeper feeling, a heady power that spread from his heat to her body. She wanted him to feel what she had. She wanted him to be lost to that unbearable pleasure. She didn't want him in control or thinking. She relaxed her body with conscious effort and moved slightly, experimentally, but his arms pulled her down against him, crushing her.

'God, Sari, please don't move, not yet,' he whispered harshly against her hair, and she realised he was trying not to hurt her. She turned her mouth against his neck, tasting the warm salt of his perspiration. He groaned and tried to move his head away so she moved her hips instead, which sent his head back on to the pillows with a gasp and surprised her with a rush of pleasure. At this angle there was just enough friction... She moved again even though he tried to stop her and another wave of pleasure ran through her all the way to her breasts. She moved, this time brushing them across his chest. The pain was completely forgotten now and the strange tension he had caused earlier, before she had exploded into that sweetness, was building again.

'Michael, please,' she murmured against his throat, feeling his groan against her lips.

'Sari, I don't want to hurt you...' he whispered raggedly.

'You're not hurting me, it doesn't hurt any more. Michael...'

She pulled away, pressing herself up and bracing her

forearms on either side of his head. He finally opened his eyes, and she saw that they were almost black, gleaming with gold from the firelight. His hands were shaking as he ran them up her arms, his eyes not leaving hers, waiting for some signal. She pressed her cheek to his hand as it reached her shoulder and closed her eyes.

He shuddered and his hands moved to her waist, over her breasts, to her neck and then pulled her mouth down to his. The rush of blood as his palms grazed her breasts swam straight to her centre and she squirmed and then he was lost. He kissed her and his hands moved down to guide her hips against his, one hand sliding between them to tease her to that edge once again. Then it was she who stifled his cry when he came. Deep inside her his warmth became a sweet wave that washed over her, draining her, and her arms gave way as she sank down weakly onto his chest. Her last thought before she slept was that she could not tell whose heartbeat was thudding in her chest.

When Michael woke it was dark. The fire had burned out and he was cold again, except for where a soft body pressed against him. It took him a moment to realise where he was and whose warm form was curved next to his. A wave of pain collided with a wave of remembered desire and he had to stop himself from groaning out loud. He had well and truly done it now. He could hardly believe it. He might not have believed it if she had not been curled up there, her head resting on his shoulder and one leg spread across his.

He shifted, sliding her off him. She murmured faintly, but did not wake, and he stood up shakily, his vision blurring for a moment. He stared down at her as his sight resolved again and then reached down to pull the covers over her. He found his clothes in the darkness, while his head pounded painfully, and half staggered naked back to his room. He lay face down on top his bedcovers, suddenly hot despite the chill in the air.

He did not expect to sleep, but when he opened his eyes again, the sun was streaming through the gap in the curtains. He raised his head painfully, groping for the small ormolu clock that stood on his bed stand. When he finally managed to focus on the hands he started in alarm. Eleven o'clock. He had to get up. His mind was too numb to fathom what he felt about the implications of the night's events, but he couldn't let her think he was avoiding her after what had happened. They had to talk.

He groaned and swung his legs out of bed. His head swam unpleasantly and his chest felt as if it was weighed down by a boulder. He was very cold and thirsty and he reached stiffly to tug on the bellpull.

'I'll send up a bath immediately, my lord,' Watson said brusquely when he saw him.

Michael wanted to ask about Sari, but his throat was too dry.

'Some water, please, Watson,' he asked instead, his voice barely forming the words.

Watson hurried to pour him some water and handed him the glass. To Michael's surprise it slid from his grasp and fell to the floor. He frowned at the spreading puddle and tried to reach for it, but his head swam again. Watson picked it up.

'Sorry, Watson, not awake yet,' he mumbled.

'Perhaps you should lie down, my lord,' the man said gently.

'I want a bath.' Michael scowled.

'Of course, my lord.'

By the time his bath arrived Michael was feeling even

colder. He staggered into it and let the warmth wash over him. He even managed to drink a glass of water, but the effort of washing and drying himself left him exhausted and he sat down on the side of the bed again. Someone was driving a hot nail into his temple with rhythmic brutality. Watson stood by, a frown now fixed firmly on his face.

'I think your lordship should rest a little now,' he said at last.

'I'm rested. It's almost noon,' Michael retorted but the light was doing strange things to his eyes, like clouds passing rapidly outside his window. He stood up slowly, leaning one arm on the bedpost. He was having trouble locking his elbow and the bed was shaking. He tried to breathe more deeply, but his lungs protested painfully against the invasion of air. He had never felt quite this bad after drinking and he wondered if there had been something wrong with the port he had drunk. He managed to bully Watson into helping him with his trousers before he had to sit down again. To his surprise he was shaking.

Watson finally stood back.

'I am sending for a doctor,' he said firmly, and Michael scowled up at him.

'A doctor? Don't be ridiculous. I merely drank too much port.'

'I am afraid not, my lord,' Watson replied calmly and walked out.

'Damn it, come back, here, Watson!' Michael called after him, or at least he tried to, but it came out hoarse and weak. He tried to stand up, but the room tilted ominously and he just caught himself on the bedpost before his knees folded and he managed to sit down again.

A gentle knock on the door made him raise his head warily.

'Come in,' he said, hoping it was someone sane enough

who could help him find the rest of his clothes so he could get up.

Letty poked her head around the door. Her eyes widened when she saw him and she stepped in.

'Watson said you were ill.'

'I am not ill, just a little worse for wear. Help me find my shirt.'

Instead, she sat down beside him and pressed her hand to his brow, only to pull it back with an exclamation of concern.

'You are burning, Michael. Oh, goodness, you must lie down.'

'Don't be silly, Letty. I am fine. Hand me a shirt,' he repeated hoarsely.

'No, you are lying down this instant.'

'Letty!' he started, but she stood up, her hands planted firmly on her hips.

'Very well, then, if you are not ill, find your shirt yourself.'

'Fine,' he retorted and tried to stand again, taking a step forward. To his surprise his legs gave out and he found himself on his knees. A sharp pain exploded in his head, tearing at him, trying to rip his skull apart. His vision blurred and the room receded into darkness. When his sight came back Letty was on the floor beside him and his full weight was leaning on her shoulder. Then Watson was beside her and together they raised him onto the bed. Michael tried to argue but now even his voice was failing him. Then someone pulled a cover over him and the lights faded.

Chapter Twenty-Two

'He fell into the Thames, you said?' asked Dr Felton, removing the listening horn he had pressed to Michael's chest and looking up at Letty's worried face.

'Will he be all right?' she asked faintly.

'I believe so. He has the heart of a workhorse by the sound of it. But even a workhorse can fall ill. He sounds like he breathed in some of the river—not the most salubrious of liquids,' the doctor said calmly. 'But quite frankly, I am much more worried by the blow to the head. I presume he is suffering from quite a serious concussion. I will arrange for a nurse and return in several hours. If he tries to get out of bed, keep him in it, by force if need be. And he is to have nothing but boiled barley water with lemon, understood?'

She followed him out and then went slowly upstairs to the guest room and knocked gently on the door.

Sari was surprised to see Letty enter. She stood up stiffly. Her mind had been numb since she had woken that morning. She did not regret what had happened, but she couldn't contemplate coming face to face with Michael yet. She knew him well enough to know that whatever the unusual circumstances of the previous night, bedding her had been a breach of his code of honour. And she might be inexperienced, but unless she had missed something, she was very much afraid they had taken no precautions to prevent conception. She knew him well enough to know that under the circumstances he would consider himself honour-bound to offer her an *amende honorable* in the guise of a proposal of marriage. And she didn't know how she would be strong enough to reject him.

She dug her fingers into her palms. She wished she could just disappear before she had to see him again; she could not stand the thought of seeing the guilt on his face, the regret. Seeing his sister only made her feel worse. Letty looked pale and anxious and Sari wondered for a shocked moment if she knew or had guessed what had happened.

'Good morning, Miss Trevor, how are you feeling?' Letty asked. 'I should have asked the doctor to see you, as well. I didn't think...'

Sari frowned at her strained tones. 'There is no need. I am merely tired. Thank you for this dress. I... What did you mean by "as well"?'

Letty shook her head, rubbing a point between her brows. 'Michael is ill.'

'Ill?' Sari repeated dully.

'Yes. He is unconscious. The doctor says it is a concussion.'

Sari stood up abruptly, her mind struggling to comprehend what she was saying. Unconscious. Concussion.

Letty focused on her in concern.

'Perhaps we should get you a doctor after all. You look very pale.'

'Oh, God. This is my fault,' Sari said hoarsely, her voice shaking.

Letty stared at her, then moved towards her and clasped her hands.

'I am sure it isn't your fault. He is strong, he will recover.'

To Sari's shame she felt hot tears spill out, and Letty put her arm around her and drew her to sit down on the side of the bed.

'Hush,' she crooned. 'Hush, he will get well, don't you worry. I know, I know, hush…'

Sari cried until her sobs were no more than dry shudders. Finally she pushed away from Letty and dried her face with the handkerchief Letty handed her.

'I'm so sorry,' she said huskily.

'My poor sweet. You care for him very much, don't you?'

Sari nodded dumbly. Denial at this point would be ridiculous. Besides, she wanted someone to know.

'Does he know?' Letty asked, giving her another comforting squeeze.

Sari shook her head and the other woman did not press further. A knock at the door interrupted them and a maid announced that Mr Anderson was downstairs asking to see Miss Trevor.

'Oh, dear,' Letty said. 'I dare say this is business. Are you strong enough?' she asked, concerned, and Sari smiled reassuringly.

Anderson was waiting for her in a small drawing room at the back of the house. He looked grim and serious, and Sari felt guilty all over again. He patted her awkwardly on the shoulder.

'Allie just told me what the doctor said about Michael and I've already spoken to O'Brien this morning about what occurred last night. I know this is difficult, but I need you to repeat everything you heard. We have very little time to stop whatever it is they are planning, and Michael will have our heads once he wakes up if we allow ourselves to become distracted the minute he is out of commission for a couple of days.'

She smiled, thankful for this common sense. He was right. She sat down, gathered her thoughts and repeated everything that had happened since her ride with Hamlin. When she finished her story Anderson sat down with a frown, staring into the empty fireplace.

'Are you sure he said "his lordship"?'

'Yes, the German equivalent. He was clearly referring to the tall man with the scarf and cane. He was the one doing most of the talking with Frey. The other two were standing well back.'

'Can you remember anything distinguishing about that man?'

Sari closed her eyes, concentrating on her memory of the scene.

'He wore a tall hat, caped greatcoat and boots with tassels. Good quality. I couldn't see his face clearly because of the scarf, just an outline, but there was something familiar... And he was holding a cane, dark and shiny like ebony, and just above his hand...a form...silvery...an animal's head, I think...'

She frowned, trying to resolve that part of the picture, but the image faded as she pressed. She shook her head.

'That's all. I know it's not much. They were too far away,' she said ruefully.

'We know he is a titled gentleman of some sort, not used to this kind of activity, and we have a broad description and a connection to Hamlin as well as to this mysterious man from the park. We also know something is supposed to happen within the week. That's a great deal more than we had yesterday, I would say.'

'But because of me we didn't succeed in following him.

And because of me Michael is ill.' Her voice cracked. 'I can't bear it.'

'Because of you O'Brien did not find himself on the wrong side of Junger's blade. I have heard what that man does to his victims, Sari, and I assure you O'Brien is very grateful! to you. As for Michael, I am sure he will be better well ahead of our fine doctor's prognosis. Now, you are to go to Montvale House and rest, for as I understand it, you have a dance promised to Hamlin tonight and we need to increase our pressure on that young man.'

Chapter Twenty-Three

Sari could hardly believe she was capable of going to a ball that night, but she owed it to Michael to continue the investigation. It was immediately apparent that Hamlin was nervous and prattling on more foolishly than usual. After their dance Sari saw her chance, manoeuvring him into taking her to one of the curtained anterooms. Inside, she sat down with a sigh.

'I'm terribly sorry to be such a bother, Mr Hamlin, but I declare I did feel faint just for a moment.'

'Not at all, Miss Trevor, dashed crush, don't you know. Is there anything I can do?'

'Oh, no, do sit down. You have already been quite gallant…' She was about to begin her probing when to her surprise the curtains parted and Lord Edgerton stepped into the room. She thought for a moment he would withdraw, but to her surprise Hamlin stood up with a start.

'Ah, Hamlin, I believe Shaftsbury was looking for you,' he drawled.

Sari watched as resentment warred with another emotion in Hamlin's face and then he bowed stiffly and withdrew without another word. Edgerton watched him disappear.

'Are you not well, Miss Trevor?' he asked tonelessly.

'I admit to feeling a bit faint, my lord,' she replied calmly, plying her fan and cursing him silently for having spiked her guns. 'I'm afraid the crush was too much for me. Mr Hamlin was kind enough to find me a quiet corner for a moment.'

To her surprise Edgerton sat down in the place vacated by Hamlin.

'I had not realised any corner with Hamlin in it could be quiet,' he said with a touch of asperity, and Sari gave a stunned gurgle of laughter.

'One makes do with what one has to hand, my lord,' she returned.

'Indeed,' he replied. 'I was rather hoping I would be somewhat better fare than our young friend there. If you prefer I could send him back,' he offered quizzically, but there was a challenge there.

'No indeed, he can be a bit...wearing.'

'Wearing. Yes, but as you said, he has his uses.'

Sari felt a quickening of interest at the undercurrent in his tone. It was obvious Edgerton was jealous of her attention to the younger man, and yet for a moment she had thought there was perhaps something more.

'He seems an enthusiastic young man,' she offered, testing the water.

'Enthusiastic. In what way? In his courtship of you? I am sure anyone would be enthusiastic in such a task.'

She flushed and shook her head. 'No, I was thinking of his political convictions; he presents them with such vigour.'

Edgerton's eyes narrowed. 'His political convictions...' he repeated slowly. 'What does he know of politics? All form and no substance. A mere vessel for the words of others.'

'Still, he presented their case with much spirit.'

'What case?'

Sari appeared to think this over.

'I think... Well, he was talking about how the government was not doing nearly enough to prevent the growing hold of radicalism in Britain. At least that's what I remember. Not so far perhaps from your own ideas, my lord?'

'Not so different in form, but he is a mere parrot. That is not to say parrots are not useful, but they can be dangerous, too. Untutored minds, as they say...' He turned to frown at the curtains, and Sari watched his profile. Then he smiled suddenly and turned back to her.

'You are a most impressive young woman,' he said suddenly, and she started.

'Me, my lord? Hardly.'

'No, no, you are modest, but you must give me the benefit of greater experience. Perhaps it is the fact that you were not exposed too young to this frivolous world of ours. Your appreciation for the higher things in life is a clear indication of a finer mind. You would be surprised to find how difficult it is to find someone with such delicacy of thought.'

'You flatter me, my lord. I deserve no such encomium.'

'You deserve a great deal more. And you would make me very happy if you would allow me to try to give it to you. I believe what I am saying comes as no surprise to you?'

'I must confess, I *am* surprised.'

'Am I speaking too soon? Surely you must know what I feel for you?'

Sari shook her head slightly. 'I had thought, perhaps, that your lordship enjoyed my company.'

'And so I do. Enough to wish fervently that you will bestow it upon me in a more permanent manner. Miss Trevor, will you do me the great honour of becoming my wife?'

Sari stared at him, at a loss for words. She had half expected this, but it still shocked her. If life had been different perhaps she might have even been able to care for this man. If she had not been an impostor, if she had not been growing increasingly worried that with him all was not as it seemed, and most importantly, if she had not met Michael. She knew she had to reject him, but something in her stuck.

He laughed somewhat uncomfortably at her silence.

'I see I have indeed taken you by surprise. I would have thought by now you would be well used to proposals.'

She shook her head somewhat ruefully and decided honesty was the best policy.

'Yours is the first proposal I consider seriously since my arrival in London, my lord.'

'Well, at least you take it seriously. Is it repulsive to you?'

'Oh, no, I mean…' she began warmly and then trailed off. She could have kicked herself. She had to play this more intelligently.

'I am surprised, though you may say I am merely being coy. I am not sure what I feel. Confused, I think. I have become very used to thinking of myself as alone.'

'So have I, for rather longer than you, and yet now I find it very easy to think of myself with you.' He hesitated. 'I do not mean to press you. Perhaps we can meet and talk in a more private setting?'

'Yes, please. That is most kind of you.'

'Kind! I would rather you did not think of me as merely kind,' he said quietly and to her astonishment he leaned forward, grasping her chin lightly in one hand as he bent to kiss her. It was a brief, gentle kiss, but a sensuous one nonetheless, and Sari almost enjoyed it for its skill. No simple country bumpkin was this man. On the other hand, there was none of the animal heat that Michael could elicit from her so easily. The memory of Michael's touch spread through her, heating her from within. Edgerton, mistaking her flush, drew back with a small smile of satisfaction.

'Until tomorrow then,' he said in a low, intimate tone and left.

Sari remained seated for a moment, staring at the blank curtains. When they suddenly drew apart she thought for a moment he had come back for more and sighed with relief when she saw Lady Montvale.

'My dear child, what on earth has been going on in here? First Hamlin walks out with an expression like a thundercloud and then Edgerton walks out looking suspiciously *aux anges*. You are skirting the borderline of what is proper here. If anyone else had seen this, gossip would be all over the ball by now!'

'He offered for me,' Sari said dully.

'Who?'

'Edgerton.'

'Edgerton! Why, you sly little puss! You've brought him up to scratch and in a mere few weeks. Quite a feat! Many have tried since he was widowed.'

'What on earth am I going to do with him?'

Lady Montvale realised suddenly who and what she was talking to. She sat down next to Sari with a thump.

'Oh, dear, and it would have been such a coup. Besides, I know you do not fancy him. You like my dear Michael, don't you?'

Sari flushed, and Lady Montvale patted her hand kindly.

'I know; the silly boy does not know what is good for him.'

'I'm not in the least bit good for him. He almost died because of me.'

'Nonsense. You are the only person aside from myself

that actually stands up to him. Not that men necessarily
value that sort of thing, more fool them. Ah, well.'

Sari was not in the least heartened by that statement.

'Can we go home now?' she asked in a small voice.

Lady Montvale gave her a sympathetic smile.

'Of course. We can think on Edgerton tomorrow.'

The next morning Sari awaited Edgerton's appearance.
She had resolved to postpone the inevitable rejection of
his suit so she could continue to stay close enough to him
to observe him. So long as she was not certain he was involved, she could do no more.

She had asked Lady Montvale to break slightly with
propriety and allow her to meet with him alone. She had
agreed and had left on a visit to a friend while Sari went
to change into a dress suitable for the occasion. She was
just descending the steps when the knocker sounded and
she waited as the butler, Henries, went to open the door to
Edgerton. He saw her on the stairs and smiled up at her as
he handed over his coat, hat and walking cane.

'Miss Trevor. I was hoping you might be at home.'

It took her a moment to overcome her shock at what
she had seen. His smile wavered slightly when she didn't
move or respond.

'Miss Trevor?'

She shook herself and forced a smile, as she came down
the stairs.

'Please come in, Lord Edgerton.'

She led him into the drawing room and sat down on
a sofa. Lord Edgerton followed and sat opposite her, his
smile slightly flat.

'I came…you know why I came. Are you going to put
me out of my misery or into it?' he asked with forced
lightness.

Sari couldn't look at him as she said it.

'My lord, I… I would be most happy…' She faltered.

'My dear!' He moved to sit by her, grasping her hands. 'Do you mean it?'

'Yes, that is, if you still…'

'If I still? Of course I still want marry you! My dear, you have made me the happiest of men.'

He pulled her into his arms, his kiss more insistent than the one yesterday, but still smooth, practised, making it easy for her to respond without much effort, hoping he would chalk up any lack of responsiveness to inexperience.

'May I send an announcement to the *Gazette*?' he asked as he finally released her. 'Is there anyone we must consult? Lady Montvale?'

'No, I am my own mistress. Lady Montvale is my trustee, but I have already discussed this matter with her and she has given me her blessing.' Sari had no idea how they would work around the logistics of this new development, but they would think of something she was sure.

'Excellent. We must toast this.' He hesitated. 'Ratafia, perhaps?'

Sari wrinkled her nose; not even for this masquerade within a masquerade could she stomach ratafia. He caught her expression and laughed.

'I agree, it is vile stuff. Madeira, then? I am sure Lady Montvale has some here,' he said as he walked over to the sideboard.

Sari accepted the Madeira and thanked its warming properties, which made the next twenty minutes bearable as he discussed possible honeymoon destinations and extolled the virtues of his family home in Dorset. Finally, he rose to leave, claiming that despite their engagement it would not be proper for him to stay with her too long without Lady Montvale's presence.

Alone again, she sank her face into her hands. She hadn't wanted it to be him. She might not love him, but he had been kind and she had liked him. But the walking stick he had handed to Henries was unquestionably the one she had seen the stranger holding that night on the quay. She had never seen anything like it, with its silver skilfully moulded to resemble a crowned lion's head. It was too distinct for this to be a coincidence. She did not believe in such long odds. Especially not when this was coupled with his comments and his strained interaction with Hamlin. He was Frey's and Junger's 'lordship'. She still did not know what he planned, but she had to stay closer than ever to him until she did and she couldn't imagine anything better than the opening he had provided for her. She jumped up. She must send for Anderson.

She was close to climbing the walls in the half hour before she finally heard someone at the door. She burst out of the drawing room just as Henries opened the door to both Lady Montvale and Anderson. Grabbing each of them by the hand, she pulled them into the drawing room.

'What on earth?' Lady Montvale asked somewhat breathlessly. 'Let me sit down, do, child. Whatever has happened?'

'I am engaged,' Sari stated tensely.

Lady Montvale gasped and sat down heavily.

'Engaged? To whom?'

'To Lord Edgerton.' She turned to Anderson. 'He's our man.'

'But, my dear!' Lady Montvale exclaimed. 'I thought you didn't… And besides, it is impossible, how are we to get round your story? And what do you mean he's our man?'

'Are you in love with him?' Anderson interjected, confused.

'Don't be ridiculous, Anderson! He is the man from the docks. His cane. He came to offer for me and I saw his cane. I swear it is the same, a crowned lion's head, silver on an ebony cane. I know it is him.'

Anderson sat down, then stood up again as he realised she was still on her feet.

'Impossible. Not Edgerton. He may be conservative but… If you had told me it was Shaftsbury, or Mannering, maybe. But Edgerton? He is as straight as they come.'

'"An upright citizen?"' she quoted Frey's words.

Anderson paled somewhat, but still shook his head. 'I cannot believe it.'

Lady Montvale stared at Sari as well.

'Sari, dear, I am afraid I agree with Anderson. It is too outrageous.'

'I know it sounds incredible, but it's not just the cane. You've seen how he is around Hamlin. It's not just jealousy, I'm certain. And there were the things he said to me about the dangers to England and how the current government is exacerbating them. I know none of it is conclusive, but together…' Sari said desperately. She had been so certain.

'But what happens when he discovers you aren't an heiress?' Anderson asked.

'By all the saints and their sandals, of course he won't find out because I am not going to marry him!' she exploded suddenly, and he took a step back in surprise.

She paced the room, trying to calm down.

'I am engaged to him to try to find out what he is up to. That is all. They said something is to take place next week. If, as you say, he is nothing more than an innocently rabid reactionary, then I happily jilt him some weeks down the line and no one is the wiser. But if he is our man, what better way to track his activities?'

'You are mad,' Anderson said after a moment.

'Of course I am mad. Do I have your approval or not?'

Anderson turned to Lady Montvale with supplication in his blue eyes. The lady was inspecting Sari with some concentration.

'It is not quite as mad as it seems,' she said finally, and Sari gave a sigh of relief. She needed one of them at least to believe in her.

'Oh, I wish Michael were well already. All right,' Anderson said resolutely. 'I'll put a detail on to follow him, but it won't be easy. We are getting stretched thin between keeping an eye on the lot of them and our search for the man with the broken nose, and now Hamlin has disappeared into thin air. We can't find a trace of him anywhere. All right, this might be a wild goose chase, but at least it is a chase!'

Chapter Twenty-Four

Lady Montvale put down her second cup of morning cocoa and picked up the note from the platter held by her stoic Henries.

'It is from Letty,' she told Sari as she urgently unsealed it and spread it out. 'Oh, thank goodness! Thank goodness! Michael recovered consciousness last night. She says the doctor is quite satisfied and has allowed him downstairs providing that he rests. She is sending for Anderson and says I may come if I wish, but that she thinks it best to keep this between us. Dear, sensible Letty. What a stroke of luck that she is here to take care of everything. Henries, do please have the barouche brought round, we shall go over presently.'

'We?' Sari asked, caught between elation at his recovery and fear of facing him again after what had happened between them. She knew sooner or later she would have to face the consequences of their actions and she had no idea if she would be brave enough to do what was right. At least if she met him first with everyone present, she would be able to gauge his mood, prepare herself.

'Of course, my dear. You know Michael. He will want to be brought up to speed as soon as possible. This is no time to be overly proper!'

* * *

When they entered the drawing room at Crayle House, Michael was propped up on a long sofa, with Alicia and Letty seated on chairs on either side of him and Anderson standing near the fireplace. He looked pale and drawn, his face more angular than usual, but he was smiling faintly at Letty. To Sari he looked beautiful. All the noise and colour of the room seemed to fall back, mute. *He is all right*, a voice said inside her, and some of the deep scrabbling fear calmed. *He is all right.*

He looked up as they entered and smiled at Lady Montvale.

'Margaret, *et tu, Brute*? Come to crow over my weak remains?'

'No, silly boy. Come to make sure you are obeying the doctor's orders. You gave us all quite a scare.'

He leaned his head back slightly.

'I am sure I will disobey them once I can stand up without falling over. They tell me I fell in the Thames, but I can't remember. Anderson says I am not to talk shop in front of the girls.'

Sari stood somewhat behind, not quite sure what to do or why he was ignoring her. Perhaps he really could not bear to look at her after what had happened. She was almost ready to leave rather than stand another minute of this silent torture, when he glanced over at her with a slight frown.

'Good evening, my lord, I am glad you are better,' she said breathlessly.

'I am sorry,' he replied, apparently bemused. 'Have we met?'

For one stricken moment Sari thought it must be a cruel joke. Although it was completely out of character, she wondered whether he might be punishing her. But that thought receded immediately, replaced by another, as clear and sharp as an icicle snapping and falling to the ground——he really didn't recognise her. He had turned her inside out, shaken every cell in her body to its core, and now he did not even recognise her.

The rest of the company turned to stare at him, but the puzzled look on his face merely grew at their surprise. Anderson took a step towards her, taking her arm and guiding her closer to the sofa. She followed numbly, caught between shock and outraged denial. *How can you not know me?* a voice kept hammering inside her head.

'Michael, this is Sari... Miss Trevor. Surely you remember her.'

Michael scanned her head to toe and back with a frown of concentration, then gave up with a weary sigh and rubbed his forehead absently.

'I am sorry, my mind is still murky. Are you related to Lady Montvale?'

He looked so tired, Sari thought suddenly. A wave of concern pressed back the surges of pain and fear that were swamping her. He was safe and that was all that mattered for now, she told herself. Everything else must be endured.

'It does not matter. I am glad you are better, though.'

He frowned and his gaze swept over her again, but then he only shook his head once more and closed his eyes.

'Sorry, I am more tired than I thought.'

Letty herded them all out into the hallway, where they all stood staring at Sari. But she just gazed at the intricate design of the carpet beneath her feet as a maelstrom of thoughts and emotions tugged at her, conversely pulling her deeper and deeper into a numbing haze.

'The blow to his head, could it have done this?' asked Lady Montvale after a moment.

'But he knows all of us,' Anderson replied.

'We had best send for Dr Felton,' said Letty, ever practical. 'You should all stay until he arrives. We'll wait in
the blue room.'

Twenty minutes later the doctor finally arrived, a frown
of concern on his face.

'What is wrong, has there been a relapse?'

'No, he seems well enough,' Letty said reassuringly as
she showed him into the blue room. 'At least… Well, he
did not remember some things.'

'What things?' asked the doctor, his frown deepening.
'Did he not remember you?'

'No, he remembered all of us, except for Miss Trevor.'

The doctor turned to Sari, and she forced herself to try
and remain present.

'Were you well acquainted before the accident?'

She shook her head, stammering slightly. 'He remembered me right after…well, between the blow and when
he fell ill, but…'

If the doctor found anything strange in this admission
he showed no sign of it. 'And for how long have you known
him?'

'Just under two months,' she replied, suddenly shocked
that it was only that long. Surely it must be more than that?

'And does he remember anything else from this period?'

They all looked at each other.

'We don't know,' Letty admitted. 'It did not occur to
us to ask. He said his head hurt and that he was tired so
we left.'

The doctor nodded.

'Miss Trevor, if you could come with me for a moment.
And perhaps Lady Letitia…'

Letty glanced at Anderson. 'I think it would be best if
Mr Anderson accompanied you.'

The doctor raised his brows, but assented. 'Very well.'

They followed him towards the drawing room, but he stopped just outside the door, lowering his voice.

'It is not uncommon for a blow to the head to result in temporary loss of memory, but did something occur at that time which his lordship may prefer not to remember?'

Me, thought Sari, but she said nothing.

The doctor inspected their faces with a frown and continued into the drawing room. Michael was still propped up and though his eyes were closed he opened them as they entered.

'Ah, Doctor, come to see if I have stuck my spoon in the wall yet?'

'I have no concerns there, my lord. However, I would be interested if you would tell me the last thing you remember before you became ill?'

Michael closed his eyes briefly, the lines between his brows growing pronounced. 'I remember I was going to take Allie to a ball, at the Stanton-Hills.'

'That was two months ago,' Anderson said resignedly.

A slow look of shock spread across Michael's face.

'What the devil do you mean, two months ago? That's impossible.'

The doctor laid a soothing hand on his shoulder.

'Calm down. This is not unheard of. You received a rather severe blow to the head. It may take time for the mind to recuperate. It is likely your memory will return and possibly very soon.'

He turned again to Anderson.

'Do you know if something of import occurred during that period?'

Anderson shifted uncomfortably; there was no way he could reveal what had truly happened.

'I believe they were held up by highwaymen on the way back from the ball.'

'Ah!' said the doctor portentously. 'And what occurred? Was anyone hurt?'

'No one but the…highwaymen. Michael chased them off.'

'That may explain it, then,' said the doctor. 'It is most likely that as you recover from your concussion, your memory will return, my lord.'

As they turned to go, Michael's voice stopped them.

'Anderson, if you don't mind…' he began, his voice deceptively calm.

Anderson cleared his throat, turning to the doctor.

'I believe Miss Trevor and I should have a few moments with Lord Crayle, Dr Felton.'

The doctor hesitated, but the obdurate look on his patient's face convinced him it made more sense to give him these few minutes than allow him to fret.

'Very well, I will go and speak to the ladies. Ten minutes,' he said warningly, and Anderson nodded.

As soon as the door was closed, Michael leaned forward.

'Two months, Sinjun? What the hell has been going on?'

He noticed Sari was still standing there.

'Look, I do not mean to be rude, and I apologise for not remembering you, but I need to speak with Anderson. Alone.'

'Michael, Sari is here for a reason. You want to know what happened two months ago? Well, in brief, Miss Trevor here was one of the, ah…highway robbers that held you up that night and you convinced her to join the Institute. For the past few weeks we have been tracking Junger and Frey, trying to discover what their plans are in London and who they are working with. Miss Trevor has been involved in all of this very closely. In fact, it was to save her life that you jumped into the Thames in the first place, after she saved O'Brien from Junger.'

After a moment of staring at Anderson and Sari in bemusement, Michael burst into laughter.

'It is not funny!' Sari said adamantly. It was outrageous, but not funny.

'It is preposterous,' he gasped finally. 'Anderson, you cannot be serious.'

'I most certainly am.'

'Come, now. I think I would have remembered being assaulted by a female.'

A sudden burst of fury scattered Sari's numbness and pain. How dared he? First he bedded her, then erased her, and now he ridiculed and belittled her? She took a step forward, her hands fisting.

Michael returned her glare with an amused smile, his eyes inspecting her flushed face appreciatively. He wondered what on earth had made Anderson concoct such an outrageous story. The thought that this girl had been a highway robber was too ridiculous to credit. He wondered if the tale was some trick to try to jog his memory.

He did remember they had discussed finding some actress for occasional work at the Institute. If it were true and she did indeed work for them, she was probably an actress Anderson had recruited, and by the looks of her not a very good one. She was pretty enough and seemed spirited, but she looked like she had the devil of a temper, which was not a good asset for an agent.

Still, something Anderson had said rang a bell. He glanced up.

'You said Junger and Frey are definitely in England already. Is that part true?'

Anderson nodded.

'Damn it. They are not here for the weather, I presume. What have they been doing and what did they have to do with my midnight swim?'

Anderson nodded again. 'I told you, you jumped in to save Sari when she was forced into the water after distracting Junger from O'Brien. You were at the docks to try to find out who they were meeting. It appears they are plotting something with some titled gentleman here in London. Given Junger and Frey, we presume it will be an assassination attempt, we just don't know who the target is.'

'Damn Metternich,' Michael muttered, then glanced up at the young woman again. 'Sinjun, do you mind sending her away? I don't care what kind of…arrangement you have with her, but she should hardly be here while we discuss this, don't you think?'

Anderson looked slightly shocked at Michael's insinuation of a relationship between him and Sari. 'You're quite wrong, Michael. Miss Trevor has been with us from the beginning on this case. In fact, she was the one who led us to the meeting with Hamlin and this unknown lord.'

Michael stared incredulously at the girl, who was continuing to regard him haughtily. He wondered if Anderson was besotted with her and that was why he was treating her with such privilege. He sighed, deciding to ignore her for the moment.

'Tell it to me from the beginning.'

By the time Anderson had recounted what had happened on the quay, Michael's head was pounding painfully.

'We'll talk more later, Sinjun. Come back later,' he mumbled, pressing a hand to his forehead, and his friend nodded and led Sari out silently.

* * *

Lady Montvale had been right that mayhem would follow the announcement of Sari's engagement in the *Gazette*. It just kept getting worse. Montvale House had been bombarded by visits from well-wishers, disappointed suitors and the plainly curious. The one positive effect of the commotion, as far as Sari was concerned, was that it distracted her from her wretched internal monologue and the constant urge to go and see that Michael was safe.

When Lord Edgerton invited her to go for a ride in the park in his curricle she forced herself to accept warmly and prepared herself to endure an hour of discussing their marriage plans, but to her surprise even once they had made their way out of the city traffic and into the quieter lanes of the park he remained silent. Finally, he turned to her and smiled slightly.

'Forgive me, I have been wool-gathering.'

'Not at all. You need not entertain me every moment of the day. I do not mind silence.'

'Thank you. It is a compliment to you that I feel comfortable being quiet with you.'

'It is nothing serious, I hope?' Sari asked gently, on full alert.

'Nothing for you to worry about, my love. Only I am afraid I will not be able to attend the theatre on Thursday. I have…an important guest I must entertain and there are some constraints…in short, I have been forced to bring forward our dinner date to this Thursday. But we shall still be able to attend the show at Vauxhall on Wednesday.'

Sari smiled, outwardly serene. 'Of course.'

'You are truly a jewel among women,' he said softly before he turned the carriage.

* * *

Sari tried to contain her agitation until he let her down at Lady Montvale's. Luckily the lady was at home and she glanced up as Sari hurried into the blue room.

'Quick, we need to find Anderson.'

'I believe he is at Michael's place. He just stopped by on his way not half an hour ago,' she said calmly, tugging on the bellpull to order the carriage.

Sari almost stopped her, but then just sat down to wait, staring at her clasped hands. Part of her didn't want to have to bear another round of Michael's antagonism and dismissiveness, but it was crushed by a surge of anticipation at the thought of seeing him that was so powerful she wondered it didn't just spill out of her for all to see.

Anderson and Michael were seated in the study and rose as Sari and Lady Montvale were announced. Sari found it was still hard to meet Michael's eyes as she walked in and she was surprised when he addressed her once they were seated.

'I hear congratulations are in order. Allie showed me the announcement of your betrothal in the *Gazette*.'

'Thank you, my lord,' she replied warily, unsure what to make of his languidly mocking tone. There was something harsh underneath it which made her uneasy. She had no idea what Anderson had told him about Edgerton.

'So you should, since I perceive it is our funds that are paying for your courtship. I am not quite sure what return on our investment we are receiving, unless the Institute is to share in Edgerton's spoils as well?'

'Michael, wait,' Anderson interjected, evidently shocked by Michael's bluntness. 'I was just about to explain about Edgerton...' he added, turning to Sari.

She swallowed her hurt, angry at herself for allowing Michael to affect her like this.

'Never mind. I have something important to tell you. That's why I came here—I think whatever Edgerton is planning is scheduled for Thursday night. I know you think I am wrong about him, but humour me. He seemed very troubled today and begged off from our visit to the theatre on Thursday, saying he had an important guest to entertain and that he had been forced to bring the date of their engagement forward.'

Michael frowned.

'Wait one moment! Sinjun, do you mean to tell me you had her get engaged to Edgerton in order to spy on him?' He sounded incredulous, and Anderson flushed a little.

'Of course not…' He floundered, and Sari jumped in to fill the breach.

'Anderson didn't ask me. I did it myself. It was the best way to keep track of him once I'd realised he was the man at the quay.'

Michael pressed the heel of his palm to his forehead.

'Miss Trevor, my head hurts like hell and none of this is making sense. Kindly let Anderson speak.'

Sari gritted her teeth against a childish urge to shout. Fine. Let the big brave men deal with it.

Anderson explained briefly Sari's account of Edgerton's possible involvement. Michael listened grimly, not looking at her. As she watched him Sari's frustration was once again swamped by a sudden wave of sheer misery. How could this man have made love to her as he had that night and now regard her as nothing more than an inconvenient nuisance? She had never deluded herself into thinking he might care for her the way she did for him, but to be so…obliterated… This was worse than anything Hector had ever done to her. She had a sudden urge to walk over and slap him, hard, and demand he remember. She looked down at her clenched fists and opened them slowly.

When Anderson finished speaking Michael nodded.

'It is tenuous but we have to look into it. Get a tail on him and O'Brien should get what he can out of the servants. Margaret, do you know what Edgerton's social activities are over the next couple of days?'

'I know he's dining with the Shaftsburys tonight because he wanted to cancel so he could join us at the opera. But we agreed he would join us tomorrow at Vauxhall instead. And as you heard he is engaged Thursday.'

'Fine. Sinjun, what about Hamlin? Anything more on him?'

'No, it's strange. He hasn't been seen for the past couple of days. Either he's gone to ground or—' Anderson broke off suddenly as Sari gasped.

'I had forgotten,' she said in shock. 'On the quay, when they were talking, they said his lordship was tired of Hamlin asking for more money, that he wasn't trustworthy.'

'There is no need to jump to conclusions,' Michael said. 'We'll meet back here tomorrow morning at eleven. Anderson, tell O'Brien to come as well, I want to hear what he finds out at Edgerton's. And have Morton check with Bow Street about Hamlin. Discreetly.'

'Check if a body has been found, you mean,' Sari said tensely.

He glanced at her, then his grey eyes flickered downwards. He didn't answer.

'I had forgotten,' she said, swamped by sudden guilt. 'Perhaps if I had remembered earlier...'

'I said don't jump to conclusions,' he repeated brusquely. 'You seem to have a rather inflated concept of your ability to influence events, Miss Trevor. It's not a healthy trait.'

The gratuitous cruelty of his words given the circumstances shocked her almost as much as being forgotten by him. Before she could even think of what to say, Lady Montvale spoke up.

'Michael, that was completely uncalled for. You should apologise to Miss Trevor!'

Michael flushed slightly at the rebuke.

'Very well. Miss Trevor, I apologise.'

His grudging apology was more than Sari could bear. She stood up.

'I'll wait for you in the hall, Lady Montvale,' she said as calmly as possible. 'Good day, Mr Anderson, Lord Crayle.'

Lady Montvale stood up as well, but waited until Sari had left the room. She turned to Michael, who was staring at the closed door, frowning.

'I will make allowances for you, Michael, as you have been ill. But I think that once you are in fuller possession of your senses, you will see you owe Miss Trevor a rather more gracious apology than that and not merely for your last comment.'

Michael raised his hands, caught between guilt and annoyance. He had no idea why he had been so harsh on her. He had spoken before he had even thought.

'Fine. I've already made a habit of apologising to her, one more won't make a difference.'

Anderson's head snapped up in surprise at his words.

'What do you mean "a habit"?' Lady Montvale asked shrewdly. 'Does this mean you remember apologising to her in the past?'

Michael stared at her, suddenly confused. He had no idea why he had said that.

'I…I don't remember. You know I don't.'

Lady Montvale raised one shoulder. 'Very well. Enough for now. I will see you at the opera tonight.'

Michael groaned. This he had clearly forgotten.

'I hate the opera.'

'Now, now, you promised to accompany Allie. She and Letty will be disappointed if you don't. Really, Michael. I never understood how someone who likes music as much as you doesn't like opera.'

'It's not the music. It's the wailing. All right, I'll come.'

Anderson grinned.

'I have another engagement or else I'd take your place, man. Good luck. We'll all convene here tomorrow morning.'

Chapter Twenty-Five

That evening as they entered the foyer of the Opera House Michael was stopped often by acquaintances, wanting to know the origin of the cut on his head. They had kept the news of his illness quiet and he passed his injuries off with a joke about a riding accident. Since he was known as a first-class equestrian, that provoked some amusement, but he took it in good humour. Sari was careful to seat herself as far from him as possible in the box, taking the seat in the shadowed corner slightly behind Alicia. Not that it mattered. Within minutes of the curtain rising, Michael quietly stood up and, with a rueful grin at Lady Montvale, left the box.

Sari sat for a few more minutes, struggling with herself, then stood up as unobtrusively as possible and left the box as well. She had no idea where he might have gone but as she followed the corridor which led away from the entrance she noticed they had opened the balcony doors which overlooked a small fountain in a garden below.

He was leaning on the high parapet, looking down into the garden, and she stopped, wondering what on earth she was doing. She could hear the relaxing rush of the water from the fountain beneath. Behind her the music continued, high and beautiful. She breathed deeply, tasting the faint, surprising scent of honeysuckle that mixed with the more acrid smell of the city. Her nerve failed as she stood there and she was about to return to the box when he turned suddenly and saw her. She squared her shoulders and moved towards him.

'I would like a word with you.'

Michael took in the determined look in the young woman's eyes and repressed a smile. She looked like a fiery little amazon, even in the civilised and admittedly flattering silvery gown she wore. He was beginning to understand why Anderson had so obviously knuckled under to her. She was apparently used to getting her way.

Fine, he wanted to have a word with her, too. He didn't need Lady Montvale's admonition to realise he had crossed the line of civility with her. His only explanation was that her role in this story worried him and he couldn't afford to be worried at the moment. She was the one piece in the puzzle they were trying to unravel that he couldn't get his mind around and that was dangerous.

He had spent the day at the Institute talking with Anderson, O'Brien, Morton and others involved in the case, trying to cobble it all together into some kind of coherent picture that would patch over the gaping hole in his memory. He had been surprised by how often her name had come up. Not one of the other men seemed to regard it as suspicious that a young woman who had no particular training and who had been part of the Institute for less than two months should have become central in such a sensitive case while also becoming engaged to a man who was possibly a traitor.

Of all the critical information regarding this case which he had managed to collect, she was the most incongruous and disturbing. Somehow she had managed to earn the goodwill of everyone closest to him. Nothing about her made sense.

He had to be on top of every aspect of this case if they were to stop Junger and Frey. And that apparently meant he could no longer afford to ignore her involvement. She wanted to talk? Fine—so did he.

He moved past her, reaching out to detach the silken rope holding back the balcony curtain, and it swung closed, effectively shutting them off from the rest of the world. Then he turned to her.

'Very well. Have at it.'

She glanced around, as if surprised by his choice of venue.

'Here?'

'Why not? Everyone is inside listening to Bertolli massacre Mozart.'

Amusement flashed in her eyes, and the hint of a dimple quivered before it was rigidly suppressed. Something not quite a memory flickered in him. More of a familiarity. Then her determined look returned.

'I understand that you have no memory of doing so, but I joined the Institute at your invitation and at the very least you could have the decency to treat me with respect. I'm tired of you insinuating all manner of things about me that have absolutely nothing to do with reality.'

He leaned back against the pillar and crossed his arms.

'What precisely did I insinuate? I forget.' He had no idea why he was goading her. Some demon in him wanted to prod at this prickly side of her. He tried not to smile as her head dipped a little, rather like a bull preparing to charge.

'Don't overplay that card, my lord. You know full well what you implied when you said I used my role at the Institute to ensnare Edgerton... And to insinuate that I have an "arrangement" with Anderson! That is insulting to both of us.'

'If I was wrong, then I apologise, but frankly I still find it hard to understand why you saw the need to become engaged to Edgerton. Surely that is a bit extreme, even given our interest in him? Don't you think I am justified in wondering whether there is more to it than your professed loyalty to the Institute?'

It sounded reasonable enough on the face of it, but Sari felt such a blast of fury at his light, dismissive tones that she suddenly understood what drove people to violence. She wished for one moment that she could be a man and fight it out with him rather than having to stand there and try to convince this rude, unbearable person.

'Oh, perfectly justified, my lord! Why stop there? What else would you like to lay at my doorstep while we are at it? What precisely did I allegedly do to Anderson? Did I seduce him or did he seduce me or doesn't it matter in this little fairy tale of yours?'

His dismissive look faded as she tossed these words at him, to be replaced by the stony, controlled look she knew well. She knew they were entering dangerous territory, but didn't care. She didn't care about a damn thing any more.

'I like to stay as close to the truth with my fairy tales, if you don't mind. So I would wager it wasn't Anderson who did the seducing,' he said contemptuously.

Sari couldn't believe it was Michael and not someone else who had said that. If she had been angry before, now she felt quite capable of murder.

'Why not? You certainly did!' she flung at him.

The words were out before she could stop them. She clapped her hand to her mouth as if she could take them back.

In the silence that followed she could faintly hear Bertolli begging his fair maiden to love him.

'Excuse me?' Michael asked slowly after a moment.

'I am going back inside.' She started towards the curtain, but he moved to block her path.

'No,' he said grimly. 'You don't just walk out after saying something like that. Explain yourself.'

'There is nothing to explain.' she said, crossing her arms. She had no idea why she had said it. Perhaps she *had* wanted to shock him. To force him to remember. She feit pathetic and she almost hated him for making her feel so. Even if he believed her, all she would do was convince him she was as unprincipled as he already seemed to believe. Still, something perverse in her wanted him to know he was far from perfect in this whole story. To knock him off the pedestal he had placed himself on and condemned her from.

Michael looked at the young woman facing him defiantly, trying to make sense of what she had said. The implication that *he* had seduced her was ludicrous. Wasn't it? He had accepted that for some reason he himself had recruited her for the Institute and that meant that he was responsible for her. It would go against every principle he had to have an affair with her, whatever her background or her behaviour. He could not deny that she was disconcertingly attractive, but he had never let attraction overrule judgement, certainly not in such critical areas.

It wasn't true, he told himself, wondering why he wasn't convinced. He should know. Unequivocally. He should know if he had bedded this woman. His gaze roamed over her for an unguarded moment, searching for something familiar. Well, of course she was familiar, but that was because he had now known her for two rather intense days and it was hard not to notice that she had an uncomfortable effect on him. He could well understand why he might have wanted to bed her, but he couldn't conceive that he had. Perhaps it had been before she had even joined the Institute...

'If I—and I'm not saying I believe you—but if there was anything, it must have been before you came to the Institute. Right?'

'No, but why worry about it if you don't believe me? Now let me by, please. I would rather not have to explain what we are doing here together.'

He waved a dismissive hand.

'There's still plenty more of that wailing, unfortunately. We're not done here.'

'What do you want from me, Michael?' she asked almost desperately.

The way she said his name shook him, and he reached out, grasping her arms. 'Don't call me that,' he bit out.

She laughed recklessly and appeared to throw caution to the wind.

'You told me to, you know. In fact, you begged me to...'

A wave of shock coursed through him, followed rapidly by a surge of heat at the thought of her calling out his name in passion. He had no idea if she was telling the truth or lying and he had to know.

'Prove it,' he said hoarsely. 'Where did we...where did we meet?'

She stared at him, with her lips parted, uncomprehending.

'Prove it?'

His hands moved up, grasping her shoulders.

'Yes. Or can't you remember?' he said caustically.

She crossed her arms, trying to shake off his hands but he didn't let go.

'We didn't "meet". It was one time. In your home.'

His hands tightened on her and his mouth opened, but he didn't speak. She could see how hard this was for him and almost relented.

'I don't believe you. Not in my home,' he said after a moment. 'I have never... For heaven's sake, my sisters are there.'

She shrugged, suddenly very tired. 'If I were lying I'd make up a better story than that, wouldn't I? It doesn't matter. Let me pass.'

Sari tried to slide past him, but he held her easily, pressing her back against the cool marble pillar at the end of the parapet, one hand moving to tilt up her head. His eyes locked on hers, as if he could force some revelation out of her.

'I don't believe you,' he said again, but there was no assurance in his voice, just a kind of supplication. His gaze moved to her mouth. She knew what he was about to do and even though she knew she should try to stop him, for his own sake, she did not want to.

Michael hesitated before he touched his mouth to hers. He had to find out if it was true. Surely if he had done this before, he would know. The moment he brushed his lips against hers, just skimming their warmth, something else took over. A need that carried the same intensity as his resistance crashed through him, as his whole body flamed the instant he tasted her.

Despite the strength of his embrace she opened to him without hesitation, which only made him more desperate. She was so sweet his lungs constricted under the force of the desire her taste set loose. He raised her so that she was seated on the parapet separating this balcony from the next. He moved closer, pressing between her legs. It was the perfect height. He thought he could feel her heat even through her skirts. He groaned and wrenched his mouth from hers, trying to regain control.

He had no idea if she was familiar or not. It didn't matter. Nothing mattered but the heat of her legs cradling his hips, the soft swell of her breasts above her bodice. He wanted her. He wanted her naked, clinging to him, crying out his name. He bent to kiss her again, trying to drown out his betraying thoughts, but she was kissing him back, biting gently into his lower lip as she ran her tongue across it, sending a thunderbolt through his body. He grasped her skirts shakily, pulling them up, his hands sliding up her silk stockings, and when his fingers met the soft flesh above her garters he almost cried out as he slid one hand between her thighs.

'Michael, oh, God, please...' She gasped, her head arching back against the marble pillar behind her as he kissed her neck, the swell of her breasts, slipping the gown from her shoulder with one hand even as his finger slid over her heat below, making her cry out again. Her hand slid down his chest and tentatively pulled at his shirt, tugging it from his breeches, and pleasure shot through him at the simple friction. His hand tightened in her hair as he deepened his kiss, punishing her for the pleasure she was inflicting.

He increased the pressure of his fingers below, wanting to finish her before she destroyed him. But even as her tremors picked up speed, her legs quivering against his thighs, her hands pressed the shirt up, running her palms against his chest, just grazing his chest and sending his nerves into an ecstatic, undeniable dance. He tried to stop her, but with a whimper she shifted against his hand, leaning in to kiss his throat, and he had to brace his hand on the pillar behind her to keep his knees from folding.

There was an answering desperation in her embrace, in the way her fingers bit into his back as she shook under his hand. Her breathing was ragged, breaking with each slide of his fingers. She was so close, but he couldn't wait any longer. The wet heat under his fingers was too much, like the arching of her hips with each thrust. He wanted to be inside her, feel the tight slick heat... He fumbled at his trousers, no longer thinking of anything but the need to feel her fully, of guiding her destructive hands to touch him where he needed it most. He dragged her mouth back to his as he drew her hand downwards. Then her cool fingers closed on his erection, and his breath simply disappeared. Desperately, he pushed her hand away, pulling her to him as he slid her forward to guide himself inside her.

She was so hot and tight he could hardly stand. He slid one hand under her bottom, raising her, and she whimpered, locking her legs about him, pulling him inside. Then the world slid away and he thrust into her again and again, his mouth on her throat, one hand still between them, caressing her. She called out his name as she came—a deep, luxurious cry that tore at him. But he was already drowning, thrusting into her one last time, so deeply the world cracked and spilled about him and he stopped breathing.

When his sight returned he was still holding her, still inside her. His shirt was clinging to him with perspiration and he was filled with her taste, her scent. He could feel the tremors still running through her and her breathing was short and shallow, matching his own. He forced himself to withdraw, but he knew he did not want to leave.

Finally, he let her go and turned away. He heard the rustle of her skirts behind him as she slid off the parapet, but he would not turn around. He wanted to say something. He knew that whether he remembered her or not, she had not been lying. He had no idea how he had allowed himself to seduce her. And in his own home of all places. She was his responsibility. But after what had just happened—the

speed and intensity with which his body had surrendered
to desire—he knew it must be true.

'I'm sorry,' he said hoarsely as she walked past him and
pushed aside the curtain. She did not reply, and he didn't
try to stop her. He heard the applause erupt and felt unable to go back. He left a message to be delivered to Lady
Montvale saying he had returned home. Let them think he
was still unwell. He could not face anyone tonight.

Sari didn't return immediately to the box, but made her
way to the powder room. He had used her and discarded
her and his apology only made it worse. And yet, before
the return to the world, it had been utterly incredible. She
had not realised her body could achieve such pleasure. She
couldn't understand how this capacity had existed in her,
undiscovered until now.

One reality sang through her. He wanted her. He might
have dismissed her, but he still wanted her. Then another,
depressing, thought occurred to her. If she had wanted to
convince him she was no simple scheming wanton, she
had failed miserably. She had given herself to him without
reservation, without a whimper of protest. She had confirmed everything he had insinuated about her.

She sat down in front of the mirrors and inspected herself shakily. Her hair was mussed, but aside from a slight
redness to her lips she looked no different. She took a
deep breath and set about correcting the damage, at least
the external damage. Then she stood up resolutely and returned to the box.

Chapter Twenty-Six

The following morning Sari debated long and hard whether to go to Crayle House for the meeting Michael had mentioned. She felt it would be impossible to meet his gaze after the events of the previous evening, but she was damned if she was going to forgo her duties to the Institute because she had acted a fool.

She needn't have worried about the embarrassment. She arrived at the same time as O'Brien and she could tell he was burning with news. He didn't even wait until they had all sat down, but turned immediately to Michael and Anderson.

'You won't believe it, Major. I've been having a nice flirt with the Edgerton's downstairs maid and the long and short of it is that the sweet lass tells me they be busy getting ready for an important guest. You'll never guess who—Castlereagh! Wait, that's not all. Apparently the servants are all to be given the evening off once dinner is served. Only Edgerton's steward from his Dorset property is to remain to wait on them that evening.'

Sari leaned forward.

'Edgerton said... I remember he said once that Castlereagh was more dangerous to Britain than Napoleon.'

'He certainly is more dangerous to Metternich. If it weren't for Castlereagh he would have had both France and Russia under his thumb by now. I can see why he wants Castlereagh gone, but how the hell he convinced someone like Edgerton to go along with this...' Michael paused.

'He thinks Castlereagh's negotiations in Europe are opening Britain to liberal revolutionary influences.' Sari added. 'He said he has too much power, that by the time he's dislodged it will be too late. But I never thought... I mean, to actually assist in the assassination...'

'This is Metternich all over. Somehow he has convinced Edgerton that stopping Castlereagh will stop Britain from changing. Blind fool.'

'But why on earth couldn't Metternich just have Junger and Frey do it?' asked Anderson. 'Why does he have to go through all the effort of involving someone like Edgerton? Think of the risk!'

'Because he knows he can't afford an international incident. This can't be connected to Austria. He probably convinced Edgerton that Junger and Frey will make Castlereagh's death look like an accident and all he had to do was supply the venue and make sure he got them out of the country afterwards. The fool doesn't know those two will probably stage it to make it look like he did it in a fit of insanity or something and then get rid of him somehow. Either a staged suicide of a failed escape...'

'Or an accident like Hamlin,' Anderson interjected.

'What accident? You found Hamlin?' Sari asked urgently.

Anderson hesitated as Michael shot him a warning look.

'For heaven's sake, don't play coy now. Just tell me,' Sari said impatiently.

'His body was found in the Thames, caught in the piers past the West India Docks. He was...hard to identify, which is why it took us a while to track him down. They presume he fell in while intoxicated and was swept downriver,' Michael stated curtly, watching her closely.

Sari pressed her lips together. She'd had no affection for Hamlin, but the thought that he had been extinguished so brutally, that this was part of the world she had entered, shocked her more than she liked. And the realisation that Edgerton was responsible for that frivolous young man's death, even if he had not ordered it himself, woke such a fury against him that she wondered how she would mask it. She looked up, meeting Michael's hooded gaze, and raised her chin. She had no intention of turning faint if that was what worried him. He stood up and motioned to Anderson.

'Come on, Anderson, we need to speak to Castlereagh.'

Just as he reached the doorway he turned back to Sari.

'Didn't Margaret say you were to go with Edgerton to Vauxhall this evening?'

Sari shuddered slightly and nodded. How was she going to face him? This was terrible. Somehow she had still hoped she had been wrong about him. What a fool.

Michael's face hardened.

'Cry off. Tell him you are ill or something.'

'But he might… We shouldn't do anything out of the ordinary, should we?'

Michael ran his hands through his hair.

'Fine. Just make sure you don't go anywhere with him unattended.'

He didn't wait for her to respond but walked out, followed by Anderson and O'Brien.

Castlereagh grimly regarded Michael and Anderson as the three of them sat in his spacious office at the Foreign Office.

'What do you suggest?'

'Well, you obviously will have to call off the dinner engagement.'

'Won't they suspect we know the truth?'

'We cannot risk anything else at this point. We might even make it work to our advantage. If Junger and Frey realise they have been exposed, they will try to get out of England. That in itself is an admission of guilt. But it's not enough. We need Edgerton to know he is suspected. Hopefully, he will do something rash and then we will have him as well. At least enough to give you grounds for exiling him. It will have to be done quietly.'

'Yes, damn it. Unbelievable! Edgerton! What is wrong with these so-called patriots? Can't they see the world has changed?'

Michael shrugged. It was a moot point.

'The problem is that they do see it has changed, but they believe they can turn time back. Are we agreed, then?' he asked.

'Yes, blast it. Do as you see fit. Keep it as quiet as possible, though.'

'Of course. We will send your regrets and make sure Edgerton gets scent of your suspicions. Nothing concrete, just enough to rattle him. Meanwhile, we will talk to your people about having you put under guard until this is over. Just to be cautious it might be safer for you to stay here in your office for a couple of days rather than at your home.'

Castlereagh sighed and nodded.

'I have plenty of work to keep me occupied here. Go to it and keep me informed.'

Michael nodded and he and Anderson left, heading back to Crayle House.

Once they were seated in Michael's study, Anderson turned to him.

'What do we do about tonight?'

'We both go. I don't want him near any of them without protection.' Michael sat staring out of the window.

'Miss Trevor seems to have the most unfortunate choice in suitors,' he said after a moment. 'Hamlin was found floating in the Thames and Edgerton is probably a traitor.'

'Michael, enough,' Anderson said sharply. 'If it weren't for Sari we wouldn't have come this far. She was the one who identified Edgerton and stuck close to him even when we wouldn't believe her.'

Michael stood up abruptly and started pacing the room.

'Damn it! Why can't I remember anything?'

'Perhaps it's because you don't want to!' Anderson returned with equal heat.

'What is that supposed to mean?'

'I don't know. Why don't you tell me? The fact is your memory closes down the day you met her. I don't give a damn what you think of her, but you are going to have to give it a rest until this is over because I am fast losing my patience.'

Contrarily, Anderson's uncharacteristic outburst calmed Michael. He walked over to look out of the windows to the gardens beyond, which were green and cheerful and inviting. Anderson was right. Whether his memory loss was related to her appearance in his life or not, he had better get a firm grip on his behaviour. He was acting like a pathetic fool.

He pushed down his annoyance. But unfortunately there were other reactions he could not hold back so well, or frankly, at all. Even now in the cold light of day the memory of her on the balcony seared through him. He closed his eyes briefly against the rush of physical need that swept through him.

He still had no idea how he had allowed himself to go against his principles to such an extent. Even last night at the opera—he had fought it, but not nearly hard enough.

And she had let him touch her without protest. She had surrendered herself without hesitation, her body singing under his hands, her mouth sweet and hot against his…

He clenched his fists, pressing them against the cool glass. The thought that she might have given herself as easily to Edgerton was unbearable. He could not stomach the thought of another man touching her and he despised himself for his jealousy. He pressed his clenched fists together, drawing a deep, shaky breath. He wondered whether it was still some vestige of his illness that his need was so great. He had never given anyone power over him. To give it to someone like her… It was unthinkable.

'You're right,' he said over his shoulder. 'Enough of this. We have work to do.'

Chapter Twenty-Seven

Sari didn't know how it had happened. She had been certain the rest of the party was right behind her on the long garden path heading towards the famous cascade and miniature clockwork show at Vauxhall, but somehow a surging crowd of raucous pleasure-seekers had come between them, and whether by accident or design she had found herself alone with Lord Edgerton. It was ridiculous to feel fear bathed in the light of the pretty lanterns that were strung among the trees. And certainly Edgerton did not seem at all ominous. Though he held her arm firmly, he looked distracted and strained and not at all like a man who was intent on doing her harm.

They were certain to find their party once they reached the Cascade, she told herself, as they turned down another lane, joining the flow of people heading in the same direction. She tried to steer Edgerton around a very large woman in a dress with loud cherry stripes and was just about to accomplish this feat when her other elbow was grasped and she glanced up with a start into Michael's face.

'Lady Montvale asked if you could join her in the retiring rooms, Miss Trevor.'

'Of course,' she said gratefully and turned to smile at Edgerton. 'Would you mind, Lord Edgerton?'

He smiled stiffly and she sensed he was even somewhat relieved. He took her hand in his.

'Not at all, my dear. In fact, would you very much mind if I begged off from the rest of the evening? I have a long day ahead of me tomorrow.'

'Of course, please don't give it a thought. Goodnight,' she said with as sweet a smile as she could muster, some of the tension leaving her body in relief.

His face relaxed into a warm smile and for the first time that evening she felt he was truly looking at her. He raised her hand to his lips.

'Goodnight, my one love. I will see you tomorrow.'

She flushed, very aware of Michael standing just behind her. As Edgerton left she turned to follow Michael. To her surprise he did not lead her towards the retiring rooms, but rather to the room they had hired for their group where they were planning to meet for dinner after the fireworks. Once inside she sat down on one of the chairs that lined the wall and rubbed her arms. She felt tired and depressed.

'Where is Lady Montvale?' she asked.

'I have no idea. Probably at the Cascade,' he said to her surprise. 'I thought we told you to stay away from him. I hadn't realised you would interpret that as an invitation to stroll down a deserted pathway with him.'

'I... We were separated from the rest in the crowd. And it was hardly a deserted pathway!' She dredged up some anger, pulling it about her like a protective shell. 'I cannot very well just give him the cut direct, can I? We are engaged after all.'

He closed the door, and she shivered.

'I am well aware you are engaged. But that does not give you licence to sneak off into the bushes for some furtive groping.'

Sari's face flamed.

'I did not—' She cut herself off, standing up. There was no point in arguing. One way or another she always lost.

'Let me by,' she said firmly.

'Not until you give me your word you will keep contact with him to the barest minimum. I have no intention of wasting energy on extracting you from trouble.'

So, she was good for bedding, but not for expending energy of any other form.

'What a bore it must be to have to play *preux chevalier* to someone you so thoroughly dislike. You may rest easy; you won't be called on to exert yourself on my behalf again tonight.'

She curtsied mockingly and moved towards the door, but he grasped her arm, stopping her.

'This is no joke!' he bit out.

Sari realised they were utterly alone. Everyone was down in the gardens for the show and would remain there to await the fireworks. No one would come to the room now. Sudden panic hit her. She wasn't sure she could cope with being alone with him again.

'Let me go!' She tugged her arm away abruptly and to her dismay the delicate fabric of her sleeve tore at the seam.

He stared at the tear in surprise. The anger faded from his face and he looked distant again, withdrawn.

'I am sorry. I will get you another.'

Sari looked down at her shoulder, trying to inspect the damage. It would be impossible to appear in public in such a state. They would all have to return home early now.

'How kind!' she said bitingly and continued before she could think rationally enough to stop the words. 'Payment for services rendered?'

His head shot up at that and the detachment in his eyes vanished.

'Yes,' he replied simply.

'No.' She could not let him do this to her, not again. She took a step back, but he followed.

'I think so. We have already proven you are willing, haven't we?'

'Michael, please...' She took another step back and found herself against the wall and then his hands closed on her shoulders and she could feel their heat, which burned stronger where the tear had exposed her skin.

'I like it when you beg,' he said hoarsely, lowering his mouth to hers.

To her shame he was right. She did not even try to resist him. Like a starving child, she was willing to give up her pride for this. She did not even really care. He would despise her one way or another. It did not matter if she gave in or fought. And she wanted it. At least here she had some power over him. At least this way she received some measure of return. And this time she would make him pay. She would torture him as much as he tortured her, she resolved.

Michael did not even try to raise excuses this time. He knew it was madness to be doing this, in the middle of Vauxhall, with a young woman he didn't trust but who was under his protection, and just one day away from a possible attempt to assassinate the foreign minister. At the moment none of that mattered. He just gave in to the enticing taste of her mouth. He had kept away from her all evening, but her stupidity in allowing Edgerton to lead her away from the group had broken down his good intentions. He had brought her upstairs with the sole intention of taking her to task. But the minute he was alone with her, his resolution had crumbled. He wanted her, pure and simple, and he knew she would not fight him. They both wanted this. There was nothing wrong with appeasing this hunger.

He pulled her to him, feeling the length of her body against his. He took his time, imprinting the texture of her lips on his mind, feeling the smooth glide of her warm skin under his, the silky pucker of her lower lip that trembled under his mouth. Then he tasted her, touching his tongue to the parting, teasing it open, his senses drowning in the sweet warm heat of her mouth.

The satin of her dress slid beneath his fingers with a subtle friction. He ran his hands down her back and over the soft curve of her bottom. He wanted to savour this, take his time. He moved away slightly, reaching across to close the latch on the door, watching as her eyes flickered open. They were the most incredible eyes. He looked into them for a long moment, searching for the answers she refused to give, and then he pushed reason away and reclaimed her mouth.

He pulled her sleeves down, lowering her dress to her waist in a slow movement. He leant back to inspect her and then just as calmly slid one strap of her shift away to uncover her breast. His jaw clenched at its perfection, at the way it swelled and tightened under his gaze. With equal leisure he bent to kiss the taut rose of her nipple, abrading it with his lip lightly and touching it with his tongue. She cried out softly, her breath cutting off in the middle of the sound as her body twisted in the tight embrace of his arms.

'Open my shirt,' he whispered against her skin, holding her as she shivered, feeling each tremor run through the length of his body, pooling in his loins.

'What?' she asked hazily, her eyes opening again.

'Open my shirt; I want to feel you against me.'

To his surprise she moved away from the wall and for a moment he thought she might try to leave once more. But she just nudged him back so that he was against the wall now, bathed in the deep shadows. She ran her hands from his shoulders to his waist, just brushing the stiff fabric lightly, and his blood rushed down with the contact.

She undid his cravat first, pulling off the long silk cloth with a slow movement that made his nerves sing. Then she undid his shirt, catch by catch, following the opening with her lips and tongue, and he closed his eyes, leaning his head back. He was both cold and hot and every touch of her mouth pulled all his blood to one burning point.

She pushed apart his shirt and he shrugged it and his coat to the floor. She leaned against him to brush the lightest of kisses across his chest, her hipbone pressing against his erection. He groaned and threaded his fingers through her hair, loosening the pins, pressing his forehead down against hers, holding back the need to cry out her name.

She leaned more deeply against him, teasing her breasts against his ribs and he saw a smile play across her lips. He bent to catch it, to taste it. His calm was fading fast and he reached around, fumbling with the small buttons on her dress. But the fabric was bunched about her waist, and as he pulled at it he heard a few buttons clatter to the ground. He couldn't bring himself to care; the dress was already ruined. Finally, it slid away, collecting in a puddle at her feet to be followed by her stays, and he knew this was madness. They were in the middle of Vauxhall, for goodness' sake. But her silk shift only magnified her heat and he pulled her down to the floor, spreading his coat beneath him and pulling her down on top of him.

Her body shivered and stretched against his, as if unsure whether to pull away or sink into him. He kept as calm as possible, letting her become accustomed to the contact, brushing one hand lightly and rhythmically down her back, just skimming the rise of her bottom. Even with his body on fire he had an urge to just stay like that, caressing her until she relaxed against him, and surrendered every defence.

But every time his fingers brushed lightly up the slope of her backside he could feel the gentle catch of her breath against him and an answering surge of heat pulsed through him. Then her hand echoed the motion of his caresses, sliding against his side and stomach and making a mockery of his fantasy of a leisurely seduction. His blood was pounding with the rhythm of the friction and each touch of her fingers sent his nerves singing.

Then she pulled back abruptly, surprising him, and he reached up to stop her, but she only bent down, drawing her silky hair across his chest before she bit gently into the side of his neck. Just before it became painful she let go and caressed the spot with her tongue, and his body bucked under her.

'Sari, touch me,' he whispered hoarsely, and she raised herself again, her hair drawing up from a soft puddle into a curtain that gleamed in the light of the candles that glimmered in their sconces. He unfastened his trousers and pushed them down abruptly. She hesitated, then closed her hand over his erection, and he pulled her mouth back to his, kissing her until he could barely breathe.

Her hand slid over him tentatively and then with increasing assurance as she read the responses of his body. Finally, he could not bear it any longer and he pulled her hand away and slid his own between her thighs, pressing her back so he could kiss her breasts.

He wanted to taste her. He needed to taste her fully. He pushed her even farther back so that she lay on his coat. Her arms reached out, but he bent to kiss her stomach, running his lips down to her hipbone, and her body twisted under him, trying to escape the sensations this set off. But

he spread her legs and raised her knee, moving to kiss the
soft skin on the inside of her thigh, and she gasped.

'Oh, God, Michael...'

She tried to pull away from him, but he moved farther
down, raising her knees, hooking one arm about her leg as
he bent to kiss the nerve centre of her pleasure. She gave
a sharp cry, but he held her, tasting her, his breath coming short and hard.

Sari bit her lip at the impossible intensity of the feeling. A voice was chanting inside her head. *This cannot be
happening, this cannot be happening.* It was almost painful it was so good and she didn't know what to do, how to
stop it or end it or anything. Her hands clung to the fabric
of the coat beneath her and she tried to hold back the cries
that threatened to burst from her. She had wanted to torture him, but he was torturing her. Tears squeezed from
her eyes and she gasped for air.

Then he was on top of her and he was kissing her neck,
her mouth, her name shuddering from his lungs. He filled
her and suddenly she was on fire. Her body was blazing
and she found herself laughing his name, her nails biting
into his back, urging him to move faster until they were
falling and it was so sweet she knew she was crying.

Michael was flying as the world let them go, pleasure
filling his lungs so that he didn't even need to breathe. He
didn't care when the world exploded. It didn't matter—he
was soaring. He thought he had died for a while and when
he surfaced it was out of a deep calm, his mind settling
back into his body slowly. He was wonderfully light, his
blood full of air. Then she shivered beneath him, and he
shifted to take the worst of his weight off her.

'Are you cold?' he murmured, and she shook her head

slightly. He tucked his hand into her silky hair and just stayed there, not wanting to move. Then he realised what was exploding and almost started to laugh. The fireworks had begun outside.

He raised his head slightly. If the fireworks had begun, that meant the spectacles were almost over, people would start coming upstairs... He pushed himself up with a groan. It was much too soon to move, but he had to. He fumbled on the ground and found her slip. She sat up as well and took it from him, holding it to her protectively. He could not cope with talking so he found his shirt and pulled it on and stood up. He helped her wordlessly with her clothes, pulling her gown over her head as one would dress a child. He knotted his cravat quickly.

'Stay here. I'll have the carriage brought around and come back in a minute,' he said and left, allowing Sari to arrange herself as best she could. He returned after a few minutes, carrying a shawl.

'Here, put this around you.'

'Where did you get this?' she asked, bemused.

'I stole it. Don't argue.'

Sari had no energy left to argue, or to talk. She followed him meekly through the unheeding crush of people to the entrance. To her surprise he joined her in the carriage, but looking at him she could understand his reluctance to go back into the crowd.

'What about Lady Montvale?' she asked.

'I had a boy take her a message that you were not well and that I was seeing you home,' he replied. 'Anderson will see them all home.'

Sari grimaced. This would require some explaining tomorrow.

'Your shirt is fastened incorrectly,' she said, staring out of the window.

Michael glanced down and refastened it. Not that it mattered. He must look as if he had been through a thresher. And he felt like it, too. A very pleasurable thresher. His body was still humming with contentment. He wanted to hold her, to feel her warmth, but he knew the moment had passed.

He gave in to the urge and pulled her to him anyway, onto his lap, and she tucked her head against his shoulder without a word. He did not know what it was that made him crave her like this. He could hardly believe he had done what he had. It was wrong on so many levels that he hardly recognised what he had become, but at the moment he did not want to fight it or her.

'I am sorry about your dress,' he said after a moment.

'It does not matter,' she answered. Her hand touched his arm briefly. It was a simple, unconsciously intimate gesture of forgiveness. He tightened his arms around her.

He let her down at Montvale House, not daring to take her to the door, so he watched from the darkness of the carriage as Henries let her in. It would be hard to explain the dress, but he was sure she would think of something. She was nothing if not resourceful.

Chapter Twenty-Eight

'Are you all right, child?' Lady Montvale asked with unaccustomed concern as they finished a very late breakfast.

She had refrained from questioning Sari about last night, for which Sari was very grateful and not a little suspicious.

'Everything is supposed to happen today and there is nothing for me to do,' she burst out. There was no way she could share her other thoughts with Lady Montvale. Sari suddenly wished she could just go back to Pimlico, put her head in Mina's lap and cry. Tomorrow, she promised herself. Today she had to stay close by. She was sure that eventually they would remember to let her and Lady Montvale know what was happening.

'You need a distraction, my dear. Didn't you say you had some new books waiting at Hatchards? Take Tansy and go and pick them up. The walk will do you good.'

'But if there is news…'

'If there is news I will send a footman directly to bring you back, my dear. Do go. I'm afraid that whatever exciting events are occurring elsewhere, we are in for a long, dull day of waiting.'

Sari sighed and stood up. 'You are probably right. I wish I were a man.'

Lady Montvale smiled at her despondent tone. 'The fault is not in our stars but in ourselves, said the bard, and though he, too, was conveniently a man, still he had a point. I would say that you have done a great deal to exceed whatever boundaries life has set you and may yet do much more if you will but learn patience. Now go and get your books.'

Sari laughed and came to give the older woman a quick hug. 'Thank you, I will.'

She made it as far as the small side street that led from Berkeley Square towards Albemarle Street and Piccadilly before she heard a faint squeak. Tansy, the maid, had been trailing behind her, but now she was nowhere to be seen. There was nothing but a carriage moving towards her slowly. Suddenly, its door swung open and she saw the man with the broken nose. He held Tansy easily, his hands clasped over her mouth, and tears of terror were spilling from the maid's eyes.

'Step in, miss, and not a sound,' he said. 'We've orders to bring you in as gentle as can be, but I have no orders about not hurting your maid.'

'Let her go, then, and I will come with you,' Sari said urgently.

'All in good time, miss. Now, step in, there's a good girl, and no harm will come to either of you.'

Sari looked helplessly down the empty street, then gave in, stepping into the carriage.

'That's right, miss. Now have yourself a seat here and take a good long draw on this.' He held out a small monogrammed silver bottle and she stared at it, her mind still trying to think of a way to escape without Tansy being hurt.

The man leaned forward ominously.

'Don't make me force you, miss. Just drink it down, like the master said. No need to get rough.'

He shoved the vial at her again, and she took it and raised it to her mouth. She took a careful sip, her eyes on the man's broken nose. She gasped and almost dropped the bottle. She had expected spirits, but the taste was bitter and harsh. Before she could react, the man grabbed her hand and chin, tipping her head back as he forced the rest of the bottle's contents down her throat, and she swallowed before she realised what she was doing. Then she was free again and she shoved the man away, falling against Tansy, who gave a little whimper of fear.

'It's just laudanum, miss,' the man said, grinning evilly as he pocketed the bottle. 'It'll make for a more restful journey, now.'

Tansy was shivering, and Sari patted the girl's shaking hands absently. She tried to concentrate but her heart was racing and she had no idea whether it was fear or the laudanum taking effect. She had no idea what to expect. She watched the shadows of the trees flash by. They must be heading out of town.

She realised her hands were suddenly too light to comfort Tansy. They were light and warm and very soft, like goose down. She couldn't quite feel the rumble of the carriage; it was just a pleasant, calming hum. Her mother used to hum like that when she was sewing. Then everything was very warm and reddish brown and Sari was floating…

Michael twisted the dial and turned the handle of the safe in his library, happy that he had at least not forgotten the code. He wanted his best pistols within reach until this episode was over. He swung open the safe, reaching in to extract the wooden case, and froze, staring in shock at a carefully crafted Venetian masque that lay on top of it.

He stood there for a long moment, then took it out and moved to sit at his desk. He placed it in front of him, spreading his hands on the polished wood surface on either side of it. The desk was not a perfect surface, he realised. There was a slight knot that sanding had not succeeded in levelling. He could very slightly feel its contours under the pads of his fingers. It wasn't quite round, just slightly oval, and thinner at one end. It had been his father's desk. He clasped his hands together and rested his forehead on them. The mask blurred this close, becoming a swirl of pastel colours shot with silver.

He had told her to stay in the carriage. He had made her promise to stay and she had disobeyed him. Again. She had saved O'Brien and almost lost her life and he had almost lost her when the boat had struck him. His fists clenched and he pressed them to his forehead. Fear cut through him as sharp and fresh as at the moment he had stood at the edge of the quay.

He did not know why seeing the mask had broken the dam that had held back his memory, but it was swamping him now. The whole insanity of those two months crashed back down on him like a brutal flood. He felt again as if he was drowning. As he had felt that mad, frantic night. And what would have happened had she died? Had she thought of that before she disobeyed him and left the safety of the carriage? Did she think of anyone before she risked her life again and again?

She was dangerous. Uncontrollable and dangerous. Being with her would be like living through one long battle, always waiting for her to destroy herself. And him. He had wanted to stop it. He had tried to, obviously. He had erased her.

But not soon enough. Not before he had compromised her. It was bad enough that he had taken her, knowing she was a virgin, but he had not even bothered with precautions. He had never in his life taken such risks. It was incredible to him that he had forgotten himself that far. He wanted to blame his concussion, but knew that would be too easy. He had wanted her and not cared about the consequences. Perhaps he had even been inviting them. He clenched his fists furiously. His mind was raw and weak, unable to check the onslaught of images that crashed through it. She had not resisted him; she had come to him as openly that first night as the others. He had used her passionate intensity against her to betray her trust. He closed his eyes.

He would have to marry her. The thought came to him cleanly, like a cool dash of water sweeping across and dousing a fire. He owed her that at least. He sat back and drew a deep breath. It was easier now that he had decided. The strange hollowness that had settled upon him when he had seen the mask was still there, as heavy and stifling as a blanket of fog. He welcomed it. It was pleasantly numbing. He was calm for the first time in weeks. It was quite easy, after all. The day was going to be a long one and he had to focus, but first, he had to get this over with before the numbness wore off.

He found Lady Montvale at home, sorting through invitations. She looked up and smiled as he entered. The strain of the past few days was showing on her as well, and she looked fragile. He wanted to say something reassuring but the numbness still held him flat.

'Is Sari here?' he asked instead.

Her smile changed to an expression of surprise.

'No, she has gone to run an errand, why? Has there been a development already?' she asked.

'Not yet. I just need to talk to her. Did she go alone?' A sudden rush of concern threatened his calm.

'No, she took a maid. Why?' she asked again.

'I need to talk to her,' he repeated. 'Where did she go?'

'To Hatchards to pick up some books she had ordered.'

'When did she leave?'

Lady Montvale glanced at the clock and a look of surprise crossed her face again.

'Just over an hour ago. Michael, what is wrong? Is she in danger?'

'Of course not, I just need to ask her something,' he said as calmly as possible. 'I will pass by Hatchards and see what is holding her up.'

He turned and left. Trust Sari to get lost in some book at a time like this. If only she could limit herself to their pages, they would not be in this whole predicament in the first place.

He reached Hatchards in ten minutes. It was almost empty and one of the senior booksellers, Mr Shaw, was unwrapping books behind the counter. He looked up as Michael entered.

'Ah, Lord Crayle, how may I help you today?'

'I am looking for one of your customers, a Miss Trevor. I believe you had some books on order for her?'

'And so I do. Let me see.' He reached under the counter and pulled out a package. 'Ah, yes, *The Byzantine Legacy*, by Alfred Chatham, and...'

Michael stared at the books in sudden unease. 'She has not been here yet?'

'Oh, no, I have not seen her today.'

'Are you certain? You have been here all day?'

'Why, yes. I have been behind the counter all morning. I would have surely seen her had she come in. I know she was very anxious to receive these books; they arrived only late yesterday...'

But he was talking to the air. Michael paused outside the

door, wondering what to do. He told himself not to panic. She had probably merely run into some acquaintance and been diverted. She might have gone to the Institute, or back to Montvale House. He hailed a passing hackney and gave Lady Montvale's address.

The hackney dropped him at the stairs and he ran up, opening the door without waiting for Henries. The sight that confronted him was chaotic. The whole household, including Lady Montvale, was gathered in the hallway, and in a chair by the wall sat a weeping maid, with her cap askew and mud on her cheek and pinafore. Michael froze just as they all turned to him.

'She is gone.' Lady Montvale stammered, stricken.

The maid started crying again and chaos broke loose.

'Quiet!' Michael heard himself yell and silence fell again. He turned to the maid.

'What happened? Tell me slowly,' he ordered her.

The maid stared at him, tears still pouring down her cheeks.

'It's my fault, my fault,' she mumbled almost incoherently.

'It is not your fault, but I need to know what happened,' he said as calmly as he could.

'We were walking and then suddenly a carriage pulled up and someone had me by the arm and pulled me in and then they told her to step in or they would hurt me. Then he put something over my mouth and then I was on Clapham Common and a man on a cart agreed to bring me here, and… Oh, it's my fault. She never would have gone with them if it wasn't for me. I'm so sorry.' She covered her face with her hands, shaking.

'It is not your fault,' Michael repeated woodenly. His hands were clenched so hard he had to relax them by force. He needed to think. Why would they take her? Had they found out about her involvement in the case? How could they have found out?

The door knocker sounded behind them and they all jumped. Henries jumped for the door, but his face fell when he saw it was only Anderson. Anderson took in the sight of the gathering in the hall.

'What is going on? Lady Montvale, I received your note...'

The maid started sobbing again and Michael grabbed Anderson's arm and hauled him into the nearest room.

'Someone has kidnapped Sari,' he said roughly.

'Who?'

'I don't know, damn it. It makes no sense. They can't know she is involved. How the hell would they know?' He could not think that her captors were Junger and Frey. He could not allow himself to think that.

'Tell me what happened,' Anderson said, echoing Michael's earlier words.

He repeated the maid's words briefly, his mind working.

'Clapham Common. They were headed south,' he said finally. They both looked up at the same time.

'Hadleigh Hall,' Anderson exclaimed.

'Edgerton's taken the bait. He is panicking and is going to try to leave the country.'

'O'Brien is with the men watching the hall. He will stop them.'

'Tell them to stop a carriage going out, not going in. And once Edgerton has her inside, he may not even know it, but he has us as well. Come on, they have two hours on us.'

Anderson followed him at a run. Michael turned to Lady Montvale at the door.

'Margaret, if you hear anything, anything at all, send

word to the Institute. They will know where to find us; we will be with O'Brien at Hadleigh Hall.'

'Edgerton,' Lady Montvale whispered in shock, but they were already leaving.

Sari opened her eyes to a kaleidoscope, like the one her father had once given Charlie. The colours broke together only to collapse again into chaos. She closed her eyes and breathed deeply. Then she remembered.

'How are you feeling, my dear?' a familiar voice asked.

She turned her head stiffly and opened her eyes again. The face shifted and then resolved.

'Edgerton?' she whispered and something moved under her as he sat down. She was on a bed, she realised in alarm. He reached over and brushed the hair back from her forehead.

'Yes, my darling. I am so sorry about this, but I could think of no other way. If I had sent a note... I could not be sure it would not be intercepted, or that you would come.'

'My lord, what...?'

'Hush, rest a bit,' he said kindly, pressing a finger to her lips. 'I am sorry about the laudanum but I did not want you to be alarmed and it was a rather long ride. They did not hurt you, did they?' Concern entered his voice.

She shook her head. This was madness. Surely he must be mad. She tried to sit up, but he pressed her back.

'No, darling, you must rest. We have a long trip ahead of us. I am so sorry you did not have a chance to pack, but we can always have your things sent after us when we arrive.'

'Arrive? Where?'

'I have an estate on Trinidad. It is a very pleasant island, a lovely people, very welcoming. I am sure you will be delighted with it.'

Trinidad? What the devil was going on? Humour him, she told herself, and took a deep breath.

'Why must we go to Trinidad, Arthur?'

He smiled at her use of his Christian name and bent to brush his hand across her brow again.

'Some plans of mine haven't fared well, I am afraid, my love. It pains me to have you dragged in to this imbroglio, but I could not leave you behind. There was no time to explain. I hope you understand. I could not leave without you. I thought, since you are also alone in the world you might not mind too much...'

He trailed off, obviously seeking some form of approbation, and she tried to smile. She needed him to trust her.

'When are we leaving?' she asked faintly.

'On the morning tide. I have a yacht waiting in Portsmouth. We will leave within the hour.'

'Perhaps I should rest then, I am still a bit dizzy,' she said, lowering her lashes wearily.

'Of course, my love. Ring this bell if you need anything. One of my men will stay in the corridor to make sure no harm comes to you.'

In other words, Sari thought as she let her eyelids drift closed, I am a prisoner. He might not see it that way, but she certainly did. She waited until his footsteps disappeared down the hall and then sat up, inspecting the room. He had left a small bell and a single candlestick by the bedside. Other than that there was nothing in the room.

She shook the bell and a chair creaked in the corridor followed by heavy footfall as her gaoler approached. She did not recognise the man, but he looked burly, with a neck as thick as his head. She gave a small moan, resting her forehead on her hand.

'What's to do?' he asked impatiently.

'I'm terribly sorry to be such a bother, but could you

help me with my boot? I hurt my ankle and the laces are so tight, but every time I try to untie them I get dizzy…' She trailed off wanly.

He grunted as he knelt down. She had tied the knots well and his large fingers fumbled at the laces. He hit a particularly thorny knot and Sari snatched the candlestick from the table and brought its heavy bronze base down with all her force on the side of his head. It made a sickening thud and he slumped sideways on to the floor. The candle flew off and plunged the room into darkness. Sari pulled off her boots and stood up, listening. Nothing.

She opened the door carefully and stepped out. She had her story ready if need be, but thankfully there was no one there. She ran lightly to the end of the corridor and down a servants' staircase, groping her way in the darkness. It opened on to a narrow hall, at the end of which a door stood ajar leading to a back courtyard. She held herself there for another couple of minutes, listening, and then hurried outside. The courtyard lay long and empty without even shrubbery for shelter. She heard voices approaching from the corridor behind her and knew she had no choice. She would have to make a run for it. She turned, keeping close to the stable wall, and ran.

Chapter Twenty-Nine

It took Michael less than two hours to reach Hadleigh Hall. His mare was sweating and its flanks were flecked with foam, but he could not spare it any pity. The light was failing and he led it across a field towards the Hall, staying in the shadow of the trees. He reached a hill overlooking the rear of the building and heard a click behind him. He froze, hoping he had not yet crossed into enemy lines.

'Turn around slow like,' whispered a voice behind him and he turned with a wry smile.

'Evening, O'Brien.'

'Crayle! By all that's holy, you gave me a fright to knock my freckles off. What news—?'

'Have you seen a carriage go through yet?' Michael interrupted, speaking low.

'A carriage? Aye, one this morning and another round about an hour ago. What's he up to? Setting up for a siege?'

'No, bringing in hostages. He has Sari.'

O'Brien's jaw dropped. 'Sari? How? Does he know?'

'I don't think so. I hope not.'

'Then why—?' He broke off and a look of comprehension crossed his face. 'The devil. There never was such a fool as a fool in love.'

Michael could not agree more heartily. 'Tell me what has been happening,' he instructed.

O'Brien nodded. 'There's been more movement this past hour. They're preparing both carriages. Looks like they're packing to leave. I've got men set up around the perimeter. No one is getting out without us knowing.'

'They'll be leaving soon if they want to reach his yacht in Portsmouth before the tide goes out. With the ports on alert a private yacht is his best bet for getting Junger and Frey out of the country. I doubt he realises the Austrians will probably try to get rid of him once he has them safely out of England. Anderson has gone ahead to Portsmouth to prepare the excise officers if we don't manage to stop them here.'

Suddenly, they saw Sari's pale figure detach from the back entrance of the mansion and break into a run, keeping close to the walls. Before she had even made it halfway across the courtyard a dark figure surged out of the stables and with a few strides had brought her down, her skirts billowing out like a falling flower. They rolled over and she climbed to her feet and began running again, but then two other figures came towards them and they brought her down again.

Michael watched helplessly as they dragged her towards the house.

'Little fool. Crazy little fool.'

'Should we go in now?' O'Brien asked shakily.

'No. It's worse now. Edgerton won't let them hurt her.' He prayed he was right. 'We attack now and they just might kill her. I need to think.'

Sari also needed to think. She had hurt her knees and palms in her fall and it was not hard to make herself start crying. When the men had dragged her back inside the house Edgerton came running towards them.

'What happened? What have you done to her?'

'She tried to pull a runner, Guv'. I stopped her in the courtyard,' said the man who held her arm.

'I told you bringing the woman was injudicious, Edgerton,' said a languid, accented voice behind the lord. 'Just one more unfortunate twist in a singularly botched affair. This is the last time I work with amateurs.'

Sari recognised Frey and started crying harder.

'Let her go!' Edgerton ordered, ignoring the Austrian. The men did so and Sari sank down to her painful knees, burying her face in her hands.

'Sari, darling. What were you doing?'

She heard the touch of steel in his voice and knew she had to play this carefully.

'He touched me. I asked him to help me because I was dizzy and he...he t-touched me. He t-touched me and smiled and I was so scared and I hit him with the candlestick and I ran and I wanted to find you, but I fell on the stairs and... Oh, he touched me!' She started sobbing again and his hand tightened on her shoulder.

He pulled her to him and she put her arms around his neck thankfully, praying Frey would not say another word. Her salvation rode on Edgerton believing her.

'Hush, love. What an ordeal for you. You needn't worry, you are safe now. I'll not leave you again. Come, we are all ready. We will go straight to the carriage and you needn't see him ever again. Can you stand...?'

'I th-think...' she stammered. Just before they reached the servants' door, Edgerton turned to Frey and she saw Junger standing behind him as well.

'Find the bastard and kill him,' Edgerton said harshly over her head.

'That will cost extra,' Junger replied laconically, but with a certain satisfaction.

'Just do it,' Edgerton barked and Sari cowered against him. Remorse coursed through her. The man would die because of her. And she hadn't even managed to escape. She started crying again, this time in earnest, and Edgerton pulled her closer, caressing her hair as he led her to the carriages. At one carriage door he stopped and pulled out his handkerchief, bending to dry her tears. She gave a last shaky sob and raised her hands to catch his, pressing his palm to her cheek.

'Don't leave me, Arthur,' she whispered. 'Please.'

'Never, my darling. My poor love, this has not turned out at all as we had hoped, has it?'

She looked up at him. 'I don't care, so long as you are with me.'

She heard him draw a deep breath and then he bent to kiss her, brushing his lips across her eyes, her cheeks, before he finally closed on her mouth, whispering endearments between each touch. Sari thought she would suffocate. Fear and acting and a strong wish to survive had carried her thus far, but she was weakening. She could feel the disgust rise in her throat and she almost gave a gasp of relief when he finally stood back.

He smiled down at her. 'Chin up, my darling love. We will be sailing within the hour.'

She returned his smile as best she could and let him hand her up into the carriage. He stepped up beside her and pulled her head against his shoulder. She was almost glad for the comfort of his embrace when the carriage door swung open and Frey stepped in and seated himself opposite them. Within a couple of minutes they were rolling forward.

Michael and the other men had been advancing swiftly through the shadows, resolving to go in, but he gave the

signal to halt the minute he saw Edgerton step outside with
her. Michael watched from the darkness of the tree line as
she smiled up at Edgerton, as she leaned into his caresses.
He knew full well what she was doing, but still he had to
hold his hand rigid so as not to take the shot and finish
Edgerton where he stood. What mattered was that she
was safe, he told himself. Somehow the minx had turned
things around. How, he had no idea.

'No such fool as a fool in love,' O'Brien repeated in a
whisper and Michael forced himself not to react.

'All right. Get everybody to pull back and saddle up,'
he commanded.

'Can't we take them in the carriages?'

'Blind? With Frey inside and people shooting right and
left? Frey will have no qualms about slitting her throat at
the first provocation. We will have to wait for Portsmouth
when they are exposed and we can take our shots. She
looks safe for the moment.'

'Looks more than safe if you ask me, bless her heart.
What an actress.'

They all saddled up and Michael led the way across the
field. He knew these roads well and as they came over a
rise, in the moonlight they could see the carriages moving
on the dark road below. He smiled grimly. The carriages
would have to stick to the main road, but on horseback
they could gain at least half an hour going across the fields.

They made it into Portsmouth with enough time for the
men to take their positions on the quay around Edgerton's
yacht, the *Seahorse*. With help from the excise officers the
yacht's crew was convinced to remove themselves from
the premises and then there was nothing to do but wait for
the carriages' arrival.

He had been in such situations so often, the upcoming battle was almost sketched in his mind in advance. Whatever his weakness after a battle, before it he was always crystal clear and focused. He had the image of the surroundings in his head, an assessment of the forces they had to face, their firepower, their agenda, their weak points. Each of the men knew their role and Michael had little doubt they had the advantage in this skirmish. They would be as swift and as surgical as possible. Once they took out the trained assassins, the others should be easy to pick off. At least that was what his rational side believed.

But he knew this time it was different. He had never wanted to die, but he had always known it was a possibility and at times a strong possibility. The thought had usually angered him, raising a kind of frustrated rejection of that eventuality. But it had never really threatened his concentration. But now the realisation that Sari would be at the centre of this battle, exposed to Junger and Frey and to their crossfire, vulnerable... If they weren't quick enough or accurate enough... As the minutes ticked by in the dark, seemingly sleepy quay he kept repeating to himself how much depended on remaining calm, focused. But as the ship swayed gently beneath him like a great sleeping, breathing beast he knew he was as close to panic as he had ever been. With each moment that passed he became more convinced they were merely setting up the stage to watch her die. That it had always been inevitable that she would finally run out of luck. That before the sun rose he might be truly and utterly alone and it would be unbearable.

Chapter Thirty

'Chin up, love, we have arrived,' Edgerton murmured as the carriage drew to a halt. Sari's knees and hands still hurt wickedly and her side ached where she had been thrown to the ground. She wanted to scream in fear and frustration, but instead she let him hand her down from the carriage, leaning on him weakly, trying to think of some way she could still prevent this.

When the first shot rang out it sounded like a mast cracking. But then she saw one of the men crumple in front of her and all mayhem broke loose. She heard Frey curse in German just ahead of her and then a dark splash of colour erupted from his neck and he fell back before he could even take aim against the unseen assailants.

She tried to drop to the ground, but Edgerton was dragging her towards the gangplank. She pulled at his arm, but his grip was strong and she stumbled after him, trying to understand what was going on. Shots seemed to be exploding everywhere. Then they were on the gangplank and he stopped abruptly. He dragged her in front of him, his left arm tight around her neck. Something cold pressed against her temple and she snapped her head up in shock.

She was staring down the barrel of a pistol and at the

other end of it stood Michael, facing them just where the gangplank met the boat. She felt Edgerton's thundering heartbeat through her back and in the arm that pinned her to him. She knew he had a gun to her temple and for a split second wondered how he could do this to her if he loved her.

'Let us pass or I will shoot her,' Edgerton gasped above her head and she instinctively tried to pull away, but he only tightened his hold, cutting off her breath. Around them there was suddenly total silence.

'Stand perfectly still, Sari. Do you understand me?' Michael said, his eyes on Edgerton, his voice steady. He had not lowered his pistol.

'I said let me pass or I will shoot her, damn you!' Edgerton almost screamed. His arm constricted further about her neck; she could hardly breathe and the edges of her vision were fading. Her body felt thick and heavy and it seemed as if she was sinking, but she locked her knees and tried to hold as still as possible. She knew what was coming.

'I think not,' Michael merely replied calmly. 'Your pistol isn't cocked.'

Sari felt the shock run through Edgerton, but even as he raised his pistol slightly to check whether what Michael said was true the world exploded and Sari closed her eyes against the flash. Edgerton's weight drew her back and all of a sudden she was sliding. She tried to breathe, but his arm was still around her neck, dragging her with him and she knew she would hit the water, any second now.

Then her dress snapped painfully into her chest and she was jerked back from the fall and hauled roughly on to the gangplank.

'I'm not going swimming after you again, understand?' said a voice through the ringing in her ears. She nodded and to her dismay realised she was about to faint.

* * *

'Right between the eyes, Major,' O'Brien said, looking down at the body which had caught on the rigging below the gangplank, staring blankly at the sky like a life-sized marionette. He turned to Michael who was still on his knees, supporting Sari's inert figure. A look of concern flashed across O'Brien's face as he hurried towards them.

'She's not…'

'She fainted,' Michael replied, not raising his head. 'Are the others all down?'

'Aye, your first shot took out Junger. Morton took out Frey. We have the rest under control. Not a scratch on the lot of us, either. Fainted, eh? She'll not be happy about that.'

'Get the carriage over here. And get Edgerton's body up here before it falls into the water.'

'Now?'

'No, next week. Of course now, damn it!'

O'Brien hurried off and Michael picked Sari up, striding towards the road. She shifted in his arms, opening her eyes.

'Tansy, my maid…' she murmured worriedly and he tightened his hold.

'She is fine. Don't worry.'

Her eyes drifted closed. She stirred again when they reached the carriage and he laid her gently on the seat.

'Are we home yet?' she murmured.

'Not yet, soon,' Michael replied soothingly.

'Good,' she replied, leaning her head against the squabs and closing her eyes again. 'I'm hungry.'

'I am sure you are.' A smile tugged at Michael's lips despite the tension in his body. He turned to Anderson, who had come to join them.

'Get her back to London—' he began, but Anderson cut him off.

'You return with her. I will arrange matters with the authorities here. Once she's back at Lady Montvale's I will meet you Castlereagh's. We will need to write something for the morning papers. Dead bodies all around make it easier,' he said morbidly. Michael hesitated, but gave in to the urge to see her to safety himself.

Once in the carriage he pulled her on to his lap and she shifted against him with a slight murmur, but did not wake. He did not know whether to be thankful that she slept through the long ride back to London. At one point she uttered a confused, angry protest and tried to push away, but then her eyes opened and she gazed up at him, then with a small sigh just reached up to gently touch his cheek.

'You're safe,' she murmured before closing her eyes again and sinking back into sleep.

He had to stop himself from crushing her to him possessively, from waking her so he wouldn't have to be alone with this need and the accompanying waves of fear that surged up again and again as he remembered how close he had come to losing her. He was exhausted, but he didn't want the journey to end because that meant he would have to deliver her into someone else's care.

She did wake just as they reached Berkeley Square, but even before the horses had pulled up in front of Lady Montvale's house the front door opened and Henries rushed down to open the carriage door. He was quickly followed by Heloise, while Lady Montvale stood framed in the doorway, wringing her hands in worry. Within seconds Sari had been bundled into the house and Michael watched as the doors closed behind them and Berkeley Square sank again into its darkened slumber. From the direction of Bruton Street the Watch was calling the hour, and Michael returned to the carriage and gave the direction of Castlereagh's office.

Chapter Thirty-One

Sari woke up with a terrified start and realised two things. She was back in her room at Montvale House and she felt like she had been throttled and dragged for miles behind a runaway horse. The last thing she remembered was Michael's look past the barrel of his gun, focused and unrelenting. And then the flash and the weight pulling her towards the water. And then she had fainted.

'I never faint,' she moaned to herself and heard the swish of skirts as Lady Montvale came over to sit by the bed. 'What time is it?' she asked.

'You have slept the day away, my dear, it is late afternoon. You gave us quite a fright,' she added kindly.

'I gave myself quite a fright. Is it all quite over?'

Lady Montvale handed her the newspaper. 'Anderson said to give this to you.'

Sari read it quickly. It outlined a foreign plot to foment unrest implicating some Continental power up to mischief, with carefully veiled allusions to Metternich himself. Hamlin's slaying was tied in, but neither Castlereagh nor Edgerton were named. The glory was bestowed upon the excise officers for stopping the perpetrators.

'And Edgerton?'

'There will be an obituary in the afternoon papers. Apparently he was killed in a hunting accident on his estate in Dorset. You will obviously be distraught.'

Sari nodded. That much would not be hard to fake. 'So, what now? Do I retire to the countryside, inconsolable in my grief?'

Lady Montvale looked at her peculiarly, then down at her hands.

'Hardly. Simply because you have helped to resolve this one issue does not mean your role has become superfluous. Quite the opposite, my dear. As for Edgerton, there are no clear rules with regards to mourning a fiancé, but while there should be a period of quiet reflection, it will be considered quite *convenable* for you to return to normal social activities within a couple of months. Which brings me to the next point. Put simply, Anderson spoke with Edgerton's solicitors this morning. There were certain matters that had to be cleared up in order to keep this quiet. And he had some rather peculiar news. I am not sure how you will take this…'

Sari frowned. It was not like Lady Montvale to be so diffident.

'It appears that Edgerton changed his will right after your engagement and left the majority of his unentailed estate to you,' Lady Montvale said at last. 'A rather large amount. Just under forty thousand pounds. So you are an heiress after all.'

Sari stared at her in stupefaction. 'I cannot accept it,' she said weakly after a moment.

'Well, you could always give it to charity, but it is most definitely yours. Michael said you could put part of it in trust for your brother and your friends. Think of their future and I think your conscience might allow you some leeway.'

'Michael knows?' she whispered.

Lady Montvale leaned forward to pat her arm.

'He was with Anderson at the solicitors. He also came to enquire how you were.' She hesitated. 'It seems his memory has returned.'

The blood rushed to Sari's face. That meant he remembered now. He knew. She pressed her hands to her hot cheeks and winced at the pain in her palms.

Lady Montvale's gaze fell before hers. 'He left this afternoon for Crayle Hall in Devon for a few days to take care of business now that this issue has been resolved.'

Sari nodded dumbly. He remembered and he had chosen to leave rather than to face her. If she had been waiting for any sign, she had it now.

'Well, you should rest,' Lady Montvale said, standing up briskly. 'There will be a great deal of curiosity to deal with once you are recovered.'

As the door closed behind her Sari rubbed her face wearily. She was not strong enough to turn down this windfall. The thought of what would have happened to Charlie if she had been killed decided it for her. Now, if something happened to her, he would be safe. And she could provide for George and Mina. For the first time in her life those she loved could be secure. No, she wasn't noble enough to refuse it.

Chapter Thirty-Two

Michael stood at the doorway of what had once been his father's study at Crayle Hall. He had never understood why his father had used this cramped, gloomy room. His own study was in a large south-facing room so he could look out over the lawns towards the sea. But then there was a great deal he had never understood about his father. He closed the door. He should clear it out. There was no point in keeping it like this, a sad reminder of a frustrated, emotionally stunted man. He walked out of the south exit and headed towards the cliffs.

The sun cut through the poplars, lining the cliff path with golden ribbons. He was a fool not to come here more often. Except for the times when his parents had returned home, Crayle Hall had always been his sanctuary. Perhaps that was why he had escaped here after the revelation about Edgerton's will. He had intended to offer for Sari as soon as she recovered, but the unwelcome news that Edgerton had left her his money had shaken him. She was independent now; she didn't need him or anyone. He had told himself it was only fair to give her a few days to absorb this news before he made his offer, but he knew now that removing himself from London had been pure cowardice.

He didn't know what he had feared more—that she might accept him or turn him down.

He stood on the cliff overlooking the bay where he had spent so many hours with his brother and sisters. The image of her down there, with their children, playing in the sand and waves, imposed itself on the empty bay like a tantalising mirage. For the first time in his life he allowed himself to imagine a family of his own not as a burden and inescapable source of fear, but as a fountain of happiness and even comfort. But the only way this image solidified and held was when she stood at its centre. He needed her in order to make that leap of faith.

She could deal with it. She could deal with just about anything. He remembered how hurt he had been when she had tried to spread that mantle of concern over him, not wanting to be merely another brother figure to her like Anderson. He hadn't appreciated that she had been willing to fight to protect him; it had just appeared to be another source of fear and responsibility. He should have revelled in it.

He needed her. As terrified as he was of something happening to her, he would have to live with it. The alternative was worse. If he was lucky enough and she cared for him even after everything they had been through, he would fight every one of his worst instincts and trust her.

It had taken this trip back to his home to make him admit that he was a pathetic coward. The absurdity that he had actually tried to convince himself he would be better off without her... He had been so afraid of ending up like his father that he had been well on his way there already. There were many roads to take to end up emotionally withered. If he hadn't met her...

If she cared. He had no idea whether she did, beyond the obvious physical bond that brought them together with such heat. Surely that meant something. She had responded so intensely, with such elemental passion—he couldn't believe it was purely physical. He hoped to God it was more than that, although he certainly hadn't done much to merit her affection.

She would love it here. He knew that. He could almost see her turning to look up at him from the bay, smiling. The memory of her smile hit him. He loved the way it burst over him and bared him and there was nothing he could do. He would deal with the fear. He was damned if he would let it cheat him from the chance to be with her. *If* she cared, said that little voice again, the words becoming a recurring litany.

He took a deep breath and turned his back on the sea. It was time to stop running and find out.

Chapter Thirty-Three

Sari surveyed the pretty little house from across the street. The sun glinted off its windows and warmed the stone façade. It was perfect.

'Oh, Miss Sari, it *is* lovely,' Mina said mistily beside her.

'It's ours now,' Sari replied quietly and Mina glanced at her. She knew Mina and George were worried about her, but she couldn't help it. For the past few days she had been moving through a thick, smothering fog—a numbness that was only alleviated by sharp slashes of searing pain when she thought of Michael. She had done her best to mask it, focusing all her energies on acquiring a house for them all with her new wealth, but Mina and George knew her too well.

She focused on the house. It *was* lovely. She would set up a study for Charlie for when he came down from school. And George and Mina could have a whole floor to themselves.

'I should go now, Mina. I promised Lady Montvale I would be back by four.'

Mina nodded.

'Off you go, then. Now that we've seen most of the furniture brought in, we can move in tomorrow which means I've plenty to do back at the old house.'

Sari forced a smile and headed back towards Berkeley Square. Lady Montvale had not yet returned and Sari was thankful for some time to herself. She sat down in the drawing room and picked up the book she had been trying to read.

It was ridiculous to be more afraid of the future now that she was financially secure than she had been all those months ago. Ludicrous. There was no reason why she couldn't occupy herself just fine. Despite what Lady Montvale had said, she wasn't sure she was strong enough to continue working at the Institute and face Michael every day if he was not interested in her. She would miss it dreadfully, but there were limits to her resilience. His removal to Devon after recovering his memory was a very clear message and she had her pride. She refused to allow her happiness to depend solely on him or on being part of the Institute. This feeling of being a dry, withered husk around a throbbing wound would fade with time. It had to.

She was so caught up in her thoughts she did not even notice as the door opened and Michael walked in. She stared at him in shock, as if her thoughts had somehow conjured him out of thin air and he would just as swiftly disappear.

He looked ridiculously well with his face tanned, making his eyes look a sharper grey than she remembered. She could suddenly feel everything about her, the draught from the door touching her arms, the roughness of the pages under her fingers. As if he had returned her body to her with his entry. And with it came a searing wave of love and despair.

Michael stopped just inside the door, his hand still on the knob.

'Good afternoon, Miss Trevor. I trust you are well?' he

asked formally. She looked lovely and it seemed ludicrous after all they had been through together not to just walk up to her and pull her to him. But she sat as erect as any proper young woman, without even a hint of the smile he had been fantasising about, and he felt painfully unsure.

'Quite well, I thank you,' she replied, looking up briefly from the book in her hands, but not quite meeting his eyes.

'Anderson tells me you have bought a house.' He was stalling, but he needed to find some equilibrium before he moved forward. He sat down in a chair opposite her, but she didn't look up again, her fingers playing with the edges of the book she held. He resisted the urge to pull it from her hands and toss it away.

'Yes.' She nodded, then she took a sudden deep breath. 'My lord, I have been meaning to thank you for—'

'Don't,' he interrupted. 'Please, don't. I don't want your gratitude.'

He saw the pain flicker across her face and realised she had misunderstood him.

'You owe me nothing,' he tried to explain, but that was no good, either. 'I, however, owe you a very serious apology. Another one,' he added ruefully.

'No...'

'Yes, I do. What I said...what I did...was unpardonable. I can't fully explain, because I don't really understand it myself, but I want you to know that I would never—I mean under normal circumstances—and certainly not someone in your position—'

He cut himself off, dismayed at the muddle he was making of this. She wasn't even looking at him, her gaze still fixed on the book in her lap.

'Look at me!' he said somewhat desperately.

She did look up then, her eyes intent and serious. There was nothing there to encourage him and he felt the room shift slightly around him. The thought that everything he felt might stop at some invisible line between them and have no echo in her was terrifying.

'There is no need for you to do this, my lord. I understand that you feel…responsible for what occurred between us, but I do not in any way hold you accountable. There is no need to apologise and it's certainly not necessary to contemplate anything more drastic. I am my own mistress.'

'This isn't about responsibility!'

'No? Then we needn't worry, then. I am glad you are better. Was the weather nice in Devon?'

The absurdity of talking about the weather when his whole life was on the line was too much for him. He surged to his feet, his hands clenched against the need to grab her and shake her.

'Sari! This is serious! What is wrong with you? Are you even paying attention?'

Sari stood up as well, the book sliding to the floor with a thump. There was such a fierce look on her face that he almost took a step backwards in surprise.

'There is nothing wrong with me. I am well aware that this is serious. But if you think I am going to be the sacrificial lamb for your guilt you are very wrong. And if you think I would contemplate trading my freedom for a loveless marriage simply to appease your sense of honour, you obviously don't know me very well!'

Her words slashed through him. A loveless marriage. There it was, the answer. She didn't care for him. The room seemed to recede from him. Even she looked further away, like a stranger. He would have to move eventually, he knew. Turn around and leave.

She didn't understand why he was just standing there, looking blankly at her. A burning miasma of pain was crowding in her chest, threatening to erupt and swamp her. She should have known he would offer for her. Of course he would make himself pay the price for having slept with her. But she knew herself well enough to know she could not do it. She could not live every day with the knowledge that she was just another responsibility. A burden. A sop to his damn honour. She would not be so diminished, not even to be near him. It was terrible, cruel of him to tempt her like this. Pain and fury roiled inside her and she wished she could make him feel just one inch of the damage he was wreaking on her.

'Did you really think I would agree to marry you on those terms? *You* may have no problem committing to spending your whole life with someone based on some abstract concept—'

'Being in love with you doesn't feel abstract in the least. It's damned painful!' he interrupted harshly. 'Do you think I would otherwise voluntarily want to live in fear that you will drown or get shot or throw yourself over a cliff? The only thing that scares me more than something happening to you is going through life without you!'

Shock undercut her rising wave of anger. In a kind of muted cavernous silence her mind played his words again and again as if they formed an almost understood but elusive phrase in a foreign language. *In love with you…*

'You can't be in love with me,' she whispered after a moment, her eyes wide with something like fear.

'And why the hell not?'

'I don't know… I…you just can't.'

'Well, I am. Why don't we just accept that as a fact and move on to something more interesting such as how you feel?'

She dipped her head again, the way she did when she was trying to avoid the world.

'You know I love you.'

The words hit him with such intensity he felt as if he had been forcibly shoved back into his body. 'I…you… how am I supposed to know that?'

'Why else would I have slept with you? Even when you hated me and mistrusted me?'

Michael almost groaned. In her tortured logic it made sense. She was holding herself as rigidly as a statue and he sat down next to her and ran his hands up her arms gently, trying to assuage her tension, wondering how to convince her to trust him. Without thinking, he eased open one of her hands and pressed it to his chest. Against its warmth he could feel his heartbeat, hard, insistent.

'I never hated you and the person I mistrusted most was myself. You shook my control from the moment I met you and I put you through hell because I was a coward.'

She raised her eyes and to his surprise they filled with tears. She reached up and touched his cheek gently.

'Michael… I thought you left because you wanted to make it clear there couldn't be anything between us and it hurt so much I thought I couldn't survive it. I told myself of course I could, but it didn't feel like it. I wanted to know where you were and what you were doing and if you were well and everything else was just happening to me, but I wasn't really there. I never knew anything could hurt so much.'

He listened to this passionate admission with a kind of wonder. He pressed his hands to her cheeks, leaning his forehead against hers. He felt humbled and unbelievably lucky and he had no idea what to say that would prove to her that he felt the same.

'You have to let me take good care of you. I couldn't survive it if something happened to you,' he said huskily after a moment.

She smiled suddenly, beautifully.

'If you let me take good care of you, too.'

He groaned and pulled her to him with something like desperation, and then he was kissing her as a drowning man might gasp for air. For once he wanted to take her openly, without barriers or fear. He wanted her to tell him that she loved him until she was hoarse. He wanted her safe and his.

His control was slipping, his greedy side pushing through. His erection surged against her and a small moan trembled in her throat as she shifted against him, inflicting even more damage. She kissed him back, with a desperation that met his. He tugged at the ribbon that held her hair and the thick warm tresses unwound over her shoulder. He sank his hands into them, remembering how they had brushed across his chest that night at Vauxhall, warm and silky. God, he wanted her. He was already considering how best to undress her without having to move her from his lap when he heard the door open and then close again quickly. She heard it, too, and drew back with a gasp.

'The door...' she murmured fuzzily.

'I know, don't worry; whoever it was won't try that again.'

'Should we lock it?' she asked worriedly.

His groin was pounding and he was blazing hot, but he started laughing. 'This is ridiculous. We can do this without interruption in the middle of the Opera House and Vauxhall, but here some idiot has to walk in.'

'What if it was Lady Montvale?'

'She'll have to learn about it sooner or later, and if you think I have any intention of behaving around her, or around anyone else for that matter, you are very much mistaken.'

He was about to continue when a sharp knock on the door sounded and he sat back with a groan.

'This had better be important. Come, let's scare them off.'

He stalked over to the door, throwing it open. Lady Montvale stood outside, her arms folded ominously.

'What?' Michael asked unceremoniously.

'I am glad you two have finally made up your differences,' she stated. 'But Sari is still under my protection and I take that role seriously. You should know better than to try to take advantage of her.'

'I am afraid he already has,' Sari said with a giggle, feeling ridiculously happy.

'Several times,' Michael added for good measure.

Lady Montvale gaped at them.

'Now,' said Michael, taking advantage of her stupefaction, 'if we are to be evicted from the drawing room we will take our business upstairs.'

Lady Montvale snapped out of her stupor. 'You will do no such thing...'

'Perhaps you are right.' Michael sighed. 'And Crayle House would be even more improper. Back to the Scunthorpes' garden in Richmond?'

Sari gasped. 'The masquerade? You knew all along? Why didn't you tell me?' she asked, embarrassed.

'What on earth are you two talking about?' Lady Montvale interrupted in annoyance.

Before either of them could respond, the door opened and Anderson, Letty and Alicia chose that unpropitious moment to walk in. Anderson took in Sari's loose hair and Michael's tousled appearance and raised his brows questioningly.

'Hallo. What's afoot?'

'Nothing, thanks to Lady Montvale,' Michael said. 'We

were trying to celebrate our engagement, but Margaret has become annoyingly old-fashioned so I'm off to get a private licence. The sooner we're married the sooner we can get some privacy.'

'Well, you've finally come to your senses, man,' Anderson replied mildly, as Letty gave a happy squeal and hurried over to hug Sari. 'I was wondering whether I was going to have to have the men take you into a quiet corner and beat some into you.'

'Anderson! Do not encourage him,' Lady Montvale exclaimed. 'You are going to do this by the book, including the banns and the chapel at Crayle Hall. It is bad enough for Sari to be marrying so soon at all after Edgerton, but if you think I am about to allow you to run off furtively to some back-alley priest, you are much mistaken. Am I the only one with any sense here?'

'But you don't even like each other!' Alicia said, confused.

'Of course we don't,' Michael agreed. 'This is merely a marriage of inconvenience. She seduced me.'

'Michael!' Sari expostulated, laughing. 'They will have us locked in Bedlam…'

'So long as we share a cell, I am willing. We will have more privacy there than we can seem to get around here.'

Lady Montvale was tapping her foot on the floor. 'The banns, Michael, and the chapel, and that is far more than you deserve. I should make you wait a full six months.'

'The blasted banns and the chapel, and that is far more than I should be agreeing to,' Michael said with some frustration.

'Well, if you will all excuse me, the furniture has just been delivered to my new house,' Sari interjected innocently. 'I want to make sure it was all placed where it ought to be.'

Michael tangled his hand in her hair as he looked down at her, smiling.

'Furniture? This house of yours, it is in a quiet location, is it not?'

'Oh, yes, quite set back. I thought Charlie should have a quiet place to study.'

'Of course he should. A capital idea. Now, if you will all excuse us, I have to go and help my betrothed...' this was said with a pointed smile at Lady Montvale '...make sure there are no problems with her furniture.'

* * * * *